The Wrong Dame

David Lee Dambrosio

Chapter 1.

Earl, Gus, and I sat at Mo's Bar, a five-minute walk from our offices in the Grayson Building on the east side of downtown Cleveland. Our other partner, Joey, would be drinking with us, if he weren't working on the case of a guy who didn't trust his wife. We appeared to be the swells in our three-piece suits and fedoras. The hourly workers who congregated for suds and shots knew better. We wore what we wore because we were private detectives and no better than anyone else.

Talk went to the Indians having a hangover after their 1948 World Series victory. The 1949 season ended for them on Sunday, when they finished third behind the Yanks and Red Sox. It happens. The team was too stocked with talent not to win more World Series in the coming years.

The conversation moved to the Cleveland Browns and their 28-game winning streak. Would they ever lose? They had won three straight All-America Football Conference Championships, led by the best quarterback ever, Otto Graham, and probably the best football coach ever, Paul Brown.

For a city like Cleveland, its sports fans were riding high, except for the Tribe not repeating as World Series champions.

Billy Kutler, a telephone line repairman, wondered if the warm weather was *Indian summer*. Most agreed late in September didn't count. Warm weather had to happen later in the year. A tame argument about what months qualified for Indian summer withered away, as many of the working stiffs left for home.

Gus Reece kept checking his pocket watch. It seemed to cause him to drink faster. I wondered if his wife and two kids expected him home for supper soon. They might not be happy to see him if he came home with a snoot full.

Gus was the only married partner. The other three of us weren't so lucky, or maybe unlucky, depending on who was doing the thinking. A flatfoot before the war, along with Joey, Gus mildly complained. He might be a cop off the streets in a car or mostly in a chair, if he didn't enlist for the war and then for our detective agency afterward.

Complaining about his wife's spending, or maybe all dames' spending, Gus asked flatly, "Why do dames spend so much money on hats and shoes? What mug looks above their face or below their ankles?"

Depending on what road alcohol took me, happy or sad, the comment could be funny and make sense. Feeling no pain on the happier road, I laughed. Earl agreed.

"Got a bus to catch, Gus? You keep checking your timepiece," I said.

"Not a bus. I'll be driving my heap. Hope it makes it a few miles before I need a taxi. I got that insurance thing. The cripple is going out of town, so I'm following him to see how crippled he is. You might not hear from me for a few days. Why waste a few nickels to check in."

Earl skipped the phone comment and went to, "How do you know he's leaving by car and the time?"

"I snooped. Remember, it's what we do." His demeanor flipped from annoyance to laughter.

"What's so funny, Gus? Earl and I could always use an extra yuck."

"If this guy's nose was any bigger, he'd need a cane to open a door."

This time he was trying to be funny. Earl and I laughed.

He tossed down his liquor and emptied his glass of beer with the finality of leaving. "See you gumshoes, when I see you."

Like that, Gus left, leaving us in a near-empty joint. Without any dames to distract us, especially a certain woman I didn't want to talk about, we turned to business. It was either that or reliving something from the war. Neither of us wanted to do that, though a few more bourbons and beers might take us down that road.

"We need steadier work from lawyers and insurance companies. We get the leftover cabbage. Gus is thinking about leaving and going back to being a cop." Earl seemed to sober as he talked about the business.

"It's only been three and a half or more years. I think we're doing okay," I said and began to laugh like I wasn't taking Earl seriously.

Mildly offended, Earl said, "Is talking business funny?"

I laughed more fully, from my belly, while Earl, in a soberer state, became unhappy with my attitude. "It's something, well, two things, now, that Gus said in the past. Remember the shyster lawyer, can't remember his name, who wanted Gus to help cheat a couple of youngsters out of their aunt's inheritance? Gus said, 'If he was my mouthpiece, I'd get new gums.'" I laughed hard with Earl breaking down along with me. "The other thing," I started to say between laughs, "Gus said, 'Whether you call money cabbage, spinach, or salad, money tastes better than vegetables.' I'd miss Gus, if he left to be a cop again. You don't think Joey would leave with him?"

"Nah, Joey likes the divorce business. He gets a vicarious thrill out of it."

"It's early and you're pulling out your college words. Vicarious, huh?"

He ignored me and went back to shop talk. "How do we increase repeat business from insurance companies and lawyers? Sure, an individual case now and then pays off. Private clients don't stay in Dutch and need us again and again."

I added, "How many divorces can the same people have based on infidelity?"

"Maybe more security work, like we did prewar for Pinkerton. They're big. They can lose a few clients and not come after us."

"Come after us?" I repeated and tapped the 15-shot Browning in the shoulder holster under my left suited arm.

He smiled. "Yeah, Harry, they'd come with guns blazing. I'm not talking mob work. We've stayed away from them."

"That was mostly your idea, Earl."

"If we stay shy of anything criminal..."

"Like, we find someone and they end up in concrete two days later kind-of-criminal?"

"Yeah. We need more publicity."

I responded, "It takes the private out of private eye."

Police detective Ted Matthews, a burly man with a matching head, walked in alone and straight toward us with a bad news scowl on his face. He was alone, so how bad could the news be? Maybe he was looking for a free drink or six, like most coppers. We had worked with him on a few cases. But his face didn't look right, like he had eaten bad fish.

Earl probably saw what I saw, but he didn't wait to hear whatever the lowdown was and offered, "Matthews, you look like you need a shot and a beer."

Matthews pushed his hat back on his forehead and said, "Whatever you're having."

He waited until he downed a shot and washed it with half a glass of beer, before he said, "Your partner, Joey A, was murdered about four hours ago."

Not looking surprised by anything was what we did for a living. This was something else. I didn't think I looked as shaken as Earl, so I spoke, "How'd it happen?"

"He was literally caught with his pants down, at the Oasis Motel out on Route 42. Was Noah Jameson a client?"

Earl recovered enough to handle the cop question. "Yeah. What do you mean by *was*?"

Matthews raised his mitt and signaled the bartender for another shot, knowing his drinks were on us. "After pumping one in Joey A's heart and one over his right eye, Jameson ate one, right in the yap."

When Earl commented, "Sounds like he was a good shot," Matthews looked perplexed before shrugging.

I asked an obvious question. "If Joey had his pants down, who was the dame and what happened to her?"

"Vera Jameson, the dope's wife. She's a looker. Redhead. Can't blame Joey A for jumping in the sack with her, though that's the opposite of why you guys are hired, right?"

Another cop question for Earl, who said, "Yeah, Jameson wanted to find out if his wife was up to no good."

"Did Joey A turn in a report and tell Jameson the truth or a lie?"

"I don't know. I'd have to check the files." Earl said.

Matthews sarcastically returned, "It's not the way you do business, is it? Tell a dope his wife isn't cheating and then blackmail her into bed?"

"Blackmail is a strong word, detective," Earl stated with a hard edge.

After downing a second shot, Matthews said, "How about taking money under false pretenses? Does that smooth your ruffled feathers?"

The conversation had turned adversarial. Earl and I had just talked about good publicity. This would be the opposite. Still, a major question remained unanswered. "What happened to the wife, this Vera Jameson? Joey had his pants down for a reason."

"Nothing, Harry. She's the eye witness. She told us the yarn. Why do lugs murder the other guy for screwing their dame, when it wouldn't have happened if the dame wasn't in the market for it?"

"Maybe, because its love and you can't kill what you love," Earl said. "How did you find us?"

"The door was locked, so I banged hard and a nice-looking dame named Addie told me you were most likely at Mo's."

Earl told the copper she was our bookkeeper and occasionally worked late. He didn't tell, though he might have guessed, that I had a crush on Addie. Not a thing I was ready to do anything about, because I was too much of a tough guy with an ugly mug for someone swell like her.

"Let's have another setup and drink to Joey A," the copper said, thinking he would milk us for a while longer.

I said, "Set us up, Mo. Beers and shots."

Detective Matthews said, "Come down to the central station on Fourth and give a statement tomorrow. Tell your other partner, Gus Reese, so I don't have to drive to his house. Maybe he's not home. Maybe he's out, going at it with a client's wife."

I didn't like that Joey had done what he did and ended up dead. I didn't like the cop calling Addie a dame. I didn't like Matthews' loose yap. I held up my hand for Mo to wait before serving the next round of drinks. "Listen Matthews, you've been an okay cop, up to a few minutes ago. We worked together a few times and you came out smelling like a rose, with a few extra bucks in your pocket. Cut the wise talk or you'll need a dentist and new teeth."

He held up his hands. "Easy, Harry. Earl will tell you that I'm only saying what the newspapers will be saying. Sort of preparing you."

Earl said, "We may not be the smartest, but we ain't the dumbest. Go ahead and sock him, Harry. I'll bail you out." After Matthews took two quick steps back, Earl said, "You retreat quick like the *dagos* we fought in the war. Harry isn't going to hit you, not yet."

The copper took another step backward before saying, "Keep your drinks. Bring the files you have on Jameson when you come in tomorrow. You don't want me getting a warrant and going through all your files. And tell Gus Reese."

"Gus won't be around for a few days. He's working out of town on a case. We'll tell him when we can."

"Listen, I'm sorry about Joey A. Only doing my job, boys." He turned his back to us and walked out of the place.

I waved for Mo to bring the three setups; we'd find a way to drink them and a few more.

"Was I too tough, Earl?"

"You're always too tough, Harry. It's part of your charm. He'll forget it the next time a few bucks come in his direction."

"How bad is this?"

"I know you're religious enough to know Christ was crucified on the cross. It's going to be something like that," Earl said.

Chapter 2.

Stopping at the office first, we found Carla, one of our two office girls, shedding tears for Joey. Addie didn't cry, though she was sad. I'd have given Carla my handkerchief if she wasn't using her own. I'd comfort Addie more, but she had never seen me be so familiar and might take it the wrong way. She'd be right about it and I'd be wrong to get too cozy with her.

The newshawks were laying for us at our offices and at the central station on Fourth. Earl and I lowered our hat brims, gave them blank hard looks, kept our yaps shut, and may have pushed a few aside with more force than was needed.

Detective Matthews was correct; the papers ripped us to shreds. Everything was made worse when we found little about the Jameson case in the files and showed up for our statements empty-handed.

Gus Reese hadn't heard, or he would have called the office. We guessed he was somewhere beyond the reach of the local rags. He would probably be most shaken by Joey's death. They were foot patrol cops together before the war. The coincidence of the four of us, from the same hometown, becoming friends, while we waited in England for the invasion of France, was discussed like it was several strokes of good lightning.

From what I remembered hearing, within a month from D-day, a million soldiers had landed in France. Even if the number was fudged to sound more impressive, the coincidence of our meeting led to Joey's death. That kind of thinking never led to anything positive. No, the redhead and the way Joey chased skirts caused his death.

We decided not to have our lawyer, Paul Burston, present at the police station. He wasn't much of a criminal lawyer. He handled our business affairs, not our personal ones. Besides, it wasn't like we hadn't been grilled by cops before. We didn't know anything about Joey and the client's wife. Burston would cost us money for nothing. We hoped we could repair our business reputation before we went broke.

By the time Earl and I returned to the office, we weren't in the mood to work or return any calls from newshawks or angry clients questioning our integrity.

Carla, a heavier young girl, going to night school to improve her secretarial skills, handled the receptionist duties. Besides being visually shaken by Joey's death, her day was above and beyond the call of duty. Addie gave her coffee and restroom breaks. I almost wondered if Carla and Joey had done a few things. More likely, she was upset because she was young and unaccustomed to one of her bosses being murdered. Inside I was feeling the way she was showing her feelings, but I had seen so much in the war I could fake not being affected by death.

Heroic guys that we were, Earl and I left our office girls to handle whatever would come up and went to Mo's. When you can't think straight, drinking doesn't help, though it seems like the best thing to do.

Mo's was nearly empty when we arrived a few minutes after three, too early for our after-work drinking pals. Immediately, Earl went to the pay phone to call the office we had left five minutes earlier. It made as much sense to me as everything else.

Our drinks were lined up by the time he returned. I waited, not wanting a head start. Once Earl was seated on a barstool we downed a bourbon and washed the coating down our throats with beer.

"I told Addie to send Carla home, lock the door, and join us for a drink. If we couldn't face the phone calls, why should they?"

Face the phone calls sounded both wrong and right. Didn't people believe in a period of mourning? I knew people only cared about how things affected them or what was in it for them, so I shouldn't have been surprised.

Though I wasn't making much sense to myself, Earl caught me off guard when he said, "Addie will be here in a few minutes. Anything going on between you two?"

"Where'd that come from?"

"Considering the circumstances…"

"How would that have anything to do with the circumstances? What makes you think something is going on?"

"Your stupid face always looks more stupid when you're around her or someone is talking about her."

"Nothing is going on. I like her, that's all."

"You like her?"

"Yeah, I *like* her. Drop it or I'll drop you like I would have dropped Matthews last night."

Earl closed one eye and looked at me strange with his open eye. "Sounds like more than *like* to me."

"I'm not going to do anything about it. Okay? She's too good for me." What I said cured the contortion of his eye like it made sense.

As best as I could remember, Addie had never been in Mo's when I was there. We had rules about drinking with our female help. We also had a rule about not bedding the wives of clients, which Joey obviously didn't heed. He'd be alive, if he'd obeyed the rule.

Joey Alfonso was handsome in a half-Italian way. His mother was Swedish, so that half gave him a light complexion and sandy hair. Despite his hair color, he had a resemblance to the matinee idol Tyrone Power. He was what people called a ladies' man, though those ladies ended up being dames by the time he was done with them.

But Joey wasn't especially lucky with dames. Maybe he was too flamboyant and complimentary. An obvious dame hound was an obvious dame hound.

I remembered the night we were drinking heavily and this swell-looking dame was having no part of Joey's charms. She was shining up to me and told me the secret of younger women: they didn't want the guy to be better looking than them. I ended up benefitting from what she said. Later that night, the swell-looking dame and I *went to town* and stayed in town for a couple of hours, and for a few times after that. I could only guess she found someone not as good-looking as she was, but better looking than me. Or maybe she wanted to visit different towns. Some dames are the same as some guys.

A sickening thought turned the taste of my beer slightly sour. I hoped Joey had never gone anywhere, let alone all the way, with Addie. I saw no signs of it, no special looks from either at the other. If Addie had gone all the way with Joey, then she wouldn't be too good for me. I wasn't exactly sure what a paradox was, but it sounded like one.

Since Earl was smarter with words, I asked him, "What's a paradox?"

With a quick strange look, like he had moments ago, he answered, "A contradiction, like something looks sweet but tastes sour."

I merely nodded, thinking it sounded about right for what I was thinking.

Addie walked in the door before Earl could delve into questioning what my question concerned. She looked slightly frazzled as she approached us. I liked the way her legs walked. She looked good coming or going, and even better staying.

"What are you guys having?"

"Bourbon and beer," I said.

"How about a respectable Scotch and fizz water?"

Mo had heard and seen Earl nod to him. I didn't like the ease with which she said it. I said, "Scotch?"

"An acquired taste after the war. Not much Scotch during the war. Can I sit down?"

I moved one barstool over, not liking her answer. Being too good a drinker made a woman a dame. Maybe Addie wasn't too good for me.

When she sat, her skirt rose up to expose her legs up to mid-calf. I liked the view but couldn't stare. Besides, I liked her face most of all. She looked smart and innocent, like she understood more than the way her face looked.

"Do the remaining partners have a plan, if only for tomorrow?"

Shaking his head, Earl said to Addie, "Not really. We need to survive this."

She took more than a sip and less than a gulp of the Scotch and fizz water, and then said, "There are five former clients you need to phone and convince that their spouses weren't cheating on them. It's funny or something. No one called to turn that question around the other way."

Addie was also too smart for me. "What do you mean?"

"A client suggesting their spouse wasn't really cheating on them."

Earl went directly to a tough point. "If we let Carla go, could you handle everything in the office?"

She said, "I could do the best I could do. Probably. Would I, is another question."

"Would you?" Earl asked.

"Should I, is yet another question. Earl, do you think the agency can survive this?"

"I don't know. We could change the agency name. It's not like we do much repeat business. Carla is going to leave us when she finishes night school, anyway."

Addie turned to me. "Harry, do you want me to stay on?"

I said, "I do," wondering if I would ever want to use those words again, say, in a church or to a justice of the peace. I also wondered if someone ever waited to say *I don't* after someone said *I do*. I'm sure it happened. Worse was when *I do* changed to *I don't want to anymore*. Hell, it was a good portion of our business.

Something different jumped into my head that I could say out loud. "How did Joey slip up? Joey wouldn't tell the husband she was cheating and then go cheat with her. Joey would lie and give the husband a clean report. How did this sap find out and show up with a gun?"

Earl said, "Good questions, Harry."

Addie looked at me like I was smarter than my mug looked. She said, "Against my better judgement, I'll stay, if only to find out how things turn out."

Chapter 3.

When Addie left Mo's after a second Scotch, I knew I would quickly grow tired of Earl. Yeah, he was my best friend and business partner, but sometimes he talked too much.

Gus Reese had once said, "Some guys don't know when to stop yapping. So, you get rid of them by sending them for new teeth." I had stolen several of his words when I threatened the copper, Matthews.

I would never do anything like that to Earl, but sometimes enough was enough, especially when he kept saying the same things only using different words.

Despite what happened to Joey, I had work to do the next day. So, I left Earl talking to Mo, who didn't have much to do but to pretend to listen.

The next morning I felt fine not having been a lush.

When Earl talked about the agency needing more repeat business, he wasn't talking about the work I did. I was plenty busy most of the time. My specialties, or as Earl explained, thanks to two years of college and having served in France, my *métier*, was loan collection and process serving, meaning the in person serving of summons, subpoenas, and other such legal documents.

At three bucks an hour, process serving was good dough, more than most saps made. How Earl knew the average income was about four grand a year, up a few hundred from the war years, I don't know, but I believed him. If I could serve legal documents two thousand hours a year, my income would be six grand, almost half again the average. Since I provided my own transportation and occasionally slipped a legal clerk five bucks or a bottle of hooch to keep the work coming, it was something a little less, but nothing to hiss at.

I dress neat, in a suit, like a businessman. That's not what makes me good at what I do. I'm nearly six feet tall, taller than most guys, and weigh one hundred and eighty pounds. Some of it is whiskey pounds, but most of it is muscle – I exercise with weights. Besides my size, I have a mug only a mother or a very drunk dame could like. Add in the boxer size of my mitts, and I'm not someone to ignore.

If that isn't enough, the hefty Browning I pack, with the butt often on display with my suit coat hanging open, completes the package.

On a rare occasion, a guy with enough dough would tell a driver or bodyguard to get rid of me, not wanting to accept the papers. That was always a mistake. The rich guy always ended up with the papers in his hand and his servant on the ground. Usually no one pressed charges, because what would it get anyone?

One time I went too far. After I sent the bodyguard down with a left hook and right cross, I tried to shove the papers in his boss's mouth. Well, it was open and saying things I didn't like. Charges were filed against me but quickly dropped when I paid that boss another visit. I simply sneered at him with my lips tight across my bare teeth. I learned that from Bogey in *The Maltese Falcon* in '41 before I enlisted to fight the Italians and Germans.

For a mug with few talents other than being a tough guy, being a private dick made sense.

My attitude and appearance worked well for collecting debts. Not loan-sharking debts, but what a trade construction company or a lawyer might need collected. The five percent fee sounded good, except, often the people simply didn't have the money. I didn't break arms or bust jaws – the money wasn't that good. I simply intimidated and could tell a liar from an honest guy.

My biggest payday was $500. Those opportunities were few and far between. In that case, I played the go-between to help settle an issue of shoddy work.

Joey, Gus, and Earl brought in bigger dough from time to time. My cash was steady and as regular as the sun rising in the east.

If worse came to worse and the agency went bankrupt, I wouldn't starve. My repeat clients would give me enough work to earn a living without an office or swell-looking help like Addie.

Of course, when the other partners needed a tough guy to help with their cases, they called on me. When our own clients didn't pay, Addie would call on me to collect.

My day moved along as I expected without a hitch until a guy named Pierson made it into the whorehouse before I could serve him a subpoena. Just because I didn't frequent whorehouses didn't mean I didn't know one when I saw one.

Sitting and waiting in my heap, a '46 four-door Buick, I guessed I had between a half hour and an hour to wait. An hour would impress me but not make me happy. My eyes were focused on the side alley door to the whorehouse, though my mind was thinking about Joey.

Joey had survived the war. He didn't survive the married red-haired dame. Her husband shot Joey twice, killing him twice from the description Matthews gave. The husband didn't kill the dame. Then the husband shot himself in the mouth, making even less sense.

The four of us survived the Normandy Invasion. We stayed together all the way to Berlin. No easy feat. We were luckier than many GIs. We made it back to the States alive and in one piece.

Before the war, Joey and Gus had been flatfoots, while I worked for Pinkerton with Earl Griggs. It seemed a natural development for the four of us to open Diamond Detective Agency. Thanks to movies and books, the allure of being private eyes sounded better than anything else. With the war being over, it seemed every other guy was looking to make big money and dames. We were no different.

The business grew enough that, by the fall of 1949, we had four subordinate operatives in the field and two females in the office, Addie and Carla.

The door opened and Pierson came out. Forty minutes was so-so. He had maybe ten steps to make it out from the alley, too narrow for car traffic, to reach the main street. I met him there and said, "Was it worth the money?"

His surprised face said, "Huh? What?"

"Are you Gaylord R. Pierson?"

Even more surprised he answered, "Yes. Who are…?"

I put the papers in his hand and said, "You've been served." While I tipped the brim of my hat, I said, "You've already had the best part of your day."

After signing out at City Hall to receive my receipts for billing, I headed back to the office. The guy's first name, Gaylord, kept bouncing around in my head like a song phrase you don't like.

Are we stuck with first names, last names, and often middle names or only a lonely middle initial, we don't like? Why do parents name new people after old people? Do they want the new person to be a copy of the old person?

I didn't mind Harry being the nickname for Harold. My first name always made me think of the Christmas carol: *Hark! The herald angels sing*. I knew the spelling was different, but the idea someone might think I was an angel and could sing tickled me.

My middle name meant nothing to me or to anyone else. Robert or Bob, what was the difference, if no one spoke it?

My last name was a problem my parents tried to solve by pronouncing *Hamm* as *Hum*, which created a different problem than pronouncing it *Ham*, like the meat. Nobody paid attention to my parent's pronunciation, so *Hamm* like the meat, was my moniker.

As a kid I took ribbing for being Harry Hamm, like 'hairy ham,' until my fists changed all of that. You don't pick on a kid with a right hand like a hammer and a left jab as fast and powerful as a cheetah.

When the war was simmering on the back burner, everyone became interested in what heritage everyone else had. I could never understand it. If you're born in the United States, why did heritage matter? Many people were too proud of being Greek, Italian, or Irish. I could see liking the food or adopting the religion of one's heritage, although preferring Irish food seemed on the dumb side of taste.

On opposite sides of the coming war, my heritage was half-German and half-English. Simple as that, with no little bit of this or that. My father changed German to Norse, like Vikings, leaving me to wonder about Viking food and religion.

When I joined the war, I was an American sent to kill Germans and Italians – that was my heritage.

Still, when someone first knew I was Harry Hamm, they looked at me crosswise until they looked closer at my mug and the mitts hanging from my arms. Earl said my hands looked dangerous. I never got that, but he wasn't the only one. Earl had seen them fly, so he knew what he was talking about.

When I reached the Grayson Building and took the stairs to our second floor offices, I was tired and hungry. Process serving wasn't manual labor and shouldn't be tiring, but it was.

The door was locked, probably to avoid unwanted visitors. Before I used my key I called out, "It's me, Harry. Anybody home?"

After the sound of the lock tumbling, the door opened and I saw Addie's sweet and somewhat solemn face saying, "Hi, Harry."

Earl must have heard me call out, because he came walking out of his office, looking not sweet and solemn.

"Before we talk about anything, let's get something to eat. I didn't eat lunch and I'm starving."

Though Earl offered Addie the seat in the middle between us, she climbed in the back of my heap. It would have been nice to have her so near me.

I drove past the Red Sky Diner. Since Gus Reese had said, "The food might have tasted better on clean plates," none of us ate there.

The 28th Street Chop House was too long a walk and a short drive. It didn't have a liquor license, so I ordered coffee, while Earl and Addie opted for ice water. They had the benefit of coffee during the work day and had enough. On the road serving legal documents, I missed drinking too much coffee.

Everyone chose the same meal: chopped sirloin with mushrooms and onions, mashed potatoes, and all of it smothered in beef gravy. The vegetable of the day was carrots. Okay as a vegetable went. At least I never heard anyone call money *carrots*.

"I made money today. How about you two?" I said happy to contribute to the agency coffers.

"I had a fun day," started Earl. "I fired Carla and our four field ops. I talked three of yesterday's complainers out of pursuing action against us."

"Action?" I repeated as a question.

"What did Matthews call it – dereliction of duty?"

"That was in the army, Earl. I think he said something about taking money under false pretenses."

"Regardless, they're not suing and they can't go to the papers. They wouldn't want everyone to know they had questioned their spouse's fidelity. The other two were more difficult, as if they were disappointed their spouse came out clean. We're giving them another investigation for free. Gus and I can handle them, when he gets back."

"So, we haven't heard from Gus?"

"It's only been two days," stated Earl.

"Seems longer," I chipped in. Looking at Addie, though not staring, I said, "And how was your day, precious?"

Before Addie could say anything, Earl commented to Addie, "He's doing his best Sam Spade impersonation."

"I saw the movie. Don't call me that, Harry. It sounds condescending."

"I see it the other way around, but okay."

Addie said, "Earl, tell him about Joey's father and brother, first, then what I have to say will make more sense."

"Sure. They stopped in. Joey's father's English is not so good. That's what he says about it. The brother, who looks more Italian than Joey, since he has black hair, wanted to know if they had any money coming from the business, since Joey was a partner."

"Earl gave them four hundred dollars."

"I was getting to that part, Addie. I told them it was a cash business and we'd probably be broke in two months, since what happened to Joey would be bad for business."

"Two months?" I repeated as a question.

"Four months," Addie said. "That's what I did today when I wasn't answering phone calls. There were fewer today."

Earl chimed in, "We're being forgotten as we speak. It's a good thing because of the Joey thing, but a bad thing for the future of our business."

"We should have listened to Addie about putting cash away for a rainy day."

Sheepishly, Addie said, "Well I did, without telling anyone. I sort of cooked the books. Not much. Like a medium rare."

"She's very clever, Harry."

Without thinking she was the one I *liked*, I said, "You weren't planning to embezzle the money, were you?"

"It would have to be more, a lot more, for me to consider that."

Moving on, Earl said, "Joey's wake is day after tomorrow. Funeral, the day after that. Four hundred dollars seemed okay to me. Like the right thing to do."

I said, "Wish Gus was back. I could use a good laugh."

Chapter 4.

After the generous portions of chopped sirloin filled us, we weren't in the mood for another night of liquor. One way or another, everyone was tired and went home.

The next morning I felt okay, not having had booze three nights in a row.

When I saw the morning paper, left outside my rooms at the Colton Arms, I needed a drink. The paper reported Noah Jameson had hired Crown Investigation, because he didn't believe Joey told him the truth about his wife, Vera.

Crown Investigation was a competitor with four times our manpower. They volunteered the information to the cops and the news rags. It made them look good and Diamond Detective Agency look bad. It made me think of when Gus said, "She would be a swell looker, without a head."

The rumor was Crown Investigation did work for the Baccanelli family, a local mob with juice and money. Like Earl had explained, mob money for legal investigating might lead to something illegal. We were too straight to go for such tainted money. Like a good-looking dame without a head, like Gus said.

Once in the office, Earl, Addie, and I chewed on the newspaper article like a bad breakfast made with rotten eggs.

Addie gave me a list of names, addresses, and phone numbers of clients who owed money. She suggested I get right to them before we went out of business or they might ignore what they owed. She said most of those words. I was too preoccupied looking at her. Normally she wore her hair up, looking very polished and untouchable. Today it was down to her shoulders, like the tawny mane of an exquisite palomino.

When my office door was open, I could see the front office door and Carla's desk. Since Addie had moved her work to Carla's desk, I had a side view of Addie. I didn't mind working phone collections.

It was half past eleven when a hard knock on the front door caught my attention. We were keeping the door locked to keep unwanted visitors out. The knock was simultaneous with the gruff words, "Police! Open up!"

Addie walked around Carla's desk to unlock and open the door. I was coming out of my office and Earl was coming out of his office to my left, when I saw Captain O'Brien enter before Detective Matthews. They had their cop faces on, so we waited for them to speak, to pay off the hard knock and loud demand.

Captain O'Brien, a bulky Irishman with a reddish nose, like most hard-drinking Irishmen, nodded toward Addie as he said, "We should take this private."

Earl responded, "She's on our team. Let's have it."

O'Brien didn't mince words. "A body was found in an alley behind a Bolivar Street warehouse early this morning. The wife had a hard time identifying the body. It was Gus Reese."

Addie reached for the desktop for support. I took her arm and walked her around to her chair. She sat and reached for a tissue.

With a soft apologetic voice, Matthews said, "Sorry about this. I thought I recognized Gus. He took a pasting. Didn't look much like himself. We brought in his wife and she confirmed."

My hand grasped the back of Addie's chair. I could feel her spine against my whitening fingers.

Earl may have looked cool about it, but I knew he was as shaken as Addie and I were. He could pull off the unemotional look better. He said, "What happened?"

Captain O'Brien had gone through this kind of thing too many times before. "They gave him a good working over. Cigarette burns, too. They left him in his skivvies and socks, like it was a robbery. He was shot three times: gut, chest, and head. Seems it took that many to do him in. Tough bird, I imagine."

Believing in coincidences was a crummy way not to believe in the truth. My first thought was how the murder was connected to Joey's murder. Maybe the gun was the same, but wouldn't the cops have Noah Jameson's gun?

"How is this connected to Joey A's murder? Was Gus Reese involved in the Jameson thing?" asked O'Brien.

Earl coolly said, "I don't know. You tell me, you're the copper."

O'Brien's face was spreading flush, like the red shade of his nose. Matthews saw it and intervened before too much bad talk was exchanged. "Earl, two of your guys went down in a few days. It makes us curious. You know, were they on the same case? Be reasonable; we're on your side."

The intervention by Matthews didn't cool O'Brien down. He said, "Was there only enough dough in the business for two of you?"

My hand left the chair and moved to within a swing of O'Brien. "Take that back. Take that back, right now. They were our partners and friends. We killed Germans together. You bought the story the wife told about Joey. How could that have anything to do with this? So, take it back."

"Matthews warned me about you, Hamm. Says you're a tough cookie. I ain't no choir boy. Throw your best punch. I'll take it and give you four back in return."

Earl stepped in and moved me back from the police captain. "We are on the same side, boys. You can't throw accusations around like that without some kind of idea where they're going. And Harry, you're not going to solve anything by mixing it up. The problem, as I see it, is it doesn't make any sense." After I moved back behind Addie, for the cop's safety, not mine, and O'Brien's face slowly went from red to pink, Earl continued, "Gus was working an insurance scam. He had nothing to do with Noah Jameson. I'm not criticizing, only pointing it out. Bolivar is a red-light district. We know people want things a little illegal and need a place to go. Better in one area than the neighborhoods where kids play."

Matthews never lost his composure. "Earl, was Gus into something he wasn't proud of?"

"No. Not Gus. I'm not saying some of us have things we don't tell anyone, but not Gus. Salt of the earth. Maybe it was someone he knew with a serious problem that he tried to fix. Gus would do that. But I don't know who or what. How about you, Harry?"

"Salt and pepper of the earth."

O'Brien turned to Matthews. "Is that guy always a wise mouth?"

"Most of the time. Harry is Harry. He can't help it. He don't mean much by it," his subordinate returned.

I nodded. "That's me. Sorry. I don't mean nothing by it. We lost two of our own, like a one-two punch in the gut. Can't expect us to pour tea and offer scones. We were in England together for a while before the Normandy Invasion."

"I don't like you, Hamm. That don't mean we can't work to solve this thing together. When you get a bright idea, give us a call." Captain O'Brien should have left it like that, but he had to take it further. "I better not find out you had anything to do with this."

As the coppers turned and left, Earl stood next to me, in case I needed a bear hug to keep me out of trouble, not to show friendship.

Joey was dead. Gus was dead. If they weren't connected and were merely coincidental, then goddamn bad luck, as bad as the maiden and only voyage of the Titanic, was hanging over us.

If they were connected it might be worse, though how? How could Earl or I be next in line? We knew nothing of what Joey and Gus were working on that would rise to the level of a face slap, let alone murder.

Could someone believe we knew something we didn't know?

What about Addie? Was her life in danger for the same reason? I wanted to fire her, with or without Earl's agreement, but I couldn't. She might be safer with us than on her own.

Then again, it could be coincidence. Joey's murder made some sense. Gus's murder made less sense. From what O'Brien said, he was tortured, shot, and stripped half naked. Who does that and why?

Gus was supposed to be out of town, catching someone faking an insurance injury claim. Gus acted like it was run-of-the-mill, not worthy of murder. Gus was the salt and pepper of the earth. I couldn't be that wrong about him. Could I?

Chapter 5.

As Earl entered my office and reached to close the door, I saw Addie's eyes watching him from what had been Carla's desk. Her wide-open eyes and half downturned mouth showed a hurt sadness, like we ask so much of her and then shut her out with a closed door.

"Wait," I said to Earl, who stopped in mid-door-close. I moved around my desk and walked past Earl, who moved out of my way, barely in time to avoid a collision. Going up to Addie, whose eyes and mouth retained the hurt look, I said, "Your work is caught up, isn't it? Why don't you go home and we'll start fresh in the morning?"

She nodded, then said, "There's the phone?"

"I'll handle it." I leaned forward and whispered, "Don't worry, I'll tell you everything. Earl's not himself."

With her eyes and mouth looking better, Addie said, "Okay. I trust you, Harry. I hope you tell me everything."

I waited for the thirty seconds it took for her to collect her things and leave. The whole time her words haunted me about telling her everything. I wondered if she knew how I felt about her and was waiting for me to say something.

My nod and smile were no match for her nod and smile before she unlocked, opened, and walked through the door. I locked the door behind her.

"What was that about?" Earl asked.

I moved behind my desk and pulled out a bottle of bourbon and two glasses before saying, "She's one of us, Earl. You can't shut her out."

He left the door open and sat down on the chair in front of my desk. "Is that your *liking her* doing the yapping?"

As I poured the bourbon, I said, "I'm in love with her, if that works better for you. And it's not about that. It's about her being a partner."

"Since when?"

"Since Joey and Gus died and you became a jerk," I finished by taking a slug of bourbon.

He thought for a moment, took a slug himself, and said afterwards, "You're right about that. Besides, she's smarter than you are."

"You proved everything I said. Now, what's on your mind that you wanted to close the door on her?"

"That was by habit. Sorry. I have a plan."

"To solve Gus's murder?"

"Not that. I mean for us and the business. I've hired Tommy Carter back on an hourly basis to help me finish Gus's insurance claim case and help reinvestigate those two fidelity ones. He's our best photographer and develops his own photos."

Two years earlier we plucked Tommy Carter after he graduated high school. Someone knew someone. As a matter of fact, I think it was Earl. He wasn't old enough to drink anything above 3.2 beer, a stupid law passed in '35, when Prohibition was repealed. I could testify that, from the time I was 18 until I was 21, getting drunk was more about quantity than percentage of alcohol.

"We'll pay him two bucks an hour."

"A day ago, we paid him a buck fifty."

"I know this sounds strange, but he out-negotiated me. Once Tommy and I close those cases, I'm leaving for the West Coast to start a new agency. The Diamond Detective Agency is doomed in this burg. You keep doing what you're doing and collect what you can. Addie can close up the books, whatever that takes. Our lawyer, Burston, will tell you the legal ins and outs. I'll send you my new address. If anything is left for me, send it. If you and Addie become something and want to figure out how to make this a viable business..." He shrugged. "If not, come out to the West Coast and join me."

After finishing the bourbon in my glass, I poured more. "We're not going to do anything about Joey and Gus?"

Earl poured more for himself. "What? Joey is a closed case. Gus...I wouldn't know where to start. What would it get us? Maybe what Gus got."

Now I was hurt and sad. Depressed was a better description. "I know you're right about this, Earl. I knew of the possibility of us failing, but not like this."

"We should go see Gus's widow tomorrow before Joey's wake. Hell, we'll be going to wakes and funerals for days. I don't know how long it will take me to wrap things up and leave."

I nodded with growing depression. "I have some money saved, if you need it."

He read my mood, when he said, "If you want me to stay with you until the bitter end, I will." He paused for a quick nip. "I've saved enough money. I didn't spend as much as Joey on clothes, a car, and dames. Or you, drinking and chasing dames. Though I might guess those days will be over, if Addie and you… A piece of best-friend advice: don't start anything with her unless you mean it. You'd hate yourself if you did wrong by her."

"You're right about that. Believe me, it's the reason I haven't started anything with her. And by the way, I never chased dames."

He drank. A touch of bourbon was on his lips when he said, "I could never understand it. Good-looking Joey had to work his balls off to get his balls off. You, dames literarily fell into your lap. Harry, you know you're not good-looking, but you are tough. I guess some dames go for tough."

"This one broad, who chose me over Joey, told me the secret. Women don't like guys better-looking than them. Who is less good-looking than me?"

We laughed on a day when we thought it would be impossible to laugh. Two best friends staring into the possibility of being separated by a couple of thousand miles. We would drink until the bottle was empty. Maybe find something else to laugh about. Maybe we'd go to Mo's to continue until we were done for the day.

Earl was right. Whether Addie and I had a future together or not, I couldn't start anything unless I was committed to a future with her, if it miraculously did work out. If it worked out, I would only visit Earl on the West Coast. It was a long West Coast. I wondered, though it didn't really matter, where on the West Coast?

Addie and I had family and friends in the Cleveland area, though my best friend wouldn't be around. I'd end up a regular Joe with Addie, a brood of kids, and a mortgage. With everything recently happening, it sounded like a good deal.

Process serving and legitimate collections might turn into a self-sustaining business. If I could find a few mugs like me, who had some smarts to go along with tough, I could pay them two bucks an hour and pocket a buck for the business. Addie could figure it out. It dawned on me that Addie was the perfect name for a bookkeeper.

Could something good for me for life come from something bad, as in dead, for Joey and Gus?

Of course, the Titanic-sized assumption was that Addie would go for me once she really knew me. I wondered if falling for someone involved falling on one's noggin.

After drinking about as much as I could drink with Earl, I drove the ten minutes it took to get to my rented rooms in the Colton Arms, hoping it only took ten minutes.

I thought about Addie. My drunk idea was to show up at her apartment and ask her to marry me. For all practical purposes, I would be out of work soon, but had prospects. Maybe together we could figure out how to earn a living.

We hadn't kissed or even went out on a date. It would be a bad idea for her and a drunken idea for me. Think something, drink something, and you change your mind. It's why booze is called booze.

I remembered being in a foxhole waiting for dawn and the inevitable charge forward, when a Sergeant named Ames advised me to test drive the car before marrying it. He said it just like that. Six hour later Sgt. Ames was dead, though his advice lived on in me.

Once inside my apartment. I wondered if someone had test-driven Addie and decided not to marry her. Maybe more than one guy. She didn't seem the type, but most women didn't seem the type, yet I assumed most of them, if they were of legal age and single, had been test-driven. Since returning from the war, it seemed women were easier and most of the available ones were bedding down with guys. I had no real proof, but there were a lot of dames leaving bars with guys they weren't married to, although I had never seen or heard of Addie doing that.

Having reached my apartment safely, regardless of actual driving time, I poured another bourbon instead of slapping together something to eat.

What if it didn't work with Addie?

The West Coast was a long coastline from cold weather to hot weather and every degree between. Earl hadn't been specific about location. In hot weather, where does a private detective carry his gun? Under an untucked shirt in a belt holster sounded logical. I was so drunk I decided everything I thought was logical.

I made a decision. I would make it work with Addie. I didn't want to wear a gun clipped to a belt under an untucked shirt. Even more than that, I didn't want to be a private eye anymore. It was never like I imagined it, or Bogey portrayed it.

Chapter 6.

I was too hungover to drive, so naturally I drove, and picked up Earl. Since he looked like how I felt, whoever drove wouldn't have made an anthill of a difference.

On the way to Gus's house, we found the Euclid Diner. We hadn't known it existed, let alone ever eaten there. Quantity was more important than quality. Besides, it was almost impossible to make a bad breakfast. We ate what we could stomach.

Back in my car, we didn't speak much. Maybe we were afraid words would bring up our recently consumed breakfasts.

I did say, "You have the check for $400?"

"Yeah, I told you earlier. I feel better, though I want to sleep."

"Me, too. Why do we drink so much knowing how rotten we'll feel in the morning?" Earl asked.

"Because we're dumb as a box of rocks."

"Yeah, that's right."

Gus Reese's house was pre-fab, increasingly popular after the war. Many people were marrying and having kids. Homes were in short supply, leading to simple and standard styles, similar to an auto assembly line. They came in colors, though primarily in shades of white or tan. If you took away varying landscaping, they looked the same. To my surprise, I thought I saw a pink one, but realized my bloodshot eyes may have tinted my vision.

The street had a gravel berm instead of a curb. We parked two houses down. Unless you knew better, you might think there was a party at Gus's house, for all of the heaps parked near it.

Four kids were running around near the house and three men were smoking in the front yard in the warm September weather, which was nevertheless not Indian summer. The older man of the group sat on wooden front steps with what I knew as an apple style pipe. As we approached, I realized his gray full beard was white-and-black speckled, and appeared longer than most men wore.

The men eyed our approach like we might be cops. It was the way they looked at us in our suits and hats with maybe a visible bulge under our left arms.

Being more social than I was, Earl always started a conversation. "Hi. He's Harry and I'm Earl, partners and friends of Gus."

The two younger men's eyes eased out of their hard looks. The older guy sitting on the steps kept his gaze focused and unblinking. He spoke. "I'm Dorothy's father, Arthur. They're my sons and her brothers, Warren and Colin."

Nods were exchanged. A half-dozen handshakes would have been awkward and confusing.

"We came to pay our respects and see your daughter," Earl said.

"With the help of pills, she's finally sleeping." As we nodded with understanding, he was wise enough to see we wanted to have a private conversation. "Boys, why don't you go around back and let me have a talk with these gentlemen?"

Once they were walking away, Earl began right off. "We'd like to ask you a few questions, Arthur. May we smoke?"

He tipped his pipe toward us. As we went about lighting up, Arthur said, "What does my daughter have coming from Gus's business? He didn't have life insurance."

With meekness I rarely saw in Earl, he said as he held out the envelope with the $400 check, "I'm afraid this is it. It's actually a little extra… Sorry there isn't more."

The old man looked inside the envelope, heaved a sigh, and said, "That's it, after four years. Shame. Dorothy and the children are coming to live with my wife and me. I took care of her before, I'll take care of them now. Maybe she can break even on the house." His sadness deepened with each word.

"We were still a new business. After this, the publicity of this and Joey A's murder, the agency won't survive, so there won't be anything else for her later. Do you know about our other partner's death?"

"Yes. Are they connected? Were you boys doing something you shouldn't?" With a sharp edge, he added, "Were you being reckless with my son-in-law's life?"

Earl continued to speak for both of us. "We're legitimate, straight down the line. We don't see how they are connected. The cops see it the same."

Arthur scratched the wood of a front step and the head of a wooden match sparkled before it burst into flame. He held it to the pipe bowl and pulled on the mouthpiece until pipe smoke billowed. I didn't know pipe smoke, though I liked the sweet nutty odor of his tobacco.

Pipe working again, Arthur said, "Didn't like this whole private detective business. Neither did Dorothy. Gus survived the war. Do you know how hard life was for her and the children, while he was gone? The police department would have welcomed him back. He was a hero. He'd have been promoted by now. If it's anything like the movies, and I can only imagine its worse, it was not a livelihood for a married man. It doesn't seem like much of a livelihood for any man. You're responsible. You were his friends."

"Yes, sir. We know that. We're sorry. We'd like to find who did this to him," Earl said and surprised me, since we had no intention of looking into Gus's murder.

"What they did to him." Tears filled the roundness of the old man's eyes. "Did you see him?"

"Yes sir." Earl lied. "That's why we're going to do something. Can I ask you a few questions?"

"Sure. Don't know how I can help, but sure. I'll tell you this, he had promised Dorothy he'd go back to the police force. Then he postponed it, telling her something good might happen. He didn't tell her what."

My hungover eyebrows rose, and maybe my ears did, too.

"Pardon this next question, but I have to ask. Do you know of anything Gus may have been doing that he shouldn't have been doing? Like a secret bad habit?" Earl asked.

"That is an offensive question. Other than being a private detective and sometimes drinking too much with you boys, Gus was a family man."

"Drugs or women?"

"Hell no. You knew him."

Earl continued, "Could he have been helping someone with a drug, money, or woman problem?"

"You were his only friends. You and the other dead one. He should have been a better friend to my sons. All we heard was Earl, Harry, and Joey." He focused in on me. "Harry Hamm. Queer name. You look like a prizefighter. He said you were the toughest mug he ever knew." He paused before turning off me to say, "Gus was a funny guy. He liked to make people laugh. He may have acted like he didn't know he was being funny. He knew."

It was not in my character or style, but I said, "We loved Gus."

"Arthur, did Gus say anything recently about Joey?"

"No. He mostly talked about Harry."

"When do you think would be a good time to ask your daughter a few questions?" asked Earl.

He tugged on the pipe's mouthpiece long and a billowy cloud of pipe smoke drifted upward, before he said, "Probably never. I'll give you my address. Sometime after the funeral. You boys should get out of that business."

Back on the road with Arthur's address tucked in my vest pocket, I said to Earl, "Thought we weren't going to do anything about Gus's murder, and leave it to the cops?"

"We aren't. How could I say we weren't? Nice old guy. Straight. That thing about Gus postponing going back to the cops, because something good may happen. Wonder what that was about?"

"Let's have a couple before we go to Joey's wake. They will probably have good *dago* food there," I suggested, while also wondering what something good meant and if Gus was murdered because of it.

We sipped only beer, not wanting to come a mile close to drinking too much. We talked about the future and Earl going to the West Coast, not wanting to talk about the past and what happened to Gus and Joey. Earl had no idea where on the West Coast. I mentioned warm weather and where a guy could pack his iron. He said maybe San Francisco. It was cooler most of the time. Bogey's Sam Spade's office was in San Francisco.

When the doors of the funeral home opened, we were among the first inside. We wanted to pay our respects and get out before any hot-blooded types might accuse us of anything. We had been on the defensive for days, and nothing had happened to change that.

The coffin was open. I stared at Joey's face and the good job the undertaker had done with the bullet hole an eighth of an inch above his right eye. I expected to be sad, not the anger I felt. I was angry with Joey. Yeah, he played it dumb over a dame. Most pictures in the newspapers made people look worse, guilty of something. Vera Jameson didn't look like a dame to die for.

A long time ago, when I was a youngster and should have looked my best, like younger people do, I realized looks weren't important. How else could I look in the mirror at myself while I shaved? At least I could fight for my face, if someone found it funny enough to laugh at.

A less long time ago, I realized a dame's better looks didn't mean she was better at anything. I never needed or would fight over the best-looking dame in a joint. The fourth best-looking dame was enjoyable enough for me, and probably from how guys talked about the beauties, a better time between the sheets. Maybe not being handsome, or even within ten miles of it, wasn't a curse but a blessing.

I thought Addie was a beauty, but dammit I was in love with her. Maybe other guys didn't see her the way I did. I hoped they didn't. Maybe beauty is in the eye of the beholder. I hoped so. I hoped Addie's vision of me was along that line of thinking.

Joey's relatives were friendly, at least the men. The women were more the wailing types. No one came close to accusing Earl or me of anything. Everyone knew how Joey was.

After good *dago* food and a few sips from the many flasks guys carried in their pockets, we had consumed most of the work day. We didn't see Addie or any of our former employees, though Tommy Carter was back on the payroll. We guessed they might be coming later to say goodbye to Joey.

Whether we continued to drink, maybe at Mo's Bar, was a coin flip. It was the end of most people's work week. For private dicks, work weeks were often irregular. Mo's would be busy. The guys at Mo's knew Gus and Joey and would want to toast them repeatedly. Thinking about Joey's funeral on Saturday, Gus's wake on Sunday and funeral on Monday exhausted me. Thinking of hard work to come was as tiring as doing the hard work. Wakes and funerals of friends were hard work. Besides, the flasks at Joey's only postponed the hard work of recovering from a hangover.

Earl must have felt the same way, because he asked me to drop him off, since there were hard days ahead.

I was nearly at my apartment, when a thought struck me. Was Addie at work, alone? I hadn't spoken to her since the way she left the previous day. I had promised to tell her what was going on with Earl and the attempted closed door.

There was something else. She was alone. I worried about her safety. We still had no idea why Gus was murdered. Could that *something good* he was hoping for have anything to do with the agency?

As tired as one of those dogs pulling a sled at the end of a long race, I drove to our offices.

Chapter 7.

What a stupid move! How tired was I? I had seen the lights on through the frosty glass, so I'd called out, "It's only Harry. I'll use my key." If anyone was in our offices who shouldn't be, I had alerted them to my presence.

My hand was already on the butt of my Browning, when I heard, "Okay." Such a small quick word. I believed it was a female voice, though less sure it was Addie.

It didn't help and may have disappointed what Addie thought of me, but I called through the door, "Who's in there?"

I heard back, "Harry, it's me, Addie," who by then had come to the door and unlocked it.

Her hair was up and she wore a black suit with a white frilly blouse underneath it. The suit was maybe old, though looked new from her not wearing it, because it was tight and showed off her figure. I had never seen her wear it to the office, so I made those instant assumptions. Regardless, I liked the way she looked in it.

For some reason she didn't seem happy to see me. She was dressed to go to a wake. I guessed my not calling her about the wake and what Earl closed her out of had something to do with her attitude.

The door was closed and locked. She sat back down behind the desk, while I sat on a corner of the desk, too tired to stand for any length of time. I said, "Why are you here?"

"I work here. Why haven't you called me?"

"I don't know."

"Are you taking me to Joey's wake? Were you there already with Earl? What's going on, Harry? You said you would tell me everything."

I didn't know where to start or what to say, so I did the first thing that came to my mind. I stood, took a step, took her face between the palms of my hands, and kissed her softly and kept my lips on hers.

When I moved two inches away from her lips, I watched them say, "That was nice, Harry. I liked it very much. But, it's not an explanation."

"So, you want an explanation."

"After another kiss, please."

The next kiss had more force to it. It wasn't from me, it was from her. I joined her enthusiasm, which bordered on passion.

My left hand was about to reach and feel what her suit jacket nicely showed off, when I thought better and pulled away from her. I moved back to sitting on the corner of the desk. Her eyes almost seemed to be inside mine.

"I want you to take me to Joey's wake. I'm guessing you've already been there with Earl. I'm also guessing you never kissed Earl like that."

I smiled and laughed. "No, not like that."

When I climbed into my car, after I had held the door open for her, she scooted to the middle next to me, like we were a couple. My tiredness found reserve energy I didn't know I had.

We seemed to be stumped about talking about what just happened. She went to business, a safer topic, rather than what we should be talking about. "Noah Jameson had paid a $100 retainer. Joey told me to send out a bill for another $300. It was never paid. Do you think you should get the wife to pay it? I know it sounds inappropriate for several different reasons. But I suspect she came into some money. He was an accountant. They make a lot more than bookkeepers like me. It takes you one hundred hours, not counting travel expense, to make $300 process serving."

"I could try to collect. No skin off my nose. I want to see what this dame really looks like anyway. You know newspaper pictures."

"Maybe you shouldn't. Maybe she can cast a spell on a guy."

"Like you?"

"Like me?"

"Yeah, like the spell I'm under right now."

Her giggle was a female giggle like I had never heard from her. I liked it. She said after it, "I don't know what to do, Harry. I want you to kiss me more. I'm not afraid of where that will lead, which makes me very afraid. I'm talking silly, like a woman."

"Silly isn't the right word. It's more like something a guy wants to hear."

"Are we going too fast?"

I nodded toward the speedometer. "I'm going the speed limit."

"Too bad."

I pulled to an open parking spot against the curb. The city street was busy with vehicles and with people walking on the sidewalk. I didn't care. I moved and kissed her. Kept kissing her. My left hand felt what I wanted to feel and what she wanted me to feel.

After I don't know how many minutes, someone, a guy, tapped on the window and said, "Get a room."

It broke the spell or I don't know how far we would have gone with the world watching. I said to Addie, "I have rooms. Two bedrooms, a kitchen, living room, and a bath – at a good price."

"Do you rent it out, say for a night?"

That cut it. I was more serious than angry when I said, "I don't want us like that. A night. I have other plans for you that take longer than a night. I don't want this to be like that, cheap and quick."

"Christ, Harry, you could make a girl fall in love with you by talking like that."

"Yeah, when you're in love with me, because I'm already in love with you. When you're in love with me, and not one night sooner."

"I like you half-angry and chivalrous. I'll let you know when I love you like you want me to. Until then, kiss me a few more times."

We made it through the wake without kissing. Tommy Carter and the three guys we'd let go were there. There didn't seem to be any bad blood over them losing their jobs. They were smart enough to know the agency had no future for them, so they might as well move on to a job that did.

Not seeing Carla didn't mean she hadn't been there. I checked the guest registry out of mild curiosity. She had been there. From the number of names before her name and the number after her name, I guessed she had been there after Earl and I left and left before Addie and I arrived. It was a small piece of detective work solving an even smaller question.

Addie and I didn't hold hands and I didn't put my arm around her waist, though she seemed to be touching my arm or back, places she had never touched me. I'd say we looked like a couple who had only begun to date. Truth was, our first date was Joey's wake.

As we walked to my car, a distance away, since the funeral home was packed with sympathizers, Addie's arm hooked around mine and then we were holding hands as natural as could be. Her grip was firm though her hand was soft.

Inside my car, I looked around. I don't know why. I wasn't shy about being with Addie. I kissed her. Her tongue found its way to my tongue. She had been kissed before and knew what she was doing. I made myself a promise never to ask her who taught her how to kiss. On the contrary, I wanted to thank the guy. I would never ask her about anything that may have happened with men before me. I wasn't proud or shameful about what I had done. What happens before love doesn't matter, as long as it's over.

No matter how you may want to change the past, it's dead-headed to think you can. *From here on* was my way of living. What's good for me was good for Addie.

During the drive, I told Addie everything that had happened since she walked out of the office the previous evening. She echoed our curiosity about Gus's father-in-law telling us Gus thought *something good* might happen.

When she said, "The other side of something good is something bad. Since something bad happened to Gus, we should find out what the opposite of that could have been," I was glad love had nothing to do with brains or Addie would be with Earl and not me.

She told me where she left her car, so I pulled up behind it and said, "I'm following you to your apartment and then I'm going home. I have this gut feeling we should be careful."

"Do you mean what's going on between us?"

"No. Well yes. I mean Gus and a good thing turning bad."

I knew she heard me and understood, yet she said, "We could reverse things and I could follow you to your place."

"You're not supposed to say what the guy says. You're supposed to say you're not that kind of dame."

She did the giggle again as she said, "I'm not. But I might be that kind of dame for you."

When she put her hand, all grip and softness, on my thigh, I reached down and moved it away saying, "And we'll have none of that." I guess they call it a pregnant pause, what I did. The implications didn't escape me, yet I said, "Not yet."

Her giggle lost its high pitch and came more from her throat. I liked it and was afraid of it at the same time.

"Are you taking me to Joey's funeral tomorrow?"

"No. I'm going to pay a visit to Vera Jameson in the morning. See if I can squeeze something out of her. I'll meet you at the funeral."

She floored me when she said, "Just don't squeeze anything into her." Her language lost its naughtiness, and she added, "She got Joey killed. Be careful, Harry."

After more kissing and a million reasons not to stop, I playfully pushed her away. I watched her walk to her car. The tightness of her black suit and the sway of her bottom left me feeling foolish we weren't spending the night together.

After she parked at her apartment building, I shooed her away from coming back to my car. One more kiss would have tipped me over the edge. I watched her enter the building. I drove off, had a bad feeling, and drove back to the building. In the vestibule, I pushed her apartment buzzer.

The cracked sound through the speaker said *yes* in a fearful yet maybe hopeful way. I said, "Just making sure you're okay. Goodnight."

Inside the crackling noise, I heard her say, "Goodnight, Harry."

Didn't I hear somewhere that most car accidents happen close to home? I fought my exhaustion. Opening my eyes as wide as possible, I made it to a final stop and turned off the engine. It had been a long time, since after a war battle, when I felt that kind of relief.

Inside my apartment, I shed my clothes, leaving them lie where they fell. Wearing only undershorts, I poured two fingers of bourbon and drank it straight down, figuring it would stop me from touching myself while I thought of Addie.

Half falling and half sliding, I was in my bed. The bourbon worked.

Chapter 8.

The next morning, before a shave and shower, I put on a shirt, trousers, and a coat and walked down to street level and around the corner for breakfast. My hangover was gone, barely a memory. I'd forget to remember the awful feeling when I headed to my next hangover. Addie might affect my way of thinking. Perhaps fewer hangovers were in my future. Besides, not feeling the effects of a hangover on the second morning was barely an accomplishment.

I had awakened hungry and feeling good. Sure, everything was wrong, but Addie was right – I could feel it under my skin. Sure, my buddies from the war and my best friend since before the war would soon be out of my life. Two couldn't help it – they were out of their own lives. My best pal would be somewhere along the West Coast, maybe someplace like San Francisco, where jackets were often needed.

Dipping bread into a broken egg yolk was my favorite part of breakfast. I felt better and better. I had a reputation for drinking and handling hangovers. Not that it made me proud. Practice makes near perfect, or something like that. Addie surely wouldn't appreciate such a dubious distinction of 'good at handling hangovers.'

Something told me that what seemed important before Addie would become insignificant. Not that that was necessarily smart. I was a lovesick sap thinking life was fresh and rosy, despite the bad business of murders and being a partner in a business a few months from bankruptcy. I didn't mind a bit or worry how naïve I was.

Any worry about Addie leaving for another job, leaving me alone to handle the ending of the business, was gone. She'd stick with me. She'd do whatever our lawyer, Burston, said was necessary to wrap up the Diamond Detective Agency in a ribbon and toss it on a bonfire. What came after that, out of the ashes, would be simple and steady, like process serving and debt collection, and rank second to Addie. She had me going like that, like a teenager who had his first kiss and touched his first boob. I liked the feeling of washing away the grime a guy collects from being careless with women.

I walked back to my rooms wishing the sergeant hadn't told me about test-driving a woman before buying into a permanent commitment.

If I had my way, I'd collect some money from Vera Jameson, go to Joey's funeral, where I would meet up with Addie, and we would drive to where marriage was as simple as a justice of the peace. Everything from the previous night told me the car in my story would run as fine as it looked and kissed.

After a shave, shower, and a fresh suit, I felt even better. Thinking about Addie had lollygagged me through the early morning. Now I needed to hightail it out to where Vera Jameson lived without a husband. A wife was responsible for her dead husband's debts regardless of how the death occurred.

When guys jump off a ten-story building or put a gun in their mouth, did they realize the mess they would leave behind, beyond the blood? Did they realize who had to clean up what? To top it off, life insurance didn't pay off on suicides. Didn't everyone know that?

I had never been to the well-off burg twenty minutes outside of the Cleveland city limits where the Jameson house was located. A quick look at a map was all I needed for directions.

I had heard Noah Jameson was an accountant, which I knew meant money and taxes. Making money was one thing, paying as little tax on that money as possible was something else, something I didn't understand and never wanted to understand. Somewhere I had heard words like adjusted income, deductions, depreciation, progressive tax rates, deferred something or other. Remembering the words was bad enough without remembering what they meant and how it boiled down, like a chicken reused to make soup over and over. It boiled down to forking over cash to the government, and not just one government. Too many governments seemed like a bad hangover, without the fun of the booze that caused it.

From the little I knew, most accountants earned a fee to tell whatever government, in the way it wanted to be told, how much could be squeezed out of a taxpayer – not unlike a stool pigeon. The good ones deciphered the rules and used them to benefit the taxpayer. The shady ones simply lied. What kind had Noah Jameson been? From the reputation of the location of his house, he appeared to be one of the ones who made money manipulating other people's money and taxes.

Accountants and taxes were near the bottom of what I wanted to think about. I needed to keep it simple. If someone saves someone a buck, they've earned a dime. Ten dimes added up to a dollar and so on. Simple. Then I reminded myself Addie had the perfect name for someone working with numbers. How could such boring, headache-inducing work result in someone as exciting and alive as Addie? I was obviously head-over-heels in love with her and no longer playing coy with myself about it.

If I was going to collect a bag of dimes from Vera Jameson, I needed to put my mind on being a debt collector.

Good-looking Joey didn't look so good-looking in the newspaper. That was no surprise to me. Vera looked okay in the newspaper. In a macabre way, I wanted to see what Vera Jameson looked like, in real life, in the flesh. Did she look good enough for Joey to betray himself and his partners? Was she worthy enough to inspire jealousy, rage, and murder?

I knew looks weren't everything and I wasn't a prude. Sex often was everything to many guys. Some guys might choose to pay for it. A few guys had no choice and ended up murdering or being murdered because of it.

Joey being caught with his pants down told me Vera Jameson had more than sex appeal, she delivered on it. I wasn't heeding Addie's advice. I was becoming obsessed with seeing this woman and speaking with her. I told myself I was too far gone over Addie to be susceptible to Vera's charms, yet I imagined a few dames existed who could get a lug's trousers to his ankles without him having a conscious thought to stop them.

The drive to the Jameson house was too long and gave me too much time to obsess. How many feet away from her was a safe distance to keep my pants up?

The houses were wide and long, the front lawns large and green. No cars were parked on the street. So, this was the way people with real dough lived. Noah Jameson must have been good at what he did.

Swell houses didn't mean bad things didn't happen inside them.

Then again, Joey's murder didn't happen in the Jameson house. It happened in a motel out on Route 42. In keeping with their reputation of having mob connections, Crown Investigation had fingered Joey for Noah

Jameson. They would never admit to any liability, and probably had no idea Noah Jameson would go off his rocker and murder Joey and then kill himself.

The Jameson house fit in with the neighborhood. Any domicile with a two-car garage, like the Jameson's, meant someone had money. Most people were lucky to have a one-car garage.

As for my situation, I parked on the street in front of the Colton Arms when a spot was available, and not in the tight parking lot, thinking it would be easier to make a quick getaway. The fantasy of being a private eye hadn't been totally erased by reality.

Being only one story high, they would call the Jameson house a ranch, though it wasn't a ranch to me if it didn't have horses and cows.

From the outside, it looked like no one was home. Whether Vera Jameson paid the debt her husband owed or not, at least I wanted to get a look at the dame.

After I parked in the wide driveway, I walked to the front door and rang the bell. I could hear it ringing through the front door. Looking around, I saw no folded newspapers lying around.

I waited for a couple of minutes before ringing the bell again and adding four knocks on the door. I peeked through the small high door window and saw only dark. The house seemed to be locked up tight like a barrel of crude oil.

On my way back to the car, I went to the mailbox on a pole in the grass between the sidewalk and curb. Looking at someone's mail without opening it or taking it wasn't a crime. The mailbox was empty.

Several good reasons existed for there not to be newspapers and mail. Perhaps they didn't have a newspaper delivered and recently received no mail. Perhaps a neighbor was holding the newspapers and mail, because Vera Jameson was away and out of town.

The police had announced the murder and suicide as closed cases. With no chance of new news, reporters wouldn't be hounding Vera Jameson. There would be no reason for the police to tell her not to leave town.

It wouldn't look good if she went on a vacation, though understandable if she went to stay with relatives. The odds of collecting any of the debt or satisfying my curiosity about the dame were looking more like a long shot that would never pay off.

I had made the drive and wasted considerable time thinking about her and her accountant husband, so I decided to go back to the front door and try one more time. I rang the bell and knocked. Nothing.

On an impulse, I took hold of the door knob and turned it. The door wasn't locked. Suddenly, I sensed danger. I pulled the Browning from my shoulder holster and pushed the door open. Before I entered, the light from the doorway illuminated the foyer and much of the living room. The house had been ransacked.

Every sense I had was on alert as I stepped into the house. In one hand I held my revolver and in the other was a handkerchief in case I needed to touch something.

What I saw led me to the conclusion that this wasn't vandalism or a simple robbery. Sections of walls were axed open. Someone was looking for something well-hidden.

The sofa and chairs had been ripped open. Cupboards were empty, with their contents littering the floor. The refrigerator was left open and empty; its contents dumped out. I wondered how cold the items were until I saw a carton of ice cream open and on its side with the ice cream in a watery pool on the floor. Whatever happened had been hours ago.

The bedroom was strewn with men's and women's clothes. Empty closets and drawers stood open like sad sentinels to heaps of disrespected clothes. I was sure Vera Jameson wouldn't toss around her clothes and leave her undergarments on the floor.

Throughout the house, everything that had been inside something was on a floor.

The only thing I didn't see was Vera Jameson in the flesh. I stared at a better photo of her than was in the newspaper. She was a good-looking dame. I considered taking the photo in case I needed it for something in the future, though I didn't know what. The cops would make something out of a photo missing from a photo frame. I'd remember her without a photo handy. Her looks were swell. The something in her eyes and smile was something more alluring than a newspaper picture.

Back in the living room, I looked at the phone sitting in its cradle on an end table. Since neighbors had probably seen me and my Buick, I needed to call the cops or risk being considered a suspect – perhaps even for the abduction of Vera Jameson. Using the phone could be risky if someone was tapping the line. I would give my name, when I reported the crime. How interested would someone be to know Harry Hamm was at the Jameson house? I didn't want anyone to think I was involved with Vera beyond being a partner of Joey's. Reasons for not using the phone piled up. I also wanted to exit the house before I disturbed evidence.

It took me several minutes to find a pay phone in the swanky burg. I slid a nickel in the pay slot and dialed a number I had memorized, the central station of the Cleveland Police Department. I half expected an operator to ask for more nickels until the phone was answered at the other end. When I asked for Ted Matthews, I felt lucky he was in the station on a Saturday morning. Dealing with Captain O'Brien sooner or later would lead to someone taking a poke at the other guy.

Technically, Cleveland cops wouldn't have jurisdiction, if Vera Jameson had been abducted. If Cleveland believed it was connected to the murder and suicide, the posh hamlet would gladly give it over to Cleveland cops. Such whistle-stops often turned serious criminal investigations they couldn't handle to bigger city cops, and often paid for those services.

"Detective Matthews."

"Ted, its Harry Hamm. I went to the Jameson house to collect a debt. I'll explain the logic of that when I see you. The door wasn't locked. The place has been torn apart, like someone was looking for something important. There's no sign of Mrs. Jameson. I figured you'd be more interested than the locals."

Chapter 9.

When two local cop cars arrived, I knew it was more for show and to secure the premises. I was parked at the curb, leaning against my Buick, finishing another cigarette. I said, "I wouldn't go inside and trample over evidence, if I were you."

One of the locals took offense and said, "Who the hell are you?"

As I told them about the murder and suicide, about being a private dick partner from the agency of a murdered guy, about the ransacking with Vera Jameson missing, their eyes opened and their mouths closed. I showed them my P.I. ticket and my license to carry the Browning holstered under my left arm.

They left me alone and seemed to just stand in the lawn in front of the front door doing nothing and waiting for reinforcements from a more experienced police force.

Having nothing to do, I lit yet another cigarette, thinking I would probably miss Joey's funeral. In the scheme of things, it wouldn't be the end of the world. Not meeting Addie at the funeral was nearer to the end of the world. She would probably worry about me. I couldn't do anything about that. She wouldn't know my plan to find a justice of the peace, and she wouldn't know it had been postponed.

Cleveland cops arrived to do a full investigation of the house.

Detective Matthews showed a concerned look on his face when he ordered me to stick around. Obeying cops was like obeying your parents when you're a kid; the more you tried to get around it, the more trouble you got into.

Continuing to stand by my Buick, I shook loose another cigarette from a nearly empty pack. Before shaking it out, I changed my mind and decided not to smoke cigarette after cigarette. I had another pack in the glove box, so it wasn't because I was running low. I simply had already had too many in a row and whatever I was getting from them had disappeared two smokes ago. I was smoking too often and thinking about it too often.

With a slight turn, the autumn sun was on my face. I closed my eyes like I might fall asleep standing upright. Horses slept standing up, but they had four legs. Humans had a harder time with the balance part of it.

I wondered how long before the autumn sun would tan my face. If asked, I would prefer the moon to the sun. I was never the beach-and-tan type. Maybe it was my profession, in which more interesting things happened at night than in daylight. Certainly, women in ever-more-revealing beach clothes would be a good reason to put up with a beach and the sun. On the other hand, there were more women who shouldn't reveal so much than there were ones who looked good revealing more. I wondered how Addie would look in revealing beach attire. She looked fine with clothes on. What I was dancing around was wanting to be with her with no clothes on. The beach and sun were a lot of hooey. I may have been some kind of sap to act so noble last night. Weren't love and being naked the same thing?

I sat inside my car, not wanting to risk a sunburn, and closed my eyes. I think I wanted to sleep and dream, if I could dream about what I wanted to dream about.

A push on my shoulder told me I had fallen asleep.

From outside the open driver's window, Matthews shook his head while he looked at me and said, "Harry, you're some kind of strange bird to fall asleep like that, considering where you are."

"Yeah. I'm beginning to believe that myself."

He lit a cigarette before saying, "No signs of foul play in respect to Vera Jameson, but you probably saw what I did. Someone was looking for something important."

I agreed. "She wouldn't have been so disrespectful of her own things."

He nodded before saying, "You know what I'm thinking?"

"Yeah, because it's what I'm thinking. Perhaps Vera Jameson lied. Perhaps someone else shot her husband and Joey."

"It wasn't her. No gunpowder residue."

"Perhaps she lied because she was afraid of people who could do things like kill people and tear apart a house."

"Can I sit down on the passenger seat? We need to put up the windows and have an off-the-record conversation."

Nothing he'd said made me feel optimistic.

Once he was seated in my car and the windows were up, meaning his smoking would soon fill the car with smoke, Matthews said, "There have been rumors. Unsubstantiated. Maybe Joey's death didn't jibe with her yarn. Maybe Gus's murder had a connection."

"Maybe you need to keep talking."

"You didn't get any of this from me, Harry."

"Right."

"Vera Jameson, formerly Vera Burkowski, a Polish father, Irish on her mother's side, used to be Tony Bacca, Jr.'s moll."

"The heir apparent to the Baccanelli crime family."

"Yeah. Noah Jameson may have been the personal accountant for Tony Bacca, the son."

"Personal?"

"Again, it's only rumors, but the son may be dabbling in the dope business against his father's wishes. Secret-like."

I tried to remember if it was Earl or me who had wondered about the gun accuracy of accountant Noah Jameson. I didn't mention it. I said, "This smells. You closed out Joey's murder."

"That was for the newspapers. We didn't want them being a nuisance, and we had no proof of anything different. We were sort of waiting for the other shoe to drop."

"Vera Jameson disappearing?"

"Yeah, she's the other shoe. Somebody is looking for something. Perhaps Joey got in the way. More likely Joey and Gus were involved. Gus was tortured and murdered. If he knew something, which maybe he didn't, or someone wouldn't still be looking for something. This dame's disappearance was after Gus's murder, so maybe someone thinks she may know something."

"Jesus F. Christ, and I try to never take His name in vain."

Matthews almost gave me a smile. "Never would I have guessed you were the religious type, Harry."

"Only when everything else doesn't work."

"Vera Jameson didn't crack when we grilled her. We tried hard to crack her. She stuck to her story. Someone is probably trying, without laws to curb them, to crack her as we speak. Wanna know why I'm spilling the beans to you, when I shouldn't?"

I had a good idea why, but I wanted to hear him say it. "Why?"

"Because it's not right for Joey and Gus to be murdered. Cops hate murder. Cops hate murderers. I'd hate to see something happen to Earl and you. You may not know a lick about any of this, but someone might think you do, since you were partners with Joey and Gus. Be careful."

Matthews was a straight Joe. The coppers were a lot smarter than I ever believed. Their problem was that they waited for something to happen before acting.

If Earl and I were in danger, it might follow Addie was, too. "I have to go!"

Matthews nodded. "Drop by tomorrow for your statement on what you did here."

"I will. Unless you want to go with me…?"

He left my car and I drove off. I drove the speed limit until I was out of sight of the cops at the Jameson house. The other cops, especially the locals, would know nothing about what Matthews had told me. I didn't want a pain-in-the-ass local stickler chasing me for speeding.

I needed to find Addie and Earl, in that order. I would speed when I thought I had a chance to get away with it.

Chapter 10.

A backhoe was probably already dumping dirt on Joey's coffin. I didn't take a second to think about sending him any kind of mental farewell. I drove directly to the funeral reception, perhaps breaking two driving laws along the way.

Eyes were on me as I entered. I may have heard someone say, "Better late than never."

When I found Addie and Earl sitting next to each other at a table, as dishes were being cleaned away, I gave them no time to ask why I was late. "We need to go. Right now. We need to go. We're in danger."

I gave them no further explanation and said, "Back to the office. Earl you're lead car, then Addie, and I'll follow Addie. Tight formation. No one gets lost. We park at Mo's."

At almost half past three in the afternoon on a Saturday, only three cars were parked in Mo's side lot and none along the curb out front or on the side street. We weren't there to socialize, only to park.

Once the three of us were parked and outside our cars, Earl said, "I'll go check things out. Give me forty minutes." He was off walking toward our offices.

I answered Addie's curious look. "He's going to look for the opposition."

"The opposition?"

"Them."

"Them?"

"Anyone spying on our offices. I'll give Earl five minutes to get there. Fifteen to twenty minutes to look around. Another five to get back. Add ten minutes for the unexpected. If he's not back in thirty-five minutes, I'm going after him and you're driving to the nearest police station. Ask for Detective Matthews and tell him what you know."

She surprised me by asking, "How do you know how to do this stuff? Detective school?"

"Before the war, Earl and I worked at Pinkerton. We had training. During the war, we became good at it. Joey and Gus only knew what we taught them. They weren't as good at it."

"Did it get them killed?"

"Maybe."

"Better tell me what this is about, Harry. I don't know if you can hear them, but my bones are knocking against each other. You promised to tell me everything."

While I told her, I checked my wristwatch. I was done in twenty minutes, finishing by saying, "If they think Earl and I know something and you've stayed with us, while everyone else was fired, they may think you know something."

"What about Tommy Carter?"

"They probably don't know he's been hired back part-time."

Addie said, "What if they've been listening in on our phone calls?"

"It's too soon for that. Surveillance takes money and men. I suspect Crown Investigation would be used."

"By the Bacca crime family?"

"By Tony Bacca, Jr. I think Vera Jameson told him Gus knew where this something is."

"The books for the drug business, I'm guessing."

I asked, "Why would they keep books for something illegal?"

"To keep track of the money. Maybe there's a list of names, too. Bookkeeping ledgers. Maybe several of them. That's how they got Al Capone."

"How do you know that?"

As more of a question, Addie said, "I pay attention to what I see and read? Maybe I'm smart?"

"You are. The more brains on our side, the better."

"Aw, Harry, you're saying that because I'm your girlfriend."

Earl arrived back in twenty-nine minutes saying, "Nothing outside."

The front doors of the Grayson Building were never locked, meaning each business was responsible for its own security. We were on the second floor of the two story, boxy, plain building. Without a lift, an extravagance no one wanted to pay for, we took the stairs, stopping at the top of the stairs. Since leather shoes would make noise on the tiled hallway floor, Earl and I took off our wing-tips and handed them to Addie. She took off her pumps with a two-inch heel. She looked silly holding three pairs of shoes, but I didn't say anything.

Earl said, "I'll go. Stay here with Addie."

It was obvious my job was to protect Addie until she didn't need protection. If the tables were reversed, I'd do the same for Earl, so he could protect his girlfriend. It's what best friends do. I was becoming comfortable with Addie being my girl. It seemed that Earl and Addie were, too.

Earl held his semi-automatic Czech VZ 27 at his side pointing toward the floor. For safety, some guys pointed their weapons up; others down. I was like Earl, because raising a weapon to shoot made for a more accurate shot than lowering one.

From the sag of his left side suit pocket, I guessed he was also packing his Colt Model 1908, made for a vest pocket, though too big at 4.5 inches. His weapon choices seemed more about preference than utility.

A third of the way down the hall in his stocking feet, Earl pointed at the door to a travel agency. By accident over the years, I had learned someone was usually in those offices on a Saturday.

On the other side of the hallway, our offices were about another third of the way down. Earl listened at the door for several minutes before he crouched down to inspect the lock. He raised back up and listened for several more minutes.

He made it back to where I was pointing my Browning toward the floor, while Addie stood holding three pairs of shoes. He said, "There are new scratches on our lock. If anyone is inside, they're sleeping and not snoring. I'm going to stop at the travel agency to find out if they heard anything. Just in case, back me up."

I signaled Addie to follow me. She seemed shorter and vulnerable. Oh, yeah, no shoes on.

Earl knocked and entered, holding his weapon behind his back. I was near the right side of the doorjamb with Addie close behind me. Earl said, "Jeannie, working again on a Saturday?"

"A girl has to make a buck. I guess you didn't call me for dinner because of Joey and Gus. So sorry to hear about them. It must be a real shocker.

Shows us how short life is. You could come in and lock the door, if you wanted to forget about things for a while."

Addie and I shared a look, surprised Earl and Jeannie knew each other intimately.

"Next week we'll get together. I just attended Joey's funeral. I don't think I'd be much fun. By the way, did you hear anyone in the hallway today?"

"No. It's been quiet. Why do you ask?"

"I was supposed to meet a couple of guys, but with the funeral... I couldn't get a hold of them to call it off. It's not important."

"Make sure you get a hold of me next week. I'm already looking forward to it."

"I will. I better go, before I decide to stay."

"Are you sure, Earl? That time on my desk was fun."

Addie and I shared more surprised looks.

"No. I have to go," he finished and closed the door after leaving. He shrugged when he saw our faces.

Down at our front office door, Earl pointed to the lock. I could see the tampering scratches and nodded. We listened for several more minutes.

Earl took a position to the right of the doorjamb, while I was to the left with Addie a couple of paces behind me, still holding our shoes. Earl slid in his key with his left hand, not so easy when you always do it with your right hand. The key turned and the faint tumbling of the lock reached my ears. Earl turned the doorknob and pushed the door open. Guns in front of us, pointed straight ahead, we peered into the room.

Our offices had been ransacked, like Vera Jameson's house. Addie wiped a couple of stray tears from her eyes.

We congregated in my office, feeling temporarily safe. We shared one stiff shot of booze each, knowing now wasn't the time to overindulge.

"You never told me about Jeannie."

"Are you going to kiss and tell me about Addie?"

"I'm right here, Earl."

Earl said, "Harry, tell me the details of what the hell is going on."

I told him what I told Addie, who supplied her suspicion about a set of books for a dope operation.

I took the explanation back and said, "I think this Vera dame gave them Gus. When Gus didn't know anything, they went back to her. Maybe she gave us up."

"Maybe she doesn't know, so they might think our dead partners had clued us in." Earl seemed to stretch his neck as if it was stiff. "What if they shot Joey and he was the only one who knew. So no one knows where he stashed these alleged books."

Addie's breaths were faster than normal. "Should we go to the police?"

"They're waiting for the other shoe to drop before they do anything. They want us out here drawing fire. Speaking of shoes, where did you put them?" I asked.

With our shoes back on, Earl said, "We could run or stay and fight."

"Fight," Addie repeated with fear.

"No. He means figure a way out of this jam."

Going along with my line of explanation, Earl said, "Yeah, that's what I meant. We need to find out who is watching whom, then we spend the night together. Probably at your place, Harry. It's the most defensible. I need time to consider a hideout."

"Why can't we stay here?" Addie asked.

"No beds, no clothes, and no food," Earl answered. "Let's take the disguise kits when we leave. And the shotgun and ammo. Anything we might possibly need. Binoculars."

Addie asked, "What about a disguise for me?"

I said, "You're not going to be that directly involved."

Earl disagreed. "She might be right. If for no other reason than for moving around outside. Do you have any wigs at home?"

Sarcastically, I said, "How about fake mustaches? Do you have any of those?"

We went to Addie's first. No surveillance didn't mean it wasn't being arranged by Crown Investigation on behalf of Tony Bacca, Jr. She packed clothes with disguises in mind, including two wigs she said she'd never had the courage to wear. We left her car. When she chose to ride with Earl, because she was miffed at my sarcasm, I became miffed at her. Some kissing and now we had a spat. Was *spat* a form of *spit*, in case she made me angry enough to spit? Oddly, it reminded me of something Gus had said. "That dame was a real spitfire, hopefully with her own spit." That Gus. Why wasn't someone who lacked his sense of humor murdered? Aw, Gus.

The same process occurred at Earl's. He had parts of disguises at his place, like I had at mine. He packed with the idea of being disguised.

When we left, he drove his heap, while I drove mine. Addie chose to ride with me this time. She said, "Sorry, Harry, but you need to understand that I'm not going down without a fight." My silly face must have expressed my thoughts, because she changed from determined to startled, when she said, "Oh, you have a naughty mind, Harry." She giggled the giggle I liked so much. "Now you have me thinking about that. Damn you!"

Finally, we were safe in my rented rooms, at least for the time being.

With questions in her eyes, she said, "Where am I sleeping?"

It was my decision, since she was my girl. In a split second, I decided it wasn't the right time to sleep with her while Earl stood guard. "Take the spare bedroom. Don't unpack. We're moving to a hideout tomorrow, as soon as Earl thinks of one."

Grumbling, Earl said, "Why do I have to think of everything?"

My smile wasn't happy, but it was a smile. "You're the smartest at this kind of thing. Addie is probably smarter than both of us put together. Me, I'm happy to be the dumb one. Knew it would pay off in spades someday."

"You're not dumb," Addie said. "I wouldn't fall in love with a dumb guy."

It was obvious, but now it was in the open, out loud to Earl.

"When we're over this, I'll throw you a bachelor party."

"Deal, partner."

"Did you just ask me to marry you, Harry?"

"I guess I did. Did you think we were going to just play footsies?"

"I did, for a while. But I can see things are going to move fast. Okay, Harry, I'll marry you before we play footsies."

No one said it, but everyone was probably hoping we'd live long enough to see Addie and me married. "Aw, what the hell? Earl, will you be my best man?"

"Yes. Unless we're going to pick out flowers and invitations… Harry and I will switch keeping watch every three hours."

"What about me?" Addie asked.

"Do you know how to keep watch?"
"No, Earl."

Chapter 11.

Earl woke me at 11:00 pm. I had been sleeping in my bed alone. I didn't know about anyone else, but I was exhausted enough to fall right off to sleep. If anyone but Earl was on guard duty, I might have been worried and not been able to sleep.

When I peeked into the spare bedroom to see Addie fast asleep, Earl gave me a strange look. What was wrong with looking at your future wife sleeping?

In the living room, Earl said, "I thought you were going in there for fifteen minutes."

I smiled. "I take longer than you. Sixteen minutes. Why don't you get some shut-eye?"

"In a minute. When did you get the television?"

"A couple of months ago. I guess you haven't been up here lately. It settled a debt. It's a 12" Dumont. I'm getting too old to booze it every night."

"I hear they're coming out with color."

"Color?'

"Like blood would be red."

"We've seen plenty of that in real life."

"Yeah."

"I have a couple ideas about the Vincent House. Remember the manager...Edward Doran?"

"Eddie Dorn. We got him out of that jam with the sixteen-year-old. Yeah, sixteen going on thirty. Yeah, that could work."

"I hope I can get some sleep. Wake me at two." He turned toward my bedroom, then turned back around to face me. "Addie is terrific, the best kind. I'm happy for you, partner."

It came out of my mouth without any thought attached. "You and Addie never...?"

"No. I'd tell you. You'd never speak to me again, but I would tell you."

I felt bad about asking him. I wondered if he had said something had happened, if it would have mattered. I expected Addie not to be a virgin.

That would be too much expectation and probably lead to disappointment. How could I hold Addie's past against her, when I had done so much with so many? I did hope she had never been in love enough to want to marry some other guy. Temporary love was more convenient than permanent love.

It was hard not to think about Addie and stay focused on keeping us safe. At the worst time in my life for a distraction came the best distraction of my life, Addie.

Staying awake and alert by thinking about something other than Addie wasn't easy. I needed to keep moving. I decided to listen at the door for any hallway sounds and to peek out the living room window at the street every half hour; it would get me up on my feet and moving around. It made me think of my first job out of high school as a third-shift security guard at a chemical factory. I'd make half hour rounds every hour and turn a key in a series of lock boxes. I often wondered how long it would take for help to come if I missed a key box. It never happened, so I never knew.

Earl and I knew each other from back in the neighborhood. He went to a Catholic school and I went to the public school. We had closer friends from our respective high schools, but we did pal around from time to time.

My guidance teacher, well, several teachers, thought I should find a trade. They more or less said, without saying it, that I wasn't college material. I had size and strength, good for construction work or moving things. If I applied myself, maybe I could work my way into a union situation.

Well, I didn't like any of that. I wasn't lazy, but I didn't want to do back-breaking work for the next thirty or forty years.

My uncle knew a guy who knew another guy. Three weeks after graduation, my average grades were average enough, and I was working for Pinkerton

My first assignment was walking rounds at that chemical plant. Something must have been valuable, because I carried a gun, a .45 that I wore like a cowboy in a hip holster. They thought it was a good idea for me to learn how to use the gun. They didn't pay me for the time I spent learning, though they paid for the bullets.

Earl went to the city college for two years. Later, he would say most of what he learned was useless for earning a living, but he did take two law enforcement courses.

He was waiting around to get into any police academy for any city within an hour's drive, when I ran into him at a bar. Two weeks later he was hired where I worked at a higher hourly rate, because he had some college and those law enforcement classes.

After we both turned twenty-one, we pooled our money and rented an apartment. Living with our parents was crimping our sex life. Fooling around with dames in cars and finding good places to park were too difficult. We became the best of friends.

We double dated a lot. He had little success with the better-looking dames. I always ended up with the lesser looking dame. He almost married this brunette named Betty. I almost married no one.

When I started working as a guard on an armored truck, Earl had reached lieutenant status and supervised eighteen security guards. We were told our jobs were important and would keep us out of the war. Earl was still going with Betty. It seemed like I was going with all of the below average-looking dames around. We should have been feeling happy, thankful, and lucky, but we weren't. Most of our friends were in the armed services. Several had already died, which made us feel bad. No one said anything to us, but people gave us wary looks. Why were two young, healthy guys not serving their country?

Looking at my wristwatch, I saw I was five minutes late for making my rounds inside my rooms. After standing and stretching and grabbing my revolver, I went to the apartment door and listened. I looked out the peephole. I didn't rush, though no one appeared in the hallway and I heard no sounds.

At the living room window, I pulled aside an edge of the curtain and looked out to the street below. The streetlamps lit the street reasonably well. I saw nothing except the white markings on a black cat prowling.

Setting my gun back on the end table, I stretched, twisting my head and torso, before sitting back down.

Four days after the attack on Pearl Harbor, we enlisted. Betty refused to marry Earl before we left for Army boot camp. Earl was angry. Though I could understand why she refused him, I sympathized with Earl and mostly kept my mouth shut. To the best of my knowledge, I don't think Earl ever saw Betty again.

Before we knew it, boot camp was over and we shipped out.

Besides being sick most of the time, I had never been as frightened as aboard the troop carrier. Alarms would sound and rumors of enemy planes or submarines literally scared the crap out of the GIs. It was a helpless dread that we could be bombed or torpedoed and not be able to do anything about it.

Occasionally, we heard distant gunfire or bombs, sometimes from up in the sky and twice across the water. Whoever was protecting the troop ship did a good job, because we made it to England without seeing any direct combat.

The cities of England, especially London, were going through a hell of a time with bombing air raids. It was the Blitz. We felt guilty being bivouacked in the relatively safe countryside and wondered when we would see action.

While Earl continued to think about Betty, I enjoyed England. In my spare time, I helped out at a farm where the husband and two sons were off fighting the war. The farm's mother and daughter bedded me unknowing about the other, although sometimes I still wonder about it. The mother taught me what I didn't know and the daughter helped practice make perfect.

At about that time, we ran into Joey and Gus from back home. The four of us became best friends, though we were in different squads. They had left walking police beats to join up because of Pearl Harbor. Though London and the other cities were taking a pasting from the Luftwaffe, it seemed the war didn't need us and might soon be over. How wrong we were.

September 3, 1943, we were part of the invasion of Italy. Italy was like being in hell. We saw blood, guts, and death firsthand.

I never liked to think about Italy. It seemed like one long day of brutal combat. It got so bad, we didn't want to learn the names or faces of those we fought with. As men were lost, Earl and I were shifted into different squads, so we often lost track. One day the Italians retreated fast and gave up even faster.

By the time we returned to England in preparation for the invasion of France, Earl was a sergeant and Joey, Gus, and I were in his squad. It seemed Earl had more leadership qualities than I had, which was fine with me.

Time for another round to the door and window. Everything remained quiet. The war taught me quiet was good, as long as it lasted.

Chapter 12.

Waking up meant I had dozed off. With urgency I looked at my watch to see I had slept for forty minutes. Quickly, though carefully and quietly, I picked up my gun and went to the door. After several minutes, I went to the window. Everything was quiet and quiet was good.

I began to think about those days of waiting for the invasion of France.

On a four-day pass, I went to visit the farm where the mother and daughter had been so good to me.

I didn't know much about farming, but the farm looked unkempt. Little of the land had crops. As I walked to the house, I saw a one-legged man trying to hop up a ladder near a large barn door. It seemed impossible, until I saw him grab the ladder higher up and pull himself to the next rung. I had to help him.

The one-legged man was the mother's son, Nigel. Several years younger than I was, the man was more of a boy. Working together on the top hinge needed more than freshly re-screwing the hinge. It needed a partial new upper frame. He directed and I did most of the work.

Nigel had lost his leg in Italy and only recently returned to the farm. His older brother had been killed in North Africa. Their father had been a pilot, shot down over France, missing in action and presumed dead. His sister, whom I knew intimately, though I didn't tell him, had joined the nursing corps and worked at a hospital near London.

It took several hours to fix the top hinge. I decided to tighten and lubricate the other hinges. It felt good to do something constructive instead of destructive.

The barn doors swung freely and the latching bar moved easily up and down. I felt a real sense of accomplishment.

I washed up as best I could with rain water in a barrel before Nigel led me into the house. His mother sat rocking in a chair and looked much older than when I'd last seen her. She looked at me as if I was a stranger, then suddenly she smiled and looked younger.

For the next couple of days, I worked as hard and long as I could to help Nigel around the farm. Nothing happened with the mother until the late afternoon of my last day. Nigel had gone into town and his mother took me to her bed. I told her it wasn't necessary and that I was glad to help out. She was half-naked when she told me that she was doing it for herself, not for me.

I will never forget what happened next. There were shouts from outside. I finally caught the words. Nigel shouted, "Mother, it is Father! He's alive!"

She rushed to the second-floor window oblivious that she was bare-breasted.

I dressed as quickly as I could and snuck out the back door of the farmhouse. I kept low like I was trying to avoid enemy gunfire.

Ten days later, I was in a pub on my second beer, when I saw a pretty young nurse walking toward me. She found me to thank me for everything I had done for the family. Later, she thanked me in a most improper way. She had learned a lot since that last time we bedded on her family's farm.

While we waited for the invasion to begin, the four of us hatched the private detective agency idea. Our jobs before the war seemed like good beginner experience. What we didn't know we would learn.

One would think the veterans, the GIs with the most experience, would hit the beaches first. Our squad with Earl, Joey, Gus, and me were in the second wave to land. It wasn't much safer than the first wave.

Whenever I thought I had seen it all, like the hell of the Italian campaign, something more hellish came along. On a beach in France, I saw so many dead and maimed Americans that I knew something worse than hell.

Somehow, perhaps from experience with a large helping of luck, we survived the Germans and the weather. After the winter, the Germans seemed to lose their will to fight. As the weather eased into spring, the fighting almost seemed like no more than going to work each day.

We began to hear stories of liberated death camps, though we weren't involved with any of them. From what I heard, it seemed like hell had no bottom to it.

The rumor was the war would be over in a matter of days. The younger GIs believed it – we didn't. The four of us were sent to clear, investigate, and hold a farmhouse. The farmhouse couldn't actually be a farmhouse, as it looked too good and there was neither a barn nor remnants of any crop. Later we were to find out that it was a summer house – a *Sommerhaus*. Sounded right.

The house was empty of people and everything of value. A few small items of no apparent value suggested the owners had been Jewish. Who knows what happened to them.

Joey was horsing around with Gus like they were kids without a care in the world, despite everything we had been through, when they knocked over a cheap looking lamp, breaking off a chunk of pottery. Earl saw the diamonds first. We busted up the lamp and found a dozen diamonds in the hardened clay.

The diamonds weren't large, but Gus assured us they were diamonds. Gus's mother worked for a jeweler and had taught him about precious gems.

Thinking about the discovery of the diamonds gave me energy and woke me up. I made another security round with keener eyes and focused hearing, though nothing seemed out of place.

Smuggling the diamonds back to the States was easier than we thought. GIs were bringing all sorts of mementos back from the war. Everyone was so happy the war in Europe was over that no one was paying much attention to what anyone was carrying.

Our enlistments for the duration were deemed up and none of us wanted to re-up to fight the Japanese, since we felt we had done our duty fighting the Italians and Germans.

From his cop days, Joey knew a fence who could handle the ice. Whatever the ice was worth, we believed Joey made the best deal he could when we split up $24,000, a large sum of money.

After three months of drinking and trying to screw every dame not nailed down, we made our dream of the Diamond Detective Agency come true.

In ten minutes, I would make my last security round before waking Earl to relieve me.

Remembering the stash of diamonds made me think I should give Addie a diamond engagement ring. She wouldn't want me to do that. Whatever was going to happen, if we survived, we wouldn't have much money. If I knew Addie from the years at the business and the last couple of days of becoming what I had hoped we would become, she would be happy with a cigar's paper band for a ring. It could be from an expensive cigar, like from Cuba. I knew I was thinking about silly things when danger threatened any kind of future for us and Earl.

One thing I knew that wasn't silly was whatever might happen to Addie would happen to me first. If I thought it would then happen to her, I'd take her life with as little pain as possible. From silly thoughts to deadly thoughts was far too-far crazy on the day I was engaged to be married.

Chapter 13.

I couldn't remember who said it or when. I could have been at Mo's Bar a year or two ago. Sometimes too much alcohol erases faces but not what they say.

A guy said the most important and restful hours of sleep were the first three. It was all a person really needed. I wondered how he could know that or how anyone would come to that conclusion. It seemed to me the longer you sleep the more rest you got.

I remembered how many times I was lucky enough to get three hours of continuous sleep during the combat parts of the war. Somehow, I survived.

When Earl woke me at five o'clock, I had slept three hours three times. Nine hours in total plus a nap on guard duty. Did I ever get more than nine hours of shut-eye in one night? I felt okay until I realized I would wake everyone at seven, early bird and all that, and continue to stay awake until we were safely hidden out at the Vincent House, if Earl had figured it out.

I made a slow careful security round, door and windows. Maybe no one was coming after us. I couldn't allow myself to think that way; they had ransacked our offices.

When I sat down with my Browning near me on the end table, I remembered how, the now-in-shambles Diamond Detective Agency, had begun.

When we enlisted after Pearl Harbor, it was for the duration of the war. Draftees were only required to serve two years. Within a year after Germany surrendered, half of the combat troops were sent home. They must have believed the four of us had done enough and mustered us out of the Army in October of 1945. A couple of months short of four years was enough.

Some of us had more of a nest egg than the others. Gus had the least, since he was married with two kids and his wife needed more than what he sent home. With the few chances he had, Joey wildly spent his service money on drink and women.

Earl's family was better off than most families, so they saved every penny he sent home for him. His pay was higher; he was a sergeant. Joey and

Gus were corporals. I guess I showed no leadership qualities, because I made it one step above buck private to private first class. The first class part of it sounded better than the pay. My family spent half and saved half for me.

While we were in England, waiting for the invasion of France with not much to occupy us, a snot-nosed lieutenant read something put out by the War Department about how our pays were equivalent to a bank teller or bookkeeper, because so much was provided for us, like food, cigarettes, clothes, and housing. A laugh went through the ranks when he said "housing." Tents and foxholes were far from "housing."

He pointed out that we made more in Foreign Service than those stationed in the States. For me, it meant another $130 a year. Who decided being shot at or having bombs dropped on you earned an extra $130 a year? None of it sounded right or fair, but complaining about it wasn't going to get anyone anywhere.

A GI asked if someone wounded for life, like losing an arm or an eye, would mean government money for life. The lieutenant said it would, though he didn't know how much. I guessed it wouldn't be enough.

Most GIs smoked cigarettes. If they didn't in civilian life, they did once they'd joined up. Boot camp was busier, but once we went overseas there was plenty of time for jawing and smoking; the two seemed to go together. Lulls in combat were good times to light up. Of course, there were stories of GIs who lit up at the wrong time and had their heads blown off. I had never seen it, but it kept me from automatically lighting up when things were quiet.

For some who smoked more than their rations provided, there were always easy trades with those who didn't smoke. Stopping to think about it, more people smoked after the war because of a habit they'd developed during the war.

Finding cheap booze, whether hard liquor, wine, or beer, challenged GIs the most. A few moonshine stills popped up while we waited in England. Bars and taverns could get expensive. When we could we commandeered booze, meaning we stole it. In combat, whatever you found was yours, though you might have to share it with someone up the chain of command.

Some GIs drank, when they could, before combat. The four of us generally didn't, though a few times we made exceptions. We were veterans and knew a hangover was the last thing you wanted when the bombs and bullets were flying. Having some liquor seemed to heighten senses, though knowing how much was enough was a problem. We never criticized anyone who drank because they were afraid. We were afraid, too, but being so experienced in combat we didn't show it much. Our attitude was why worry about it, it wouldn't help anything. You were either lucky or not. Worry never stopped a bullet.

The worst part, other than the other side trying to kill you, was dames, specifically, thinking about dames. Joey was the ladies' man of the group. He seemed to find dames no matter where we were. He claimed he never paid for it, but none of us believed him.

Gus was true-blue to his wife. For as smart as Earl was about everything, he was shy with dames. Besides the mother and daughter from my farmhouse adventure, every few months I would luck into something with a dame. With my mug, all of us were surprised. Earl said something about dames either going for pretty guys like Joey or a mug like mine.

The one pastime no one spoke about was jerking off. If guys spent too long in the latrine, they were either sick from the food or jerking off. Of course, there were stories about GI's jerking off at the wrong time and ending up being killed because of it. I found it hard to believe a guy would jerk off in a foxhole, but, then again, it was more important to some than others.

Without a doubt, the pastime occupying the most time was talking. I assumed most of the jabbering was lies or exaggerations. If you listened long enough, you would hear most everything about everything.

It didn't hit me until I was at home, living with my parents, that I had survived the war. Considering the combat we saw, it was a miracle the four of us survived.

My dad found me on the front porch in the darkness weeping. He brought out a bottle of bourbon and we lit smokes. He talked about everyday life, since I wasn't offering anything about the war. It finally sunk in; I would have an everyday ordinary life.

"So, son," my dad said, "you're healthy and you have some money. What are you going to do with the rest of your life?"

"Earl, Joey, Gus, and I are going to start a private detective agency."

He laughed. It made me laugh. It sounded stupid, like a kid saying he was going to be a cowboy.

So Joey fenced the diamonds for $6,000 apiece. I would have to be shown proof in black and white and still I wouldn't have believed Joey took a little extra for himself.

Remembering what that lieutenant had read to us England, Earl said, "An ordinary guy makes $3,600 a year. We should keep that amount and each throw $2,400 into a kitty for our private detective business."

I half expected Gus to say something about needing more because he had a wife and kids, but he didn't.

Only I understood, when I said, "I thought we were going to be cowboys?"

The guys didn't laugh and my father probably would have thought I had lost my marbles.

Before we rented offices, bought a typewriter, desks and chairs, a coffee pot, or a single file cabinet, we armed; two guns each, a bigger one and a smaller one, one for show and one for backup. We didn't realize our minds were still in the war. Expecting to need guns was the dumbest money we spent.

Gus chose two Smith & Wesson Model 10s, a two-inch and a five-inch barrel. Except for length and weight, they were the same gun and used the same cartridges. Being a former cop, his choices made sense.

Earl gave Joey a Bernardelli vest pocket pistol he had commandeered while we fought in Italy. Since Joey was half-Italian, he knew Joey would love it. He didn't tell Joey the weapon was referred to as *The Baby*. It was so small it could fit in a vest pocket. The magazine held six rounds of .22 long or short ammunition. Since we were saving money with Earl giving Joey the weapon, I kept my wondering whether or not the firepower could knock a kid off a bicycle to myself.

For his more powerful gun, since he had also been a cop, Joey chose what Gus did, though with a four-inch barrel. Joey liked his suits trimmer and didn't want as much bulk in his underarm shoulder holster.

To my surprise, Earl had smuggled a semi-automatic Czech VZ 27 back from the war. He said he took it off a dead German officer. No one remembered him talking about it, but there was the gun. The cartridge was a

.32 ACP and it used an eight-round magazine. Something about its reliability bothered me, but it was saving the business money and Earl's decision.

Earl's other gun was a Colt Model 1908, made for a vest pocket. At a length of 4.5 inches, it seemed too big for a vest pocket. Earl planned to carry it in an overcoat or suit side pocket. It packed more wallop than Joey's Bernardelli and also had a six-round magazine.

I almost felt guilty, though no one said anything, when I bought a Browning 9 millimeter with a 15-round magazine. It was big at 7.8 inches, but it could take down almost anything with cartridges to spare. It fit its name as a Browning Hi-Power. I told this captain how much I admired his. It was somewhere in France, not sure where, but weeks past Paris. He let me try it out. When he was impressed with my strength to handle it, I was impressed.

Earl made a comment about it being a good gun for me, since I would probably be the first one through the door. What door, I wondered?

The general thought was Gus and Joey had cop experience. Plus, Joey was a ladies' man. Earl was the brains and I was the muscle. Rather than object to being the muscle, I hoped I would show I could put two and two together as well as the next guy.

I copied Gus by picking a Smith and Wesson Model 10 with a two-inch barrel for my smaller backup gun, though I doubted how often it would leave the glove box of my car. Of course, the cars we bought would be out of our own money. Later, we would learn it could be a tax deduction if the company paid for the car.

To everyone's surprise, Gus thought we should have one double-barrel sawed-off Remington 12-gauge shotgun. We bought it.

Before we had a stick of furniture or a place to put it, we had fedoras, pinstripe three-piece suits, Florsheim shoes, a slightly used Buick, 2 Fords, a Chevy, an arsenal of weapons, holsters, and ammo. If anyone was looking for a private dick or four, we were available and looked the part.

The sun was barely up when I went to wake Addie up. If she had slept the whole time it would have been ten hours. Maybe she was a long sleeper. She was never late to work that I could tell, though I was always late for work. Thinking she liked to spend long periods of time in bed was not a bad habit to me.

At first my mug frightened her, as if what had happened had only been a dream.

As she stretched, her face turned to a sweet smile. She stretched and pulled me down for a kiss. I can't lie and say someone never kissed me first thing in the morning. I can say, it was the best morning kiss ever.

Using the bathroom and getting dressed was like a Marx Brothers movie, all bustle and running into each other, while Addie tried to maintain her modesty.

Addie was dressed more casually than for the office and wore her hair down. She searched through my refrigerator and cupboards before saying, "You usually eat out, right?"

"Yeah."

"No woman has ever made you breakfast in the morning?"

Earl laughed and said, "Good question, Addie. Can't wait for your answer, Harry."

"I'm taking the Fifth."

She caught on. "Oh, at their places. Good answer. How about fried bologna sandwiches, mustard and pickles optional?"

Like roommates, we ate the sandwiches as if it was breakfast before work.

I said, "I had a lot of time to think during guard duty. I'm thinking Addie and I should go somewhere like Florida on a pre-honeymoon vacation, while you fix everything, Earl."

Addie added, "I like that plan."

"So that's how it's going to be. Addie moves into first place and I move down to second place."

"Only one team wins a championship," I commented.

With breakfast and light banter in the past, I packed, so the three of us would be able to leave for a hiding place.

We were looking at each other, waiting for someone to say, "Let's leave," when Earl started talking.

"Interrupt me if something doesn't make sense. How Tony Bacca, Jr. and Noah Jameson know each other, we don't know. They have this side dope business going on. Tony Jr. handles the product and distribution, while Noah handles the cash. Captain Nero's, Addie, is a bar and restaurant where they hung out. It's at the end of a pier, sort of Eleventh Street. This is common knowledge. Most average Joes at any bar have heard about the Baccanelli family and their clubhouse. So, Junior brings Noah to Captain Nero's. Maybe Vera is a waitress or hat check girl. She was Junior's moll, but maybe Junior is tired of her and has moved on. Noah falls for and marries Vera. Maybe Junior pushes the idea, thinking she can keep an eye on Noah. Maybe he occasionally still sees her. One way or the other, she knows what's going on. She has the bright, or maybe not-too-bright, idea to swipe the books. Maybe there's cash, too. Maybe she's angry with Junior for passing her off to Noah. She needs someone to help her with a blackmail scheme. Meanwhile, Noah wonders where she disappears to. He hires us, meaning Joey. She turns everything upside down and seduces Joey into her scheme. Joey brings Gus in, because Gus needs money. Joey doesn't come to us, because we would tie him down for a month or two, until he wised up. Same with Gus. Addie, you should know now that Harry and I may be the most honest private eyes on the planet."

I finally interrupt Earl to say, "The blackmail is the *good something* Gus's father-in-law referred to."

"Right. What screwed up the scheme was Noah hiring Crown Investigation. Joey and Vera are both good looking. Noah is paranoid about it. Maybe he complained to Junior, who uses his own personal detective agency. They wouldn't tell Noah if Junior was still seeing her, but Joey... Suddenly Noah realizes the journals and maybe some money have disappeared. Beside the books putting Junior in jail, his father would be unhappy about his son's dope business. Noah tells Junior, who knows Crown is sitting on Joey and Vera at that motel. The rest is history."

"So, who has the books and the maybe money?" asked Addie.

Shaking his head, Earl said, "Either Vera is tough enough to handle whatever they dish out, or only Joey knew, and he's dead."

I said, "Gus would have told them if he knew. His wife and kids... He would have told."

During the following silence, Earl pulled aside the living room window curtain and said, "Damn. We have company across the street, second floor above the pizza pie parlor."

Chapter 14.

Most of the plan came from Earl. He determined the various actions we needed to do quickly, since we were now under surveillance and didn't know when it might turn into an invasion. This wasn't like waiting for military minds to think of every detail and the right weather to put a million men into Normandy.

Addie wasn't a private detective and hadn't fought in the war, but she was smart and she contributed. She was the one suggesting the tack I would take at the bank.

She wrote down the various steps of the day's plan in short memorable phrases and handed the paper to me, knowing I was the best person to accomplish all of them.

Earl disagreed, but he knew he was wrong. I was the toughest, strongest, and best with fists or guns. As for the mental part of it, if I couldn't do it, I was in the wrong profession.

My departure ended any chance of a debate. I more than trusted Earl to protect Addie while I was gone. I left without kissing Addie goodbye like I was leaving for work. Someday it might be a normal thing to do, but today it would be far from normal. If she took it as a message, the message would be that I would be back to kiss her.

To the best of my knowledge, everyone living in the building was a working stiff, except for retired old man Heldorfer. Yeah, he was German, though no one seemed to hold grudges all these years later. It seemed the Germans would end up being our partners against the new enemy, Russian communism.

Heldorfer was simply old and living alone, bothering no one. I was friendly the few times I had seen him and he needed help to carry something from his car.

He was surprised by my knock on his door so early in the morning. Before he could think too much about what I might be up to, I said, "I need to borrow your car for the day. I'll replace the gasoline I use and throw in ten dollars. That includes the use of your oldest hat and coat."

Though he looked confused, he agreed. The ten dollars probably sounded good to him and I had done him favors.

Heldorfer's hat had earflaps and a brim. It was tight on my head. The dull plaid coat was tight on my shoulders over my suit coat, wide enough around the middle, and long enough. Most important, the coat had a collar that went up and covered part of my face.

At the sight of working stiffs leaving the building to go to work, I lit out, remembering Earl had said, "Don't forget to slouch, like an old man."

As I left the building, hunched and walking slow with the hat pulled down and the coat collar up, someone behind me called out, "Good morning, Mr. Heldorfer." That cinched it for me, as I merely raised a hand without saying a word.

Heldorfer's older model Plymouth started right up. I drove away.

Two blocks away, I parked at the curb and walked slowly back toward my rooms at the Colton Arms.

Within five minutes, I spotted a man in a car parked along the curb around back, so he could watch the back entrance to the Colton Arms. He didn't seem to be doing much of anything, which gave him away. I intended to watch him a while, until I saw a second man sit up in the back seat. I guessed he had been catching a few ZZZs. Watching someone didn't mean you should ignore the possibility that you were being watched. We learned during the war to spend extra time before hastily jumping to conclusions.

Earl and I had both seen the soaped-over window with what appeared to be a dim circle of light emanating from the center of the window on the second floor above the pizza pie parlor. It could have been someone who recently rented the room, but we doubted it.

Still wearing the old man's hat and coat, I walked around to the front to confirm what we believed. I moved close enough and waited. After several minutes of staring, I made out binoculars had been raised to the opening. If my living room curtains were open, they could look directly inside the room. I guessed it was a two-man team like it was out back.

To turn on the surveillance room's light, even during daylight, was a sign of inexperience. But I wasn't going to underestimate Crown Investigation because of a rookie mistake.

After spending time watching both of their positions, a check of my wristwatch told me the bank, where we did business, would be open.

I left Heldorfer's hat and coat in his car. Addie suggested a teller might give me a hard time taking out so much cash. I went straight to the bank manager, who knew me. I gave him a spiel about needing cash for Gus Reese's widow and for us to go undercover to catch the guy who killed our partner. As I expected, he had read about it in the newspapers. Civilians could be a big help in the detective business, if they thought they were helping, yet not involved or at risk.

One check each from Earl and me and a check from the company meant I was withdrawing six grand in cash. It was a lot of dough and would raise teller looks and questions, but the bank manager kept it as quiet as possible.

The fried bologna sandwich left space in my stomach, so I stopped for two scrambled egg sandwiches and coffee. I had never been in the place before, but the food was okay and the plate and coffee cup looked to be clean. The thought made me think of Gus.

Back on the road, I drove to where Tommy Carter lived with his parents. He was home and waiting for a phone call from Earl to tell him how to earn two bucks an hour. My appearance surprised him.

I gave him fifty bucks, with the promise of another fifty, for him to stake out and secretly take pictures of faces coming out of the Crown Investigation, for up to three days from noon until ten. He should develop the pictures daily. Either Earl or I would phone him and arrange to get the photos.

He had read the newspaper and knew Crown Investigation more or less fingered Joey for Noah Jameson. He also mentioned he'd heard that Crown was connected to the Bacca mob. Everyone seemed to know it. He admired us wanting to know the faces of the opposition. He was a bright kid, which was why we'd hired him. I told him I couldn't tell him any more than I had. I told him to be careful, that his assignment could be dangerous. He glommed onto everything I said. Another reason he worked for us.

Finding a public phone, I called my apartment and hung up after three rings, my signal everything was going as planned.

My next stop was Honest John's Used Cars. Every couple of months a car would go missing. The cops figured it was some kind of inside job but couldn't solve it. We did; it was Honest John's son. No charges were filed –

it was a family thing that we never knew the resolution to. Actually, Honest John wasn't so honest. Every now and then he moved a hot car, but we weren't hired to turn him in to the cops. We knew and let him know we knew. He therefore owed us a favor or four.

Later, I would swap my car for one that ran well and could near fly, if necessary. The plates needed to be real plates, not dealer plates. I paid Honest John $100 with the promise to pay $5 per day until I returned the car and swapped it back for my car. I would sign over the pink slip to my Buick in case everything went wrong. The idea didn't bother him much, making me think he continued to sell a hot car now and then.

I phoned my apartment again and hung up after three rings.

Until it was dark, I needed to kill time and perhaps get some sleep. I had already seen *A Letter to Three Wives*, because a waitress I was so-so interested in wanted to see it. Addie may have been in the back my mind, but the waitress was in front of my eyes. The movie was sappy and too contrived – the waitress was better in every respect. I figured seeing it again would help me sleep.

When I opened my eyes, my wristwatch confirmed the movie was well into another showing. It was early in the night but dark when I made yet another phone call and hung up after three rings.

Soon would come the risky part of the plan. It only needed to be night and dark. When I was ready, I would make my next move.

With plenty of time to spare, I drove to the 28th Street Chop House for another round of the chopped sirloin. Whatever Addie and Earl found to eat in my apartment, I knew the chopped sirloin was beyond much better.

My idea of a grocery list was created by my not finding in the apartment or refrigerator something I was looking for. If I didn't have what I wanted, I would buy it for the next time. While food wasn't important, toiletries were – I was more conscientious in that regard.

I thought I had some kind of cheese and a couple of kinds of crackers. Grape jelly, yeah, maybe grape jelly. Two tubs of ice cream, Neapolitan and butter pecan, were in the freezer. Thinking of ice cream made me think of the melted ice cream on the kitchen floor in the Jameson house. I wondered if I would ever see Vera Jameson in the flesh and alive.

Chapter 15.

The pizzeria smelled good from the outside. *Dago* food always smelled good. The chopped sirloin had filled my stomach. Yet, I could have found room for beer, meaning I could have found room for a slice of pizza pie. A thin man once told me you shouldn't eat unless you were hungry. He was too thin, so why give his advice any weight? Wanting to eat something had nothing to do with hunger. It was a ridiculous time to think about pizza or the thin man. What was I doing?

The door for the stairs to the second floor was next to the brightly lit and mostly glass door to the pizzeria. I guessed another set of stairs in the back of the pizza parlor were the original stairs to the second floor where the proprietor had once lived. The pizzeria probably earned the owner enough to buy a house, so the second floor needed a separate entrance for it to be rentable. How long would it take until a renter hated the smells of the pizzeria? Too much of anything good can sour you on it.

If someone wasn't paying attention or had a snoot full, I could see someone mistakenly opening the wrong door and being perplexed looking at a set of stairs.

I slipped inside the door to the steps and saw two mailboxes shoddily attached to the right wall. Light from a single bulb at the top of the rather steep stairs barely made it to the bottom step. It was as unbecoming an entrance and way up as I had ever seen.

I went up the stairs slowly and quietly without taking off my shoes, almost like a ballerina lifting and setting down each foot, hoping any creaking noise would be unheard from inside an apartment.

At the top landing I was surprised to see a hallway with three doors almost bunched together along the right wall. My guess was a front apartment, a back apartment, and a shared bathroom between. Hopefully, a Crown guy wouldn't suddenly exit the bathroom, though I was prepared to go at him with the butt of my Browning.

The hallway seemed to extend to the back of the building. When I went there, I found a right turn and four feet that went nowhere with a boarded-up window that had to be in the back wall of the building. The construction of the whole setup seemed to be thought up as it was done. The corner dead end would be perfect for a bum needing winter shelter or for someone waiting to surprise someone going to either apartment.

Through the first apartment door, I could hear them talking about the smells from the pizza parlor and how they were hungry.

Sure enough, several minutes later, I heard footsteps approaching the door and quickly moved into the dead corner space. Operatives doing surveillance moved slowly to consume boring time. I knew it from firsthand experience. His slow steps gave me plenty of time to come up behind him before he reached the stairs.

As I stuck the working end of my pistol into his back, I said, "Quiet or else." I backed off in case he had the bright idea to suddenly spin and go for my gun. I whispered like a growling bear might, "Grab air and turn slowly, very slowly."

One of the benefits of my mug was other mugs took me seriously, especially when I had a gun in my hand the size of a small cannon.

I carefully relieved him of his weapon and slid it into my side suit pocket. I backed up another two steps to investigate his wallet. The light was too dim, so I motioned him to face the apartment door, while I swung around to get closer to the light at the top of the stairs. He worked for Crown Investigation, as Earl and I had suspected. I took his seventeen dollars; it would be the least harmful thing I would do to him.

I waited a long enough time for him to have gone down to the pizzeria and come up after placing an order. It was overly cautious, but going up against two men called for caution.

When we entered, the guy at the window didn't turn. He said, "How long?"

With my Browning pointed, I said, "To live? Depends on what you do next."

Once I had them tied and gagged, I clocked them good. When you knock someone out cold, you always run the risk of killing them or leaving them with brain damage. Their heads seemed hard enough to take a clocking without permanent damage. I could tell they were both breathing. I had more to do to them.

The first one remained unconscious when I snapped his leg down near his ankle with no problem. The second one came out of it screaming into the gag when his leg broke, so I had to clock him again.

Breaking their legs wasn't in the plan, though I knew I would do it from the beginning. I didn't want Addie to think violence was too easy for me. Besides, two fewer men on the opposition made sense. On top of that, Joey and Gus had been murdered.

Once down the steps, I turned into the pizza parlor and ordered two large pies, one with pepperoni and the other with most everything offered. I smirked, thinking I would have money left over from the Crown op's seventeen bucks. After maybe crackers, cheese, grape jelly, more bologna sandwiches, and ice cream, Addie and Earl would appreciate the pies.

After parking Heldorfer's car in the tight parking lot of the Colton Arms, I took his coat and hat and went to his apartment. I paid him extra, since I forgot to refuel his heap. He shook my hand and thanked me, when it should have been the other way around.

Addie hugged me and planted a big kiss right on my lips. I must say, it stunned me for a few seconds, though I guess I should have expected it. I was new to the being-in-love business.

Since my Buick was parked out front on the street, the surveillance team in the car around the back would not be able to see us load up the car. Once my car was packed, including the back seat, Addie had to sit up front between us. I'm fairly sure she would have anyway.

Since we would be leaving Earl's car, I wondered if he wondered when he would drive it next, since I wondered when the next time would be when I slept in my own bed.

I said, "One more thing," before leaving the car and crossing the street.

When I came back with the pizza pies, both smiled.

The only one at the car lot was Honest John. He gave me a sales pitch about the dark gray '46 Chevrolet Stylemaster sedan, telling me it was souped-up and could go faster than it looked. He said he might lose fifty bucks, if he ended up selling my Buick. He wasn't asking for $50 to make the switch; he only wanted me to know. The switch went off without a hitch.

Addie was good and angry, despite having pizza to eat in the car, when I drove out of the city limits and headed south, toward Columbus. Yeah, she was on our team, but would be sitting it out on the bench. Earl supported the decision, though I had come up with it on my own. I couldn't do what I might have to do if I was mostly worrying about her safety.

Over the next several hours, she would revisit the argument and even tried raising her voice. I wouldn't argue or raise my voice. The decision was made. Finally she gave up and accepted it.

Two of our partners had been murdered and we had decided to do something about it. They had been pals. It was like the war; some of your guys died so you fought on to kill some of their guys. A dame, even as smart and savvy as Addie, might not understand it, though she probably did. We couldn't leave it up to the cops to pick up the pieces and make it work out fair. Earl and I only played an empty game claiming to each other that we weren't going to do anything about Joey and Gus. Without saying it, we knew we'd both always planned to even things up.

Earl went down to the bar in the swell Columbus hotel to give us time to say goodbye.

I gave Addie a grand and told her I would call her from time to time, when I could. I knew, and she was smart enough to know, that we might never see each other again.

Her kisses wouldn't stop. Her tears wouldn't stop. I don't ever remember a dame crying and kissing me at the same time.

"Make love to me. Earl won't mind waiting. I think that's why he left."

I wanted to as bad as I ever wanted anything. Earl and his Betty came to mind; once was better than never.

On a rainy night somewhere in Italy, Earl told me he had never consummated the love he had for Betty, though he was dying to do it before he left for the war. Betty was a virgin. The problem was he might die in the war and Betty would have given him what she was determined to give only to her husband. It was something like that; Earl told it better.

When Addie started to unbutton my pants, she could feel that I wanted what she wanted. I was a goner. A bomb falling on the hotel couldn't have stopped what happened next.

When I ordered my first drink at the hotel bar, Earl didn't want a fourth. He would never ask me what happened, because it wasn't right to ask a guy about what happened with a dame he loved, unless it was on a rainy night in Italy during a war.

Love was right, goddammit. Everything with Addie was better and more right than anything I could possibly imagine. I hoped wanting to get back to Addie wouldn't make me hesitate or play it too safe. I had a best friend to protect, two friends and partners to avenge, and the last dame I would ever be with to get back to.

Chapter 16.

After a busy day and surprising evening, I should have been tired, but my adrenaline was flowing like the rapids of a fast river.

Three drinks didn't usually impair Earl, but he seemed tired. Anyone else and I would have wondered what Addie and Earl had done all day long alone in my rooms. I knew better. I felt like I had betrayed their trust by even considering it. If you don't know what you're sure you know, better go back to birth and start over.

Addie was obviously not a virgin like Betty; Addie knew her way around a guy's body. Maybe it would have bothered me when I was younger or last Sunday, but it didn't now. Without making a noise, I laughed, thinking the test drive convinced me to buy the car I wanted to buy anyway.

From the chatter and scuttlebutt around bars and pool halls, virgins were unpredictable. It seemed some women would never like it and some would like it too much. Finding someone in the middle, who was good at it and liked it, but not too often with too many other guys, was the best you could do. With Addie, I hoped I found the perfect middle ground.

About forty-five minutes outside of downtown Cleveland, I pulled into a rest area and parked. It had been a long drive to Columbus and, nearly, back. The Chevy had plenty of gas, but I was on empty. Since Earl fought to stay awake talking to me to keep me awake, he was also on empty. The length of time it took me to think about the first three hours of sleep being all a person needed was how long it took me to fall asleep.

When Earl shook me awake, the sun was nearly halfway up in the eastern sky. After we ate the last two pieces of luke-cold pizza, relieved ourselves in the smelly cement block men's room, and reluctantly drank from an outdoor water faucet, we were awake enough to drive into Cleveland.

The Vincent House was a former mansion turned into an eighteen suite hotel, three floors of six suites, above a ground floor of offices, a bar, and a quality restaurant. Every amenity was provided at the Vincent House. It was far too expensive for us under normal circumstances. We had helped the hotel manager out of a jam with an underage girl. Earl knew the house dick through Gus, who once told Earl the retired cop could be trusted without making any joke about it. In the private detective business, you made either friends or enemies. Hopefully, your enemies would be in prison or too afraid or too dead to be a problem.

Earl talked the hotel manager, Eddie Dorn, into two suites across from each other, one where we were registered under the name of Mr. and Mrs. Spencer Washington. Knowing Earl, I suspected he took time to come up with the name, though he told me it had no meaning whatsoever. I would have cracked wise about the Mr. and Mrs., but those few hours of sleep left me wanting more sleep. I decided needing only three hours of sleep each day was hooey.

We would actually be staying unregistered in the room across the hall with a sign about remodeling on the door. With the two-room scheme, Earl came up with a new dodge I had not heard of.

The hotel manager was uneasy thinking gunplay might damage his hotel, but he went along knowing the underage girl, who was of age by now, could have her memory helped along by photos we had stashed away. A complete lie. Still, he was too petrified of the consequences not to go along.

The hotel dick was a good Joe, who was so bored that a little action sounded good to him. No action inside the hotel sounded better to us. If any action happened inside the hotel, we would probably be on the wrong end of it.

Woodrow "Woody" Blanton was our Joe, older and retired from the police force, with an easy-as-pie job. Having been a cop, he seemed to have the goods to tell if bad actors were nosing around. Earl gave him a C-note with a promise more would find their way into his pocket. He seemed to pay more attention to my mug than Earl's, though Earl did the talking. Needing more sleep, a shave, bath, and fresh clothes, I probably looked like a bad guy on the lam. If it got him off the idea we weren't a couple of guys weak in experience and shy to violence, my silence did what it was intended to do. Earl did the talking.

The posh suite included two bedrooms, a living room with a fireplace, and a large bathroom with both a shower and a bath. The availability of room service meant any kind of kitchen was unnecessary. Rich folks don't store and make their own food. Earl was joking when he wondered out loud whether the fireplace was big enough to burn a body.

I appreciated Earl's humor in the face of impending danger, but I needed sleep and not jokes. For a split second I wondered if I would dream about good things, like Addie, or bad things, like Joey and Gus.

I must have needed the ten hours of sleep, because that's how long before I woke up. I didn't remember dreaming. I was hungry again. No matter what was happening, eating needed to be thrown into the mix.

Earl had worked out that room service would deliver the food to the door across the hall, knock, and go away. Whatever Earl arranged with the hotel manager about tips was unimportant to me.

Earl must have slept less than I did, because he went on about possible action as we ate a good steak. The apple pie at the end of the meal was even better.

He basically said we could try to find the stolen books and money, which the opposition had so far been unable to do. Having the goods on Tony Jr.'s powder operation, we could turn it over to his father, who would thank us and let us go our own way. It sounded too civilized.

Making a deal with Tony Bacca, Jr. might be a better option. How exactly would it work, with what ironclad guaranties? Would Tony Jr. allow us to go back to our normal lives, if we returned the books and money? If I were him, I'd send us on a permanent sleep. Besides, how would that avenge Joey and Gus?

What would the father do, if we proved his son was in the powder racket and slabbed three people to keep him from finding out? The father might scold his son and send him to bed without supper and think we knew too much to continue breathing.

Since the war, we had not killed anyone, rightfully or wrongfully. While I wasn't sure Earl could stomach it, I was sure I could. If the State couldn't find a way to end Tony Jr.'s life, I could, at only a cost of a half-dozen bullets. If you're going to shoot someone to death, do it right, with enough bullets.

If I decided to murder Tony Bacca, Jr., I wouldn't discuss it with Earl or Addie. They might guess, but would never know. I would do it, if it was the only way out for us and it avenged Joey and Gus.

The father would want to avenge his son's death. Someone at Crown Investigation might want a reward and would tell him about how we disappeared and I broke a couple of legs in the process. We would be high on the list of persons worthy of torture and what inevitably follows a confession. I was tougher than Earl, I thought, but all men have a breaking point. I knew; I had seen war.

The problem with every option, especially murder, was unintended consequences.

After we pushed the food cart in front of the door across the hall, I said, "You wanted to go to the West Coast. We have some cash, maybe we should go." Running away with Addie had become very appealing to me.

"And someday, a bullet parts our hair in the back. I have a better idea. If we find the books, we send him a copy of several pages, saying if anything happens to us the original books go to the state's Attorney General and a copy to his father. I'm mostly sure money was also stolen. We keep half and give him back half to show we're straight up reasonable guys. Then, we grab, or maybe you grab, Addie, and we head to the West Coast. Everyone might just be happy enough with that."

"Sounds about right. So, we don't avenge Joey or Gus. You seem to go back and forth on that."

"We could leave that to God. Vengeance is mine and all that."

Much of what I believed seemed to be changing every five minutes. If the choice was between a life with Addie or vengeance, I would take Addie.

The tasty apple pie gave me an idea that sounded smart in a simple way. "First things first. Without any apples, you don't need a cart or a horse. So, who hid the apples and where? You can't make apple pie and give it or a slice of it to anyone, if you don't have apples."

Earl looked at me like he wanted to make a wisecrack about my apple logic. Maybe it made more sense as he thought about it, because he moved on without a wisecrack.

"Don't you think Joey or Gus would have done something to protect themselves? Hell, facing a bullet, wouldn't they give it up? I think it came at them too fast, before they had things set up. They would never have anticipated Crown's involvement. They ended up in the soup before it was in the pot."

"I say apples. You say soup."

"I think the broad stole the books and money, but never turned them over to Joey, who probably planned to turn them over to Gus, who would hide them. That would be Joey's safeguard. Maybe she didn't like the idea of handing over control to Joey. Maybe all she wanted from Joey was enough protection to get out of town and then to act as a bagman for the blackmail of Tony Bacca, Jr. Maybe Joey told her about Gus. When everything fell apart she gave up Joey and Gus, though they didn't know where the books and money were, leading Bacca to abduct her. The only way she stays alive is to repeat that she doesn't know and it was their fault they couldn't get Joey or Gus to talk. That's what I would do."

"If she were to get free of Bacca, she'll be looking for another sap to do her dirty work and be her go-between. A guy like me or you."

Earl said, "She must be something in bed. Tony Jr. didn't knock her off and trusted her to tell that cockamamie story to the cops of how her husband and Joey got dead."

"You know I'm in love with Addie. So, Earl, you're going to have to fall head over heels for her, if we rescue her."

After a shrug and a nod, Earl said, "All we have to do is find her, bust her out from wherever she's being held, and let me get alone with her to work my magic."

He expected my laugh when he'd said, "Work my magic," but I didn't oblige and said instead, "I'm just thinking, Earl. How wrong is this dame? She double-crosses her husband and a mob boss, watches guys getting murdered, lies about it to the cops, probably takes beatings and worse without cracking, and fucks every other guy along the way."

"You rarely say that word."

"This dame deserves it." I paused before saying, "You know she ain't no Jeannie from across the hall. Be careful."

"If we don't rescue Vera, remind me to call Jeannie for dinner sometime this coming week."

When I smiled, he smiled. I said, "I'll drive down to Columbus and pick up Addie. We can double date like the old days."

Chapter 17.

If a disguise was intended to fool someone for more than several minutes, then a Hollywood makeup artist, voice coach, and acting coach would be needed. We only needed to fool someone who had seen a photo of us long enough for us to walk past them without them thinking, "Isn't that Harry Hamm? Isn't that Earl Griggs?"

Fake beards and mustaches. Wigs. Eyeglasses with plain glass in them. Clothes we would normally never wear when introducing ourselves as ourselves. We rarely used disguises, but we would be hanging around a hornet's nest and needed to look like anyone but ourselves.

We had already missed Gus's wake on Sunday. We weren't going to his funeral on Monday. Most wouldn't know us. A few might take note of our absence. His father-in-law, Arthur, might wonder if we were busy tracking down Gus's killer.

The worst place for us to show up would be the funeral, because Crown ops would look there first. We had disappeared, and I left two of their men with broken legs. Finding us and returning the favor had to be at the top of their list.

We took the day to try on disguises, rest, and eat. It gave Tommy Carter another day, a Monday, to photograph and develop pictures of Crown Investigation employees. I grinned at the thought of seeing two ops in leg casts, though if I had done my job correctly, neither would be going to work for some time.

Earl showed off his college when he said, "Socrates said to *know thyself.* He should have said *know thy enemy*."

My response was, "Sock-ra-who?"

We considered the idea of a new assignment for Tommy Carter. He could take photos of people coming out of Captain Nero's. Going in were the backs of heads. Coming out would be the faces.

We nixed the idea. The last thing we would want would be Tommy's blood on our hands. Earl also pointed out that Feds or local cops might be watching the joint. We had to be careful ourselves.

Since we were disguised as working stiffs, using the swanky hotel's freight elevator seemed like a good idea. Yeah, we were the ones doing the supposed remodeling of the suite where, in reality, we were hiding out. Earl thought we shouldn't use the hotel phone. He worried phone companies could do more than the general public might know when it came to tracing calls and having a record of who called who. Once you put those kinds of ideas in your head, you could take the next step and wonder who could pay who to do what at the phone company. Another step further led to a certain distrust of coppers. Maybe someone like Detective Ted Matthews was okay for what our business had been, but that didn't mean others weren't in the pocket of the Bacca mob. As we saw it, the biggest problem with coppers was too many knowing too much.

I said, "Loose lips sink ships. That's ah…John Paul Jones." When Earl smiled, I said, "He was the only one I could think of. Not sure why I thought of him. Something about he wasn't done fighting, I think."

"They said it in boot camp and never mentioned who came up with it."

"Sometimes you're annoying, Earl."

"I know."

We drove out to Tommy Carter's parent's house. When he came to the door after we told his mother we were there to see him, he looked confused for several seconds, which was about the length of time it would have taken us to pass him in the street, coming and going time.

"Jesus, guys. Good disguises. My mom asked me if a couple of working guys were here to offer me a job." He paused. "That's the best she could think of. Okay. I'll get the photos."

We walked to the front yard fence and Tommy joined us with the photos. I leafed through them first. As I expected, the two ops from above the pizza parlor weren't among the photos.

Tommy said, "There was a lot of activity on Sunday and Monday. A few are duplicates. Was it you guys that stirred them up?'

I nodded. "Yeah."

"A couple of them look like hoods, not private investigators. Does that make any sense to you?" asked Tommy.

I repeated. "Yeah. I saw the ones you mentioned." I handed the stack to Earl. I went in my pocket and counted out fifty dollars and handed it to Tommy.

Earl said, "Good job, kid. I think this is all we need."

"What else can I do? I'll do anything."

"Don't wait by the phone," Earl said and continued, "but we'll leave a message when we need you next."

"I suppose you're not going to tell me anything more."

"You suppose right." I followed with, "You're a smart kid. Stay smart."

At a cigarette and candy store, we bought cigarettes and changed folding money for coins to make phone calls at a public booth.

Since we didn't know who was being watched or having their phones tapped, Earl decided to call Clark Simmons, a newspaper reporter, whom no one knew Earl knew, not even me. So, he was Earl's secret source of information and how we leaked information to the press when we needed. Simmons never used his byline, so no one tied him to the Diamond Detective Agency.

Earl explained to me how he paid Simmons and kept him off the books. Keeping Simmons as his secret inside-the-press guy made Earl more valuable to the partners. I was only beginning to know Earl's mind ran far deeper than mine. Continuing to keep the secret inside guy from me didn't make sense now, since we were the only ones left and in trouble. Earl used a pay phone and set up a meet.

Though we were disguised so well I didn't recognize either of us, we took no chances and met Clark Simmons in the children's clothes section of the department store on Ontario and Euclid. It seemed like the last place where we would run into anyone from Crown Investigation or Tony Bacca, Jr.'s mob.

We circled around and watched Simmons, a heavy older guy with wire-rimmed glasses. I wondered how Earl knew him for a minute, then thought Earl would tell me if he thought I should know.

Earl finally approached Simmons by saying, "Clark, its Earl."

Simmons did a double take and seemed to forget to breathe. "Christ, you scared me. Are you sure you're you? How much trouble are you guys in?"

Earl introduced me as his partner without using my name.

That didn't last long, since Simmons put two and two together. "Oh yeah, Joey Alfonso and Gus Reese. You must be Harry Hamm. Are those murders connected? Are you guys next? What's the real story?"

"Stop being a reporter for a minute."

Simmons' stronger voice surprised me, "No, you wait a minute. Two partners are dead and you're disguised so your mothers wouldn't recognize you. I need to know what's going on, before I get involved, if I get involved."

Earl seemed to ignore the question and say, "We need to know everything you can get on the Tony Baccanelli mob, especially Tony Jr., and Crown Investigation."

Taking a step back, Simmons said, "No. Answer my question. Better yet, don't tell me anything else. I'm leaving. Don't call me again."

Earl gave me a look. Since I was standing closest to Simmons, I took hold of his arm with my strong mitt.

With quick words Earl said, "Tony Jr. is in the powder business. Noah Jameson, the dead accountant, handled the books and cash."

When Simmons covered his left ear with his left hand, I thought it odd, unless he was deaf in his right ear. I stepped behind Simmons and grabbed his left arm, pulling it from his ear.

Earl took a quick look around to see if anyone was paying attention. He seemed satisfied and continued, "The murder and suicide over Jameson's wife was a lie."

"She lied?"

"Straight through her lipstick."

"Don't tell me anymore."

I whispered to the back of Simmons' left ear, "What kind of newshawk are you?"

"A live one."

"The wife lied because she never stopped being Tony Jr.'s dame. Incriminating drug ledgers and money are missing. Gus Reese didn't know, and they plugged him. The Jameson house was torn apart. We had two teams from Crown Investigation watching us. We gave them the slip."

"So far."

"Yeah, so far."

Simmons asked his wisest question. "Do you know what they think you might know?"

"No." With a friendly, though unfriendly, smile that I rarely saw from Earl, he said, "And now you know enough to be involved."

I felt the tension go out of his arms.

"Okay, it's going to cost you."

"Better hope it doesn't cost you."

Back in the car, Earl was driving toward Captain Nero's for our first look-see, when I said, "Once we're on the West Coast, you won't need Simmons."

"That's the way I saw it. He'll do the job. He knows too much not to. Plus, I think you almost made him piss his pants."

I completed his logic. "All we have to do is drop his name and what he knows to the wrong people. Criminals try to never kill cops, but they love killing reporters. We've graduated to blackmail."

Earl said, "We've graduated up to everything except murder. And maybe that, if it's us or them."

"We killed our share in the war. At least we have experience on our side."

"The other side of that is how much experience they have on their side. I'm not too worried about the Crown guys. Mob guys are another story."

Chapter 18.

At the end of a long wooden-planked pier with parking on both sides sat Captain Nero's, a restaurant of Italian cuisine specializing in Italian fish dishes. The front façade was the side of a ship's hull attached to the building. On the roof was a cabin, captain's bridge, and a mast. It was legendary for fine dining, if you didn't mind rubbing elbows with mob types. One might call it a colorful experience.

I had eaten at Captain Nero's twice. Both times I chose the more familiar pasta dishes, instead of the fish dishes with names I didn't know. I found the food delicious and watching the Italian mobsters sprinkled throughout the joint kind of comical. They tried too hard to live up to the reputation of a *dago* mobster.

The story I'd pieced together over the years, after several bar and pool hall conversations, was the restaurant and bar areas of Captain Nero's fronted the back rooms where mob business was conducted. During Prohibition, more than Lake Erie largemouth bass, white bass, bluegill, and catfish were brought into the lakeside part of the building. Canadian hooch was only fifty miles across the lake.

I didn't know who actually owned the joint. Everyone knew it was the hangout for the Baccanelli mob. Perhaps if the diners knew what happened in the back rooms, the food wouldn't taste as good. The rumors about the joint ran the gamut from prostitution to gambling to murder. From my private eye perspective, the place was too well-known by too many for many criminal acts to occur, other than maybe cash changing hands and hoods bragging and acting like hoods.

A part of me wanted to walk in and have a meal. Our disguises gave me confidence. Wouldn't it be the last thing they would expect?

Earl thought it was a bad idea. "Let's say we walk in and lay our cards on the table. We say that we don't know anything and promise to forget what we do know. Wouldn't pieces of us be fed to the fish in Lake Erie?"

"I meant to check out the place. That's all."

"Oh. I thought you had gone soft in the head."

"Thanks, partner."

"Sorry, Harry. I don't want Addie to be a widow before she's even a wife. That happened fast. Addie."

"For a year or so, I've been thinking I want a couple of kids, meaning I would need a wife. I've been thinking about Addie for almost that long. The two thoughts recently came together." I paused. "When we get to the West Coast, maybe we should get into a different line of work. I'm thinking of Gus Reese, his wife, and kids."

"Me, too."

We parked about a quarter of a mile away. The closest we could have parked to the pier was half that distance. We wanted to slowly walk our way there, watching.

Trying not to be obvious or hang around too long, we looked at windows and for men in parked cars. We didn't see anything that would lead us to believe Captain Nero's was under surveillance. Men sitting in parked cars would be the dead giveaway, if someone were going to follow someone. Seeing activity in windows that shouldn't have so much activity took more time to spot, but sooner or later someone would gaze too long from a window.

After pushing our presence in the area to a half hour, we drove away to find a bar we had never been to before. We planned to have a beer or two and go back and look again in an hour.

We sat at a round table away from the few other customers. Just two working stiffs having a beer and a smoke. We spoke soft and low, so our words would go no further than each other's ears.

Earl laid it out. "We're going to need another car, if we're going to follow someone by leapfrogging. It's a shame we have two perfectly good cars parked and doing nothing, mine and Addie's."

"Maybe we should find out if anyone still has eyes on my place and your car."

"I'm wondering what the cops are thinking."

"How so?" I said and took a sip.

"Do you think they think we're missing?"

"Hadn't thought of that, but, yeah. We've suddenly gone missing, haven't we? They might think we're dead and they haven't found our bodies yet."

"There's nothing in the papers, but I'll bet they have APBs out on us. Maybe we should call Matthews from a pay phone to let him know we're alive and working on things. Nah, he went out on the limb telling you what he did," Earl stopped to light one up before saying, "I can't see him pushing the other cops to not look for two gumshoes like us and let us solve this for them. Matthews has been more than okay, but we don't really know him."

"Not well enough for me to invite him to my wedding."

Earl gave me a look like I was thinking too much about Addie and not concentrating on what we were doing.

"It was a joke. Don't worry about me. It would be bad news if the news said we were missing. On another note, how much can we trust Simmons or someone like Honest John, if they heard we disappeared and might be dead? If Honest John gives up the car and plate number, it could be worse than having the cops after us. Some copper would leak it to Tony Bacca, Jr."

"I agree. We need to dump this car and buy another one."

"Don't we need a driver's license to do that?"

"I don't know. Wait a minute. Cars are for sale in the newspaper. You think someone is going to ask someone for a driver's license over a few hundred bucks? We'd need plates."

Since Earl was having every idea, I felt some accomplishment when I said, "Police vehicle impound lot. Remember the guy who had his car impounded because they caught him drunk driving?"

"I don't remember."

"Maybe I didn't tell you or any of the guys. He had stolen merchandise in the trunk."

Wide-eyed, Earl asked, "What did you do that you shouldn't have done and didn't tell anyone about?"

"The impound lot on Shaft Road has a cliff, maybe fifteen feet high, at the back of the property. There's no fence. Only a lunatic would try to steal a car by driving it off that cliff. We didn't do that, but we climbed the cliff and grabbed the stuff. I'm still surprised the cops hadn't looked in the trunk." I shrugged before saying, "He was my Aunt Celia's boy, my first cousin."

"What else have you done that I don't know about?"

"Maybe I'll tell you when this is over and we're on the West Coast. Anyway – the point – there are cars not quickly claimed and those cars have license plates. We should swipe a few and use them – disguises for the cars we drive. What are the odds anyone would spot them missing? Cops look for stolen cars, not stolen plates. Besides, we could change them every couple of days."

"I must be going as looney as you, because it makes sense."

I had another idea. "Remember when we were spotters in Italy? We went to the highest point. Often the climb wore us out. We were outside of... What was that town? It doesn't matter. It had a tower. So, I'm thinking the observation deck at the Terminal Tower. I'll bet you can see Captain Nero's from there without using binoculars. If we identify Tony Bacca, Jr.'s car, we might be able to see where he's stashing the dame, if it's not too far away."

"Even with buildings getting in the way, it sounds feasible. Captain Nero's can't be much more than a mile from the Terminal Tower. He lives someplace, right? Simmons will get us that. It's when he doesn't head in that direction. Let's say we lose him at Broadway and 93rd and he's not headed home. We camp out there and wait to pick up his tail the next time. If he's worried about being followed, won't he feel safe after a few miles of not being followed, so he doesn't pay attention any longer?"

Earl had to explain it two more different ways before I understood him. I had the idea, while he figured out the details. Partners.

Jameson's wife was more missing than we were, because the papers knew about her and not about us. If she was dead or kept out of town without Tony Jr. visiting her, we were behind the eight ball. But if Tony Jr. had her stashed nearby, we had a chance.

He said, "Maybe we're going about this all wrong. Maybe we should be asking ourselves where Vera Jameson hid the books and money."

"I have no ideas on that. Not in her house. That I know."

"If they think this dame knows something, they're not going to kill her, if she doesn't tell them. She would know that. She'd hold out, no matter what they do to her. I don't want to think about that."

We were walking over old ground, but it was important to repeat where the landmines were located.

"Then we sweep in, like knights in shining armor. You do what you have to do to sweet-talk her, or whatever it takes, to make us partners, only we're smarter than Joey or Gus. Once we have the books, and, we're still assuming, some cash, we give it back to them and make a deal to walk away, like we've been working for them the whole time. Well, that's one option."

"If that works, her life won't be worth a plugged nickel."

"What are Joey and Gus's lives worth? She made her bed. Sounds like with several guys. She'll have to sleep the long sleep in it."

Pushing back until the front legs of the chair were off the ground, I leaned my head back and shook my head. "Maybe we should take the money we have left, skip town and disappear," I said, probably too loudly, walking over more old ground.

Earl commented, "It still may come to that, if things get too hairy, Harry."

That was almost good for a laugh, but not quite. I knew Earl was right; we shouldn't feel bad for the dame. Our lives mattered more, or, at least, our lives didn't deserve to end over this. We hadn't done anything, yet, to deserve the long sleep.

Our plan to save her sounded good up close. From a longer realistic view, it probably looked like a field of landmines. Take the wrong step and *BOOM.* There was nothing we feared more in the war than landmines.

Chapter 19.

What was the old saying? *In for a penny, in for a pound.* Was it about money or meat? From my time in England, it could have been about money.

With a flathead and a Phillips screwdriver each, flashlights, and small cans of lubricant, we followed a path I had used before to climb up the cliff. The steep cliff was made easier by the path that kids had made.

When we reached the top, sometime after midnight, Earl saw what I knew. The police vehicle compound was wide and long with several hundred vehicles parked in ragged rows.

The front of the compound, on the far side, was well-lit. It had what looked to be a guard shack just inside the metal fence and near the gates. Everything looked quiet. Even if a police tow truck pulled up with a vehicle, there wasn't any room to drop a vehicle where we were, where the longest-impounded vehicles were.

Finding plates with the right 1949 date caused us to cut the distance to the guard shack by a third. Vehicles passing on the street gave us plenty of cover to mask the sound of what we were doing.

Each with a stack of Ohio plates and a couple of out-of-state plates, we were done and down the cliff in less than two hours. Earl had suggested out-of-state plates were more difficult for the police to check than Ohio plates. I'm not sure how it would come into play. If we were stopped and were with or without our driver licenses, the game was over, regardless of which state's prisoners made the license plate.

The next day, after a third pay phone call, Earl drove to a house on West 38th Street, not nearly as rundown as most of the houses on the street.

Tears were in his eyes, as the guy, maybe a decade older than us with a patch over one eye and a gimpy leg, talked about his black convertible 1942 Packard Clipper 8, now for sale. He seemed to know everything about it. It was one of the last vehicles produced before the line closed down civilian production for the war effort. The chrome had been blacked out, but he had it restored in '46.

I was less impressed than Earl. It was a two-door with limited trunk space. I wondered how many guns and bodies we could haul in it, though I said nothing.

Earl was his normal friendly talkative self. The guy had fought in the Pacific, where he lost the eye and got the gimpy leg – his monthly disability check wasn't worth what the war had done to him, though he wasn't bitter about the war. What needed to be done was done. Naturally, Earl told him how we were in Italy, France, and Germany. The man made a comment about how we should have worked with the Germans because the Russian communists were worse.

Though the man rarely used the car – its mileage was under 25,000 – he kept it well-maintained, but now he couldn't afford to maintain it. The original cost was about $1,600. He was asking $600. I was thinking $400. Earl agreed to the $600. I didn't balk. The disabled vet needed the extra $200 more than we did.

Cash and signed-over title were exchanged. The man was in tears and told us to just drive it away and toss away the license plates when we were able. He couldn't bear to see the car one second longer. The man turned his back and dragged his gimpy leg toward his front porch and door.

Earl and I shared a look. We had used the recently stolen plates for the Chevy from Honest John. We wouldn't need stolen plates for the Packard, though our shared look said we would switch plates. We wouldn't want the disabled vet to get in Dutch because his vehicle was used in a criminal activity. Other than stealing the plates and me breaking a couple of legs, who knew what else we might have to do that was outside the law.

We drove both cars and found a pay phone on 45th Street. Earl called Simmons and set up a meeting late in the afternoon to get whatever information he had for us. I overheard it was set for four at the same place in the department store.

After Earl hung up, I picked up the phone and announced I wanted to call Addie. Earl looked like he wanted to object but said nothing.

After putting in the coins the operator requested, I heard a click and then a phone ringing. I gave the desk clerk Addie's room number and waited.

"Hello."

"It's me."

"Thank God, I was going crazy. You're obviously okay because you're phoning. Earl okay, too?"

"We're fine."

"Harry, I can't do this any longer. I've been thinking. They know I'm involved from being at your place and then disappearing like you guys. If they kill you guys, don't you think they won't feel safe until they track me down and kill me, too? Would I ever feel safe, besides kind of not wanting to live without you? I dyed, cut, and permed my hair. It's more my natural color, which you know, because of…you know. I have these curls now. I may look like Shirley Temple's mother, but I could more easily wear a wig. I hope you still love me as much as I love you. Pick me up at the downtown bus station at four this afternoon. See you then, bye."

Without her saying another word, she hung up the phone and I said to a very curious Earl, "You're probably not going to like this, but I have to pick up Addie at the bus station at four. Before you throw a fit or anything, I had no say in it. She's coming back to town. I can't leave her walking around in the open on her own. She's in this with us. If they get us, they're going to want to get her. She's like us, she wants a fighting chance to save herself."

After taking ten steps away from me, Earl lit a cigarette with his back to me; I could see smoke, fairly sure it wasn't coming out of his ears.

He walked back to me and said, "Know what pisses me off? Before we die, you're going to get laid and I'm not."

I was smiling as I said, "If you wouldn't have spent so much on the Packard, you could have spent it on several pro skirts."

He laughed. "You're right. Wait, she must have most of the grand we gave her left, plus we still have plenty of cash."

Nodding, I said, "I think Addie will go along with what I think you're thinking."

"Alright. I'll meet with Simmons. You pick up Addie. Tomorrow we put eyes on Tony Bacca, Jr."

"We'll have three sets of eyes."

Nodding positively while frowning, Earl uttered, "Yeah. I have a feeling the papers are going to announce that we're missing and wanted by the cops for questioning. Soon. After your talk with Matthews, you believed the cops were using us as bait. I think you're right about that. We should brace up the hotel manager and drop more cash on the hotel dick. And don't even look happy, you lucky son-of-a-bitch."

"Yeah, I'm real happy. The woman I love will be bait like us. Real happy."

When I spotted her I was happy to see her, as long as I left my thoughts at that. "Hey lady, need a ride?"

She expected the voice and not the hairy face, only my Harry face, but she gave me a hug and kiss. She whispered in my ear, "I need a ride," before backing away and saying more loudly, "I don't like beards."

Once two people have gone as far as they can and enjoyed it, the words they say have meanings beyond what they are saying.

She matched my normal walking pace, though I think we both wanted to run and get to the hideout's bed. One time together and everything had changed. I heard love could be like that, though I had never experienced it.

I said, "Your hair. You look like…Shirley Temple all grown up."

"You look like her father."

"Now I have to get that thought out of my bean."

Expecting something else, she was about to walk past the Packard, when I said, "This is us. Surprise."

Addie sat next to me as I drove, her hip against my hip. I wished we were going to a movie or dinner, not to a hideout, though a hideout would end up better. Why couldn't this be happening without the danger?

On the short ride to the hotel, I explained everything that had happened and not happened. When I was done, it didn't seem like Earl and I accomplished much.

More impressed than I expected, she said, "Good. Playing it slow and safe is smart. If I think we should go away and disappear, will you listen to me, regardless of what Earl thinks?"

"Yes," I quickly said. I had a growing motivation not to fix what couldn't be fixed. Earl might be the monkey wrench that could make me change my mind. Could I let Earl go it alone, while I skipped off into the sunset to the West Coast with Addie? Wasn't Addie a kind of monkey wrench between Earl and me? Her grip on me was growing tighter.

Walking down the hallway from the freight elevator, I nodded to a room and said, "We're registered there, but we're staying here," and I led her to the room across the hall.

She quickly picked up on it. "Smart. Your idea?"

"Earl's."

Inside the hotel room, she said, "Nice digs for a hideout. Two bedrooms?"

"Yes."

"Take me to ours."

"Earl might be back from meeting Simmons at any time."

Her looks told me everything. Earl knowing we were sleeping together had no significance considering our precarious situation.

Inside the bedroom I had been using, I asked, "Beard off or on?"

She said, "If you can get it off in a few seconds…"

"I have protection for this time."

Without pausing, as she took her clothes off, she said, "If it matters to you. It doesn't matter to me."

I didn't have time to think about what she said until we were done making love. If we lived long enough to have a child together, it would mean everything worked out okay. If she lived long enough to have my child, but I didn't, she'd have something left from me. We picked the worst time to fall in love, though picking had nothing to do with it. It happened and there was nothing we could do about it, except have what we could have, and do everything humanly possible to keep having it.

We dressed slowly as if neither of us wanted to be dressed.

"Earl is jealous of us. He's going to feel lonelier now that you're back. Is there anyone…?"

"Men and their pals. Considering our situation, would female companionship help Earl continue to be smart?"

"I don't know. It doesn't make me smarter, but it makes me more motivated."

The dimples in her smile enhanced her grown-up Shirley Temple look.

"How about that professional skirt you guys helped out of a jam? She had a guy's name, spelled different… Sounds like Sid. Yeah, C-Y-D."

"Yeah, her. I think it might be round two for Earl."

"With a client?"

"Not certain, but I think client went both ways."

"It shouldn't matter. It was in the past. Harry, did you…?"

"No. I'm cheap. I want it for free."

Her laugh went low, then she said, "Harry, nothing's for free."

When I came out of the bedroom wearing pants and the sleeveless undershirt that was tragically called a wife-beater, Earl was seated on the couch looking at pages. "From Simmons?

He nodded and said, "Did you hear me out here?"

"No."

"I heard you in there. The detective in me tells me Addie is back."

I grinned a grin that would make any guy jealous. "Hey, remember that skirt named Cyd? Addie brought back most of the dough we gave her."

Earl's shrug, in a positive manner, filled in the words I didn't have to say.

When Addie came out of the bedroom wearing all of her clothes, Earl said, "Shirley Temple, all grown up."

Addie said, "Earl, aren't you supposed to take Jeannie from the travel agency to dinner this week?"

"I forgot about her," he said.

"Not good, Earl. Don't ever tell a woman you forgot about her," Addie cautioned.

With my best smile and sneer, I said, "You could take her to Captain Nero's and try one of those crazy Italian fish dishes. If they recognize you, maybe they won't make you pay for the meals."

"Addie, are you sure you want to be with him? He's very strange."

"Pretty sure."

Chapter 20.

As Earl read a page he would hand it to me. I read the page and handed it to Addie to read. We were a team, only the game we were playing didn't necessarily mean someone went home and had another game to play in the future.

At six foot two, Tony Baccanelli, Jr. was four inches taller than his father. He was taller than I was and taller than most men. He weighed about a hundred and twenty pounds less than his fat father. He was said to be spoiled, quick to anger, and reputably quick to violence. He might have been good-looking enough to be a movie star, a gangster movie star.

He lived in the best part of Shaker Heights with his wife and two kids, a boy and a girl. From his reputation, his wife was married to him but not necessarily the other way around.

He ran Captain Nero's and was his father's second-in-command on everything else. Since Simmons mentioned nothing about Tony Jr.'s side powder business, it must have been a well-kept secret. He never went anywhere without at least two hoods at his side. He was questioned by the cops six times and arrested three times, though nothing ever stuck.

The father, Fat Tony, was old school, a mustache Pete. He was implicated in four murders without any consequences. Speculation of prostitution, loan-sharking, gambling, unions, and robberies never lead to a successful prosecution. Layers of underbosses, below his son's level in the criminal enterprise, insulated him. No one called him Fat Tony to his face.

One unsubstantiated story was an argument where Tony Jr. went after his father with a steak knife. He was held back by two of the fat man's bodyguards. Rumor had it that Fat Tony put a slug in his son's leg, while the two henchmen held him and he said, "I'm Boss, you're only my son." Nice family. Probably a barrel of laughs during holidays.

The information on Crown Investigation wasn't anything we didn't already know. They mostly kept their private eye business private.

A couple of glossies of a mostly-dressed Vera told what the newspaper photos hinted at; she was a sexy redhead with a look that could back up everything her body promised. She was a dame guys would fight over and die for. She was as wrong as a dame could be. She was the kind of dame who left a guy's heart in his throat and wondering if he had been a fool.

I think everyone was thinking the same after we read everything Simmons gave us. We were up against too much. Maybe Earl and Addie were smart and I was tough, but was it enough to stay alive? Maybe we would be lucky, luckier than Joey, Gus, and Vera's husband.

Out of nowhere, Addie stood up and looked around. "Doesn't anyone ever clean up this place?"

"No, but they clean our place across the hall," I said thinking she might have forgotten what I told her, or maybe it was something humorous to say.

Before Earl and I visited the hotel manager, Eddie Dorn, we put our disguises back on. No place was safe outside our hideout, including any other place inside the hotel.

Earl asked me to stand behind him and look tough. In other words, my normal look. Since Dorn was a nervous type, I could have looked half the part and made him afraid of me.

Inside the manager's office, Earl said to Dorn, "Don't sit down, this won't take long. Sometime soon the papers are going to say we are missing and wanted by the cops for questioning. The story is a plant; we're actually working undercover with a few cops who can be trusted. Don't be civic-minded and tip off the cops. They might be the wrong ones and put us in a bad situation, meaning you would be in a bad situation. Your secret will stay safe with us. If you were to play any part in things going wrong, they will go wrong for you as well. We've entrusted things to someone who won't be touched by any of this. Once that person starts things in motion against you, no one could stop what would happen to you. *Capisce*?"

He nodded and meekly uttered, "I understand." His fingers twitched as if there was something stuck to them.

"One more thing. His wife is now staying with us. Anything happens to her…"

He was scared before Earl added the last part. Double scared might be how we left him.

As we walked to find the hotel dick, Woody Blanton, I said, "My wife?"

"Except for a justice of the peace and a cake, is it much of a lie?"

"What happens if she's mentioned in the paper as missing and not as my wife? He might think you lied about several things."

"Next time I see him, I'll tell him your marriage is common law."

"Sounds like a bigger lie. I never understood. The *common* part of common law doesn't sound right. Why do people get marriage licenses with common law marriage being so easy?"

"Churches and lawyers and divorces, I imagine. Don't worry about Dorn, the underage girl would destroy his life; he'd have to kill himself."

We found Woody Blanton in the hotel bar more than looking at a tall glass of beer. For a split second, I thought he thought we were trouble coming to interrupt his beer drinking.

With the remaining portion of the second, he recognized us and said, "Not bad looks for shamuses."

Again, Earl did the talking. "We won't be here long enough to leave an impression. I guess having a beer is a part of your job."

He shrugged. "You came here to say something, say it."

"We're going to be famous soon. Missing and wanted for questioning. We're working with a few of your old honest friends."

"Both of them," he said with a slight smile. "Don't tell me anything else. Once I read about Gus Reese, I figured the murder and suicide over the dame was malarkey. I'm guessing *wops* are involved." He started, "Why else…" and stopped. He looked at me. "I saw you bring the dame with the curls in. Permanent or visiting?"

"Permanent," I said.

Earl said, "Don't bring trouble to us and another C-note will end up in your pocket."

Blanton expelled air like a whistle with no sound to it. "Better give me half now, just in case."

After Earl rather openly gave him fifty in cash, which he tucked into his vest pocket, Earl said, "If everything works out, I'll give you what I have on Eddie Dorn. You'll have the easiest job in the world, for life."

"It was already the second easiest. First is dead and nobody wants that job." He nodded once as if he had nothing left to say and turned back to his beer.

Cops, private dicks, and hoods cracked wise, especially to each other. Wherever you fell on the line from lawful to criminal, you cracked wise. Sounding off wise and being wise were different and had no real connection. Gus Reese once said to me, "I've been a cop and a private detective, so I know how to talk like a hood. It's like a trifecta of smartass, half smart, half ass, and halfway to being any one of three."

I remember wanting to counter wiseass by saying something about three halves is one half too many. If I did, it would only prove his point. So I kept quiet.

On our way back to our room across from the room where we were registered under an alias, I asked, "That last part with the house dick bought more than money can buy."

Back in the unregistered suit of rooms Addie had made more presentable in our absence, we decided to order room service. I wondered if we were paying for the suite and the food or if Dorn was taking care of the tab. It didn't matter enough for me to ask Earl.

I asked Addie to write down the food orders, then wondered if I was being too bossy. It wasn't like we were at work at the agency. When she took the food order without cracking wise, I knew she wasn't one of us yet.

To show her how it was done, I walked her over to the suite across the hall and phoned in the order. Dorn had told us room service could tell which room was phoning in orders.

The choice, as I explained, was to wait in the suite for room service, but not answer the knock. They were told to knock and leave.

Or, we could go back across the hall and wait to hear the knock on the opposite suite's door.

She said, "So they never actually see who's in the empty suite. Okay, got it. It's simple enough, but I wonder what they will think about bringing three meals instead of only two?"

We were eating, when I asked Earl Addie's question about three meals instead of two.

He cracked wise and said, "Mrs. Spencer Washington is with child and eating for two." When we both looked at him incredulously, he said, "Every little detail can't be perfect. I promise you that won't get us killed."

I responded, "I take no comfort in that, Earl."

By the time we ate and wheeled the two room service carts in front of the door across the hall, I faked a yawn and said, "I'm beat. Big day tomorrow. I'm going to bed."

Addie faked an even bigger yawn, almost laughing as she said, "Me, too. See you bright and early in the morning, Earl."

My last look at Earl told me he wished he could trade places with me. That would only happen over my dead body.

The word *dead* seemed to fit into just about everything I thought about. The only good thing, if you could call it that, was you would be the only one who didn't know you were dead. If I weren't about to climb into bed with Addie, I might dwell on it.

Chapter 21.

What I learned by morning was spending the night with Addie was better than drinks at a bar with pals or watching a 12-inch television. Being in bed together for so long gave us time for everything, including enough restful sleep.

As I pulled on pants and slipped on a shirt, I watched her sleep. I preferred her hair before the curly Shirley Temple style. How old was Shirley Temple? I remembered seeing her last year in the western *Fort Apache* with John Wayne and Henry Fonda. She had grown from a curly-haired cute kid into an attractive young woman. The curls were mostly gone. She would have round cheeks and dimples forever. Addie bore no resemblance to her.

In the living room, Earl was writing something down on paper. For early in the morning, after an event-filled bedtime, I must have felt like a wise guy, when I asked, "Last will and testament?"

Earl wasn't amused. "Writing things down helps my memory. There's coffee and the morning paper on the room service cart."

"How long have you been awake?"

"For some time. I'm been thinking we should use the '46 Chevy from Honest John and change those plates to out-of-state ones. Why would Honest John help out the coppers? What would he have to gain?"

"Maybe a reward?"

"We made the morning papers. It seems we're missing and wanted for questioning in the murder of Gus Reese. A reward isn't mentioned. We don't look good in the pictures."

After pouring myself a coffee, I looked at the front page pictures of Earl and me. After a sip of coffee, I said, "It makes me look worse. That's not an easy thing to do."

"Harry, you're not that bad looking. I've only picked on you because you think you are. You landed Addie, didn't you?"

"That was sweet, Earl, like I like my coffee. Addie will be pleased to know I landed her like a fish."

"Maybe I was thinking of her as a plane?"

For a moment I thought about his quick comeback. "That makes no sense, unless it has a dirty meaning I've never heard."

"I don't know what I meant. Just being obstinate. So, Honest John would know we would give up his stolen vehicle business. Nah, he won't bite and do his civic duty."

"Is that another of those minor risks that probably won't get us killed?" I didn't wait for a wisecrack response from Earl and said, "There's nothing about Addie. That makes sense. They'd only know about her if the opposition tipped them off."

It was strange for me to have Addie sharing the bathroom and dressing in the bedroom. I could only imagine it was stranger for Earl to be a roommate to a couple in love.

We decided it didn't make sense to think Tony Bacca, Jr. would be at Captain Nero's early in the morning; he wouldn't be punching a timeclock card. After a leisurely late breakfast and donning our disguises, Addie and I took the Chevy, while Earl drove the Packard with the ragtop up. The day was slate gray and chilly, more like fall. Top-down convertible season was over, unless there would be an Indian summer.

No mention was made of Addie being a limited partner of the team. In truth, Addie was in as much danger as we were. She was into it up to her eyeballs. I may have smiled thinking I was into her up to her…heart.

It was late morning. We were in a safe position, about a hundred and fifty yards away from Captain Nero's with only two sets of binoculars. The first time I passed my binoculars to Addie to watch, it felt odd. Her being only an office worker no longer applied. We also weren't a romantic couple sharing binocular looks at a romantic blue moon.

Several mob types in expensive cars, fedoras, and overcoats arrived between 11:30 and noon, but none were Tony Jr. or his father, Fat Tony. At just after noon, I was on the binoculars and saw a smaller, thin-faced thug, wearing what I thought was a too-big overcoat, arrive and stand outside his car. I guessed he was armed to the hilt under the overcoat.

"I'm leaving to get a better angle on the car's license plate of the short guy who just arrived."

To that, Addie only nodded with pursed lips.

Seeing the New York license plate made me immediately think he was a torpedo brought in from New York. It was a hunch. It took a pro to make the death scene of Noah Jameson and Joey look like it did. It was the precision of the shots killing Joey. It took a pro to torture and shoot Gus that way. My white-hot urge was to do to the torpedo what he had done to Gus. Addie hadn't taken the animal instinct out of me. I wouldn't hesitate to plug someone who deserved plugging.

On the other hand, the short guy in the big coat could be a dinnerware salesman from Poughkeepsie.

From the photos supplied and the description of his red Caddy by the newshawk, Simmons, we saw Tony Bacca, Jr. arrive at a quarter past noon with a driver and two bodyguards. The driver and thugs provided a perimeter while Tony Jr. had a private conversation with the guy from New York. The magnification of the binoculars took me close enough to watch Tony Jr.'s lips move. If I ever had a chance to be a private detective again, I would learn to read lips. Why didn't any of us think of lip-reading, before we bought weapons and suits?

It looked like Tony Jr. was giving the guy instructions before he passed him a thick letter-sized envelope. My gut ached that I was right about the short man being a professional life-taker.

My gut begged me to tell Addie to go to Earl's car, while I tailed the car with the New York plates. Beating the short man until he admitted to killing Joey and Gus would be like a Doberman pinscher tossing around a rag doll. My gut told me he was a coward without a gun. I could end his career with my gun, but more likely I would do it with my fists. A bullet would be too quick and easy. He deserved to be beat to death. I wouldn't tell Addie what my gut told me to do or she might think I wasn't civilized enough for marriage and kids.

My gut lost the argument with my brain, though I decided to shoot the son-of-a-bitch if we ever came face to face. No talking, just shooting.

When Tony Bacca, Jr. and his goons entered Captain Nero's, Earl came over and climbed into the Chevy, moving Addie next to me. I only then realized she hadn't been sitting next to me. I guessed it had something to do with being partners on a team and not a couple.

Earl asked, "Know what's behind us?"

I said, “Ohio.

He said, “The Terminal Tower. Some call it the Cleveland Union Terminal because of the trains. At 52 stories high, it’s the tallest building in the world outside of New York City.”

“New York, again,” I thought. Though the Terminal Tower was my idea in the first place, I didn’t mention it. If I tried to impress Addie, I’d have to live up to that for the rest of life, however long that might be. I asked, “How do you know all of that?”

“After I met with Simmons, I went to the library. From the observation deck on the 42nd floor – on a clear day – you can see for 30 miles without binoculars. There are tours, but anyone can go up there on their own.”

“Now that we’ve spotted Bacca’s red Cadillac, let’s meet up on the observation deck.”

“I think I should have tailed the short guy from New York. You saw his car plates, right?”

“I know what you’re thinking, Harry.”

“I saw that guy. What are you guys talking about?” Addie asked.

Earl answered, “There’s a good chance he’s a New York torpedo Bacca hired to kill Joey and Gus.”

“Torpedo means professional killer?”

“Yes. Harry is thinking he could get him to confess to the cops what he did and who hired him, if he had ten minutes alone with him. Anytime cops, judges, lawyers, and hoods with big money are involved anything can go sour and turn out wrong. Since Harry also knows that, he’s not going to follow him and we’re going to follow our plan.”

Earl knew I was thinking a couple of slugs into the guy from New York would leave nothing to chance. He was being my best friend by not telling Addie everything he knew I was thinking.

Somewhat addled, Addie said, “I never thought private eyes had so much to think about, so much to consider. Is it because we’re in a dangerous situation or is it like this for normal detective business?”

After some thought, Earl said, “It’s usually not dangerous like this, but we do think a lot. We read a lot into a little.”

Addie turned to me. “You’re quiet, Harry. What are you thinking?”

“Not much about anything,” I lied.

Chapter 22.

The observation deck at the Terminal Tower was windy and cold. Tony Bacca, Jr.'s red Caddy was easy to spot at Captain Nero's. Picking up the Caddy between buildings didn't seem like it would be a formidable problem, given the color. The flashy red reflected his reputed personality. I was thinking about the torpedo and Tony Jr., when I thought, "Live by the sword, die by the sword. Drive a flashy red car, expect to be watched wherever you go." The idea was smoother not put into words.

Because of the wind and chill, we decided to alternate on the observation deck every twenty minutes. Actually, Earl and Addie decided. I didn't like the idea of Addie being alone and trying to track Tony Jr. She was smart, though being in love with me meant she wasn't that smart. She wasn't a professional.

While Earl took the first watch, Addie and I rode the elevator down to find a cup of hot java. The strangest thought came to me. If someone was going to commit suicide by jumping off a building, the Terminal Tower would be the tallest building outside of New York City. My next thought was about concentrating too much on watching and accidently falling. Perhaps the *Terminal* Tower was aptly named.

Once we were seated with cups of coffee in our mitts, I said, "I'm not crazy about you taking a watch. Don't be so obsessed with watching that you get too close to the rail."

"Obsessed," she repeated. "You mean *preoccupied.* You're the only thing I'm obsessed with."

"You're a scary dame. What if it's the sex and only the sex?"

"I'm sure it's more than that. You're not difficult to read, Harry. I know I know you. But, if it's mostly the lovemaking to start, not a bad way to start."

I lit a smoke and exhaled. "I feel like I'm out of my league with you."

Addie said, "That's because you're in love for the first time."

"How do you know that?"

"A woman knows. I know you, Harry."

"So, I'm in love with you."

She was nodding as she said, "And I'm in love with you. Don't worry. I'll keep reminding you if you forget."

Sometimes twenty minutes can seem like an eternity, especially if you're keeping your head down in a foxhole while shells are looking to take your head off. Twenty minutes with Addie, now that she explained what I was feeling was love, was like five minutes.

During my first shift on the observation deck, I wished I had doubled-up on socks and worn gloves.

The other visitors, whether on the tour or not, didn't pay much attention to me. Most were simply scared and awed at the same time by being up so high. The red Caddy hadn't moved. Tony Jr. was warm and probably eating and drinking. Maybe he was plotting how to find us and eliminate us from whatever the equation was that murdered three people. Whatever we knew was too much for him to worry about.

No one else was on the observation deck when Addie relieved me after my third rotation up top. She kissed me. Her warm lips weren't on my cold lips long enough.

She said, "I can't wait to be in a warm bed with you."

I had to leave her quickly or a bed wouldn't be necessary. "Stay away from the railing."

After I used the men's room, I found another coffee and found Earl at a table. I said, "What day is today?"

Temporarily stumped, Earl finally said, "Wednesday."

"Do mob guys work on the weekends?"

"I would imagine, if there's work to do."

The coffee was warm going down. I leaned back and said, "If you haven't noticed, I'm growing a real beard under this fake beard."

"What does Addie think?"

"She doesn't like it, but she likes me anyway."

Earl repeated as a question, "Likes?"

With open eyes, I said, "I'm lousy with reasons to give this up and disappear."

"The reasons are all named Addie." He paused, looking away as if the thinking were easier if you weren't looking at someone else. "You know, if things get too dangerous, Harry, you can take her and leave. I might even go with you."

"If you don't, I'll kidnap you and take you with us. I wonder what this Vera dame is saying, if she's still alive. You don't think she fingered us to throw suspicion off herself?"

Flatly, Earl said, "I don't know. I would."

"Is she tough enough to take beatings, and maybe more, without giving up the truth? Where would you hide the books and cash?"

Earl was quick to say, "A safe deposit box or maybe a locker at the bus terminal, so there would be only one little key to hide."

"She wouldn't hide it on her or in her." When I said, "I imagine they've looked everywhere," I didn't need to be more specific. "Outside of finding the key, remind me again how our plan works?"

"We rescue her. We become her new partners in her blackmail scheme. Maybe I get close to her and she trusts me enough to tell where she's hidden the key. Something along those lines."

"Would I hurt your feelings, if I said the chances of that working aren't very good?"

"Yeah, I know," Earl said and then sighed.

"Jesus, Earl. Let's get out of this and disappear."

"Not yet. Maybe soon, though."

"Have you thought about murdering Bacca and the guy from New York before we leave?"

"As much as you have. We might get to that. Not yet, but we might get to that. Let's see what happens before that."

What happened was a lot of nothing. Our cold turns on the observation deck ended when Tony Bacca, Jr.'s red Caddy drove to his Shaker Heights home at eight at night, during my watch. In the dark, visibility was reduced. The car's red color was now washed out. Seeing the lights of his car arrive at his house confirmed my eyes followed the correct car lights. From my spotter experience during the war I guessed his house was about eight miles from Captain Nero's.

After the long cold day into night, we were tired, cold, and hungry when we returned to our hotel hideout. Earl wondered if the fireplace actually worked but didn't have the energy to find out.

After we ate from room service, which to our pleasant surprise only stopped serving from ten at night until six in the morning, I took a hot shower and climbed into bed. Addie said she was going to take a bath. I imagine she chose not to wake me, because I didn't wake up until the morning. I supposed too much of a good thing was too much to expect every night and might make the good thing less good. Being alone and needing sleep trumped all.

The next day, Thursday, was uneventful. Tony Bacca, Jr. didn't leave his house and arrive at Captain Nero's until 6:00 p.m. The observation deck closed at 9:00 p.m. and it was near midnight by the time he was driven to his home. We had used both cars to leapfrog and follow him. Addie rode with me.

Since room service would be closed for the night, we had a quick meal at the 28th Street Chop House. By the time we arrived at the hotel hideout, I couldn't remember what anyone ate, including myself.

Earl wondered, "Do you think the chop house is a place we're known to frequent?"

"It's a little late to think of that. Looks like it was one of those little details that didn't get us killed."

Too tired to shower or bathe, Addie and I went to bed. We weren't too tired to find something left to do before we actually went to sleep. What Earl did alone, I didn't care to know.

After a quick goodnight kiss from Addie, I kept my eyes open long enough to wonder if Vera Jameson was dead and whether what we were doing was worth anything. After that, everything closed and went to sleep for me.

Chapter 23.

Friday, the growth of a real beard under the fake beard itched to high heaven. During the war, I had many days in a row of not shaving. When it was safe and practical, I'd shave using cold water if it was all I had. I wasn't a hair-on-the-face kind of guy. And I knew Addie preferred me clean-shaven.

The thought of growing a disguise made me think of more. A beard would hide my less-than-good looks. I suspected I was overly critical of my mug. Didn't Earl say my mug wasn't as bad as I thought? And Addie demonstrated the opposite of being repelled by me.

I told myself that trying to scratch my itchy face through the fake beard might cause it to itch more. I'd do my best to live with the itchiness.

Being a private detective was rarely fun and games. Being a private detective was mostly boring and uncomfortable. Staying sharp and on target was an acquired talent.

Holding the binoculars a couple of inches from my eyes meant my eyes weren't as cold as they could be. Why did we leave one set in the Chevy? They could be warming up between shifts and not the same damn cold pair passed from one shift to another.

When Addie relieved me, I would get the other binoculars from the car. Most often you can't think of every little thing until you wish you had thought of it.

I lowered the binoculars and held them under my arm on the other side of where my iron was holstered. I suddenly realized it was a bad idea, totally defeating the purpose of the binoculars.

When I quickly raised them back to my eyes and trained them on Captain Nero's, I saw the red Caddy was on the move. How would I have explained to Addie and Earl that I almost missed the Caddy leaving because the binoculars were warming under my arm?

Traffic was heavy at rush hour. Maybe more rushed on a Friday before a weekend. From the previous couple of days, I learned rush hour in downtown Cleveland lasted for nearly two hours.

Following the red Caddy, even when a building got in the way, was easy.

Since the vehicle was moving slightly southwest and Tony Jr. lived southeast, I knew he was not going home. It looked like he was coming directly toward me! I watched. He was!

Why didn't we have walkie-talkies? I thought Earl was smart. Now I thought we were a couple of dumb private dicks playing way out of our league.

How much time would it take for Tony Jr. to park and get to the ground floor elevators compared to the time it would take me to go down in an elevator 42 floors?

As the light bulb for the nineteenth floor lit and unlit, I rationalized Tony Jr. might be going to see a lawyer or something like that. He wouldn't stash Vera in an office building, would he?

On the ground floor, I took time to look around to see if I could see Tony Jr. and his hoods. Nope.

I almost went back up to my post on the observation deck, when I saw a big clock on the wall. My shift was over, so Addie might be on an elevator going up to relieve me. She wouldn't see me or have the binoculars. Would she think I had fallen off the Terminal Tower?

She might have to worry about me for a few minutes, while I went to find Earl and tell him what had happened.

The moment he saw the binoculars hanging from my neck, Earl almost jumped out of his chair, bumping his knee on the table when he did. His curse described a son and his mother.

I spoke fast, like a machine gun shooting bullets. "The red Caddy came here! Despite her curls, floppy hat, and fake eyeglasses, Addie looks mostly like Addie. We need to find her now. It's possible they have her!"

Taking hold of my arm, thinking I was about to run toward the bank of elevators, Earl said, "And look where – on which floor? I'm sure she's safe on the observation deck wondering if you fell off the building."

Walking fast like one of those walk racers, we were almost to the elevators when a door opened and Addie was alone in the elevator and alive.

She playfully, well, stronger than that, slapped my arm, "Why did you leave the observation deck, you lug. Wasn't it bad enough, or maybe it wasn't bad, for me to ride on an elevator with him and his goons? They got off on the twelfth floor."

"They didn't recognize you?"

She gave me that stupid-question look. "He gave me a card and said to stop in at Captain Nero's sometime if I wanted to empty a bottle of wine."

Earl smiled a smile I wasn't happy to see, when he said, "Our boy made a pass at your girl."

How many coffees and smokes had I had during the day? Too many? But one more of each wouldn't hurt that much more.

We could see the elevators and felt safe they wouldn't spot us.

"Did you know the building has a couple of hundred one- and two-bedroom apartments?"

"Thanks, Earl. Seems you should have told us that bit of information when you told us that other stuff," I said with controlled anger.

Addie wanted to interrupt where my anger was dragging me. "How can we find out if he has her stashed here in an apartment? One thing, it's convenient to their clubhouse."

"Window washer scaffold," I suggested. "It's only the twelfth floor. I'm not afraid of heights."

"Odds are the curtains would be closed. Wait here. I'm going to go nose around."

"It's a big building, Earl. Highest outside of New York City."

"So, it might take me some time. If you see them leave, go back to the observation deck and watch where the Caddy goes. Better go together. You seem to be joined at the hip anyway."

"What if they're taking the dame out?"

"Shoot everyone but her. Harry, better do that alone."

When we were alone and Earl was off who knows where, Addie asked, "Was Earl serious about you shooting them?"

"Sure. Why not? I'm a good shot."

"Seriously? If you love me, you should tell me the truth."

"Are you sure about that?"

Addie kept talking about what had happened and how she had been worried when I wasn't on the observation deck. I let her talk. When you love someone, so much time is for talking and much less is for intimate things.

When she was out of words, I asked, “How many guys with him on the elevator?”

“Three,” she cautioned.

“Nothing wrong with trying to figure out how I might do it.”

“Kill them?”

“If I’m going to shoot them, I might as well kill them. Vera might trust us more if I did.”

“You’re joking. Right, Harry?”

“Sure I am,” I said with minor conviction. I was thinking about it. If I killed Vera, too, since she deserved it, the whole thing might be cleaned up and over. It’s the reason I packed a 15-shot Browning. The coppers and a jury might go easy on me for doing a good deed for mankind. Wouldn’t Addie wait for me, if I had to do a ten- or twenty-year stretch? I wasn’t confident my behavior in the big house would be good enough to get me an early release. I had a feeling my fists would get me into trouble, though keep me out of bigger trouble.

As the idea seemed plausible, I wondered if I might take a slug or two. The worst that could happen was the worst that could happen; I could get myself killed. Addie wouldn’t like it. I wasn’t crazy about the possibility, though if it saved Addie and Earl’s lives... Yet, how could I be certain of that. Wouldn’t Fat Tony go after them?

“Stop it, Harry.”

“What?”

“You’re quiet, so you’re thinking about shooting them.”

“Nah, I was wondering what I would order from room service tonight. I’m damn hungry.”

If we lived long enough, I imagined I would see her look of believing I was lying a few times in our future.

Nearly an hour passed before Tony Jr. and his boys walked off the elevator without the dame in tow. My response was to half stand up, before sitting back down.

“I’m warning you, Harry, don’t fuck with me like that.”

The f-word surprised me. “To think I kiss that mouth.”

On the observation deck, I watched the red Caddy return to Captain Nero's through the binoculars, while Addie's arms were around me to warm us a degree or two.

We watched night come to the city and darkness become deeper, until the sky had no color. We watched the streetlamps and business signs light up. The changing pattern of lights was impressive. The few scattered lights north of the pier and Captain Nero's had to be boats out on the lake. I would never go on a boat again after the boat ride I took across the Atlantic going to the war. The plane ride home from the war was so much quicker. I decided I liked planes and not boats.

When Earl joined us on the observation deck, I was at least half frozen. I had even sent Addie away to warm up a couple of times. Earl was like a parent with a secret, while Addie and I were like kids waiting for Christmas morning to open our presents.

Chapter 24.

We were parking at the hotel, our hideaway, before the Chevy's heater threw real heat.

Taking liquor into our bedroom, Addie and I changed into warm clothes. Seeing how the cold affected her nipples almost made me want to lay down with her, but the constant cold had left me somewhat deficient, though I knew she knew what I was like at room temperature or warmer.

Before we thought about food, Earl talked while we listened. "Finally, I found the right maintenance guy. I joined him for a couple of drinks after his shift was over. The alcohol and a double sawbuck loosened his lips. At the far end of the twelfth floor is an offshoot hallway leading to the biggest apartment the building has to offer. Around the same time as Vera disappeared and you found her house ransacked, two cops have been stationed outside the room."

"Coppers. The cops have her? Tony Jr. has something going on with the cops?"

"Part of what took me so long was waiting to see two uniformed cops take the elevator up and two come off it several minutes later. Shift change. I recognized two of the four as Crown ops."

"Christ, that's smart," I said.

"So, what's your sleepiest part of what day, not counting bedtime?" asked Earl.

Without interrupting our thinking, Earl waited, until I finally said, "Late Sunday afternoon. I doze off, can't fall asleep that night and start Monday tired and grouchy."

"Yes, me too," Addie agreed.

"Okay. Addie, tomorrow you're going to buy a used wedding dress with a veil and lots of folds in the skirt. Harry, you need to rent a wedding tux. Make sure the sawed-off shotgun is ready to go to work Sunday, late afternoon."

I often say dumb things. "We're not actually getting married on Sunday?"

"Not this Sunday," Addie said with a smile. "Maybe in a few months, when it might be a shotgun wedding."

"You're not...?"

Her laugh shook her whole body, before she said to Earl, "He doesn't know much about anything that doesn't have bullets or fists involved, does he?"

While Earl shook his head from side to side, I thought of something to say to redeem myself. I didn't quite have it figured out, but it had something to do with my bullets and pregnancy. I decided to let them share making fun of me and not be crude. It wasn't much skin off my nose and it was my girl and my best friend, so I didn't crack wise.

Carrying the dinner selections written on a slip of paper and the morning's newspaper, it was my turn to cross the hall and phone the order to room service.

Earl always seemed to be adding more to what we did. He was attempting to take any risk out of the least thing that probably wouldn't get us killed.

Messing up the beds in the other suite, flushing the toilet enough times to use up toilet paper, leaving the newspaper in disarray, and anything else I could think of – I made the place look lived-in. In the off-chance someone would bribe a maid, they wouldn't be saying the place looked like no one lived in it. We even left bed clothes lying around. I didn't need bed clothes.

Earl's plan to put the fake cops at ease by a recently married couple going to the wrong room sounded good. I wondered what extra thing he would think of before Sunday afternoon. There always seemed to be something else.

My face would be disguised and the wedding veil would mostly hide Addie's face. When I wondered if they would wonder why the veil was down after the marriage ceremony, Earl replied they wouldn't have enough time to think about it. Of course, Earl would be around the corner, armed and prepared to back my play.

Bothering me the most was Addie being involved. If Addie was hurt or killed and I wasn't, someone would pay a high price. I kept telling myself it was too late to not involve her. They knew who she was. Whether she knew anything or not, they could use her as leverage against me. She was safest with us, yet wasn't she *too* with us?

After a knock, a voice called, "Room service."

I looked through the door's peephole and everything looked right, though I was prepared to reach for my Browning if it didn't.

Even after waiting, I peeked around the doorjamb to ensure the hallway was clear of people.

Upon opening the door, everything was right. Since Addie was staying with us, the meal cart was packed high with metal covered plates. Often there were two carts, but this time only one.

I carefully wheeled the cart to our room across the hall. The food was always a little less warm than it was when it was delivered, though we weren't starving and were being cautious.

The observation deck and everything else during the day caused Addie to sleep throughout the night. I knew because I slept little, though I was tired. What if Vera Jameson wasn't in the room? Someone needing to be guarded was in the room, but who could it be, if it wasn't her? Would we be taking risks for nothing? And why had I not demanded Earl concoct a plan that didn't involve Addie? Though, I have to admit, I thought it was a good plan. If it had involved any other woman in the world, even Shirley Temple, it would be a better plan.

Saturday started slow and easy, but picked up pace. I took Addie in the Chevy, while Earl was unspecific about where he was going in the Packard.

What sounded easy wasn't so easy. Renting a tuxedo I wanted to take with me raised eyebrows. Addie diverted the salesman's curiosity by saying something about needing to be married as soon as possible, before the pregnancy started to show. I blushed along with the salesman; we were both thinking how lucky I was to be sleeping with such a swell-looking dame.

Finding an inexpensive used wedding dress, because we might need our cash to last longer than we expected, was more difficult than renting the tux. Fit was important to Addie, until I whispered and reminded her that we weren't actually getting married Sunday.

I overhead the saleslady say maybe I shouldn't be shopping with her, because it was bad luck for the groom to see the bride in her wedding dress before the ceremony. Addie said something about us already having bad luck because she was pregnant. For all we knew, maybe she was. At least Addie was consistent with her lies. Was that a good trait in a woman?

A used veil was more difficult to find than getting Addie into a wedding dress that sort of fit. I didn't want to start considering why a bride would give up her dress to be resold, yet keep the veil. Also, I wanted the veil hiding her face.

Eventually, a veil was found. I thought the ordeal was over, until Addie said she needed white high heels. I didn't understand; the bottom of the dress brushed the floor. Addie took me aside and explained her walk into the guarded hallway would expose her shoes. The wrong shoes would instantly tell the guards something was wrong. It made sense.

Someday, if we lived long enough to get married, we would be doing what we were now doing. She would buy a new wedding dress, veil, and shoes on her own. I would rent a tux on my own, maybe with Earl tagging along, if he lived long enough. It was so odd, I wondered if eloping without a wedding dress and tux wouldn't make more sense. The possibility also existed we might have disappeared into new identities. If our names weren't our real names, would a wedding be legal? Ah, common law marriage. Okay, no real problem.

On the way back to our hotel hideout, I bought two bottles of bourbon and one bottle of Scotch.

In the Chevy, Addie acted cute and said, "Are those for the wedding celebration tomorrow night?"

"They're for tonight and part of tomorrow before this charade goes down."

"Don't you want to be stone-cold sober and not hungover?"

"No. I need to be a little soused to go through with this."

Actually I didn't mean more than a bracer and spine stiffener on Sunday. I remembered from the war that drinking too much alcohol before a battle was asking for the worst kind of trouble. But that was for tomorrow. Tonight I felt like getting drunk. The worst part of a hangover would be gone by late afternoon tomorrow.

When Earl hadn't returned or phoned by seven, we went ahead with the room service process. I tried not to show Addie I was worried about Earl.

We had been together a lot, so she read my hidden concern. "I'm worried about Earl, too," she started. "What do we do if something has happened to him?"

"We skip town with the wedding clothes."

When a key unlocked the door and the door began to open, my gun was already in my hand.

By looking at his face and seeing his body movement, I knew what had happened to Earl. We had known each other for a long time and knew each other as much as we knew ourselves.

An angry Addie said, "Where the hell were you? Why didn't you phone? We were worried to death."

Her saying "death" sounded strange and appropriate.

"Harry, tell her where I was."

Addie turned on me. "I thought you didn't know, Harry?"

"I didn't. From the looks of him, I'm guessing he found Cyd or someone like Cyd, in case tomorrow doesn't go off as planned."

"A prostitute? Why not Jeannie?"

Earl plopped on the couch. "I didn't want to have to explain the beard to Jeannie. One of those little details that might or might not do us in. *Yes* to a prostitute and *no* to Cyd. An expensive stranger made perfect sense. Harry, do you think some of that bourbon could find its way into a glass for me?"

"Not without my help."

By eleven, Addie had heard enough of our stories, whether pre-war, war, or post-war. I'm not sure if she understood we needed to get drunk and remember our lives. The plan wasn't going down until late afternoon; we would have plenty of time to recover and get focused.

She asked, "Are you coming to bed?" as if, if I wasn't, she might not be so agreeable when I did.

"In a while."

Once we had another drink and Addie had been in the bedroom for some time, Earl said, "Are you going to give her the drunk test?"

"You mean walk a straight line and touch her nose?"

"Not that. That doesn't make any sense. I mean whether you can come home drunk and she is still willing to do what you drunkenly want her to do. If she does, you will have a good marriage."

"How in the hell would you know?" I asked slurring several of the words.

"It's kind of logic sense. If it makes sense, it makes sense. I think it makes sense," he said, slurring nearly every word.

"You're the thinker, Earl. Maybe one or two more drinks and I'll find out."

"If you can remember by then."

"True. She's a good dame, Earl. If this thing doesn't work, I'm going to blame you. I won't kill you, but I'll beat you up. What do you think the odds are?"

"Good. Good odds. Better than even money."

"Good. What if this Vera dame isn't there?"

He scrunched his face with another sip of bourbon, before he said, "We'll take whoever is there. I'm sure they would come in handy for something."

"Isn't that kidnapping?"

"Then we won't. I wonder: if we kidnap someone who was already kidnapped – what's it called?"

"Double kidnapping. Maybe."

Earl slurred his way through, "Maybe the second one cancels out the first one."

"That can't be right. If it's her, we're going to hold onto to her, aren't we?"

"True. Probably is double kidnapping."

"When we took prisoners during the war, was that kidnapping?"

"Harry, I think it kind of was."

After that, I don't remember what we talked about.

When Addie woke me near noon of the next day, I knew my head hurt and my stomach was queasy. I had slept on a chair in the living room, so Addie never was tested whether she would comply with the requests of the drunk she loved.

When Earl sat up on the couch, where he had slept the night, we looked at any empty bottle of bourbon and then at each other. I felt as bad as he looked. It was déjà vu all over again.

When Addie said what she said, she had every right to say it the way she said it. "Are you assholes going to be okay to do what we have to do today?"

Probably without any thought Earl said, "Are you sure you want to marry her? She curses."

"Shut up, Earl."

Chapter 25.

When we exited the hotel freight elevator, I saw Woody Blanton, the hotel dick, out of the corner of my eye. I knew he saw me in my disguise and a tuxedo, and Earl in disguise and a suit. He probably guessed the woman under the veil and wearing the wedding dress was the same woman who had been staying with us. To the best of my memory, I don't believe we told him her name. Why would we?

I'm guessing Earl felt half-crummy like I did. We learned from the war that feeling half-crummy gave us the edge we needed to kill the enemy and not let the enemy kill us. It made no sense, but being too sober and too well-rested can result in over-confidence, taking too many risks and hesitating when it came down to actually killing another human being.

The ground floor of the Terminal Tower had few people moving through it. The few did a double take seeing me in a tux and Addie in a wedding dress.

If the changing of the guards in front of the object apartment kept to the same schedule as on Friday, we had nearly two hours to snatch Vera, if she was being held there.

What if the changing of the uniformed fake cops guarding the door was different on Sunday? Maybe we should have checked it out and made our move on the next Sunday. Waiting a week would have been too long. Vera could have been moved or killed by then. The coppers or Tony Jr. might find our hotel hideaway if given another week.

Halfway down the twelfth floor hallway, Addie and I started jabbering, like we were a little drunk and excited to find our room and consummate our marriage.

We said things like *oh, baby, let's hurry and find the room* and *do you know how long I've waited for this?*

Once I looked down to see her step forward. I saw her white high-heeled shoe. She was right about that.

When we turned the corner, I saw only one fake cop standing guard. If the other one was inside using the bathroom or something like that… No time to turn back.

The sole guard smiled like he envied what I would soon be doing. He was in midsentence saying, "You have the wrong…" when the sawed-off shotgun came out from where I held it in the back folds of the wedding dress. I put my finger to my lips for him to be quiet, as I motioned for him to raise his arms.

Earl came around the corner pointing his gun and holding a finger to his lips. He took the guard's gun.

I whispered into the guard's ear, "Play ball and you'll live to see tomorrow. Where's the other guard?"

With the thumbs at the end of his raised arms, he pointed behind him to the door. He was smart enough to whisper, "He's in there taking a turn. It's not locked."

I had a good idea of what he meant. I was sure Earl understood it. I wonder what Addie thought it meant.

The second fake cop's gun was on the dresser. His pants and undershorts were down to his knees, as he rutted on top of a woman with her arms and legs tied to the bed. From what I could see she was naked and had red hair. Vera Jameson.

I hit the cop hard with the side buttstock of the shotgun without worrying whether it was too hard. Rape boiled my blood.

When the cop fell off to the side of the woman, I saw the woman, whom men had died for, was completely naked. Except for bruises, cuts that had bled, and what might be cigarettes burns over a portion of her body, she was a beautiful dame from head to toe.

The look from Vera's face, especially her eyes, showed relief and fear at the same time. A man in a tuxedo had come to save her, do worse to her, or maybe kill her. Her eyes expressed all of those things. Then, she seemed to look past me. I half-turned and saw Addie in the wedding dress behind me. Whatever expressions Addie had on her face was covered by the veil. For each person who might see what we were seeing the reaction was probably different. In general, I wondered if a woman feels different from a man seeing another women so abused.

While Earl and I hog-tied the two phony cops, Addie decided we could get Vera out with the least curiosity if she was wearing the wedding dress with the veil covering her battered face.

When Addie came out of the bedroom wearing Vera's clothes, probably what Vera wore when she was abducted, they looked tight but passable. The wedding dress looked okay on Vera. Side by side, Addie was a little bigger than Vera.

I had found a bottle of gin and offered it to Vera. She lifted the veil, took a mouthful, swallowed, and coughed. Unless she said something to Addie in the bedroom while they dressed, I hadn't heard her speak a word.

Addie and Earl refused my offer of the bottle of gin. I took a good swig.

Earl said to Vera, "Go along with this. Try to act like his bride. No one is going to hurt you. I promise you."

As the three of them went through the door, I lagged behind. I said, "Be right with you. Keep going."

I went back to the hogtied men. One already had his pants and undershorts to his knees, revealing his genitals. So I made sure the other guy was equally exposed. They were private dicks from the Crown Investigation, working for Tony Jr. They had done things to a helpless woman. When they were found hogtied with their dicks exposed, it wouldn't be bad enough. I kicked one and then the other in the ribcage, certain I felt and heard ribs crack. Their screams were muffled by the gags. With broken ribs their breathing would be difficult.

If I stayed one more second, I would punish them for their possible hand in murdering Joey and Gus. Then I remembered the New York torpedo. Still, whether they had hurt our friends or not, I could kill them just for what they did to the woman, whether she was a wrong dame or not. I didn't stay one more second, so they continued to live.

I ran to catch up to Addie, Earl, and Vera as they reached the elevator. If the elevator doors had taken one more second to arrive, I might have gone back and filled those guys with lead.

As we walked, Vera seemed to walk better. We might have looked like a tired and not-so-happy bride, groom, and two witnesses.

When we reached the Chevy, I still thought of going back and killing the bastards. Once we were in the car and started the engine, I continued to have murder on my mind.

Finally, we reached the hotel and parked. Most of the murder in my brain was gone. Some might always be with me.

Earl said, “Give me ten minutes to find the hotel dick and get him away from the service elevator.”

As long as Earl continued to think of everything, even if some of it was later, I thought we might live long enough for Addie and me to tie the knot. What knot? Who thought stupid sayings should have a life of their own?

I regretted not killing the Crown guards half-dressed in Cleveland Police uniforms. I wished I had Simmons’ phone number and had called him. A newspaper photo with blacked-out genitals would still only give them part of what they deserved. I still wished I had shot them in the head, like Joey and Gus had been.

Chapter 26.

In Earl's bedroom, I switched out of the monkey suit into slacks and a shirt, while Addie and Vera put on different clothes in the other bedroom. Addie's clothes were a little big for Vera. It didn't matter; Vera wasn't going out anywhere soon.

Doing the best she could with a first aid kit, Addie patched up Vera. Having seen too much in the war, Earl and I thought Vera's physical torture was superficial. It was meant to inflict pain, not long-lasting injuries. Questioning her would give us some idea of her mental injuries. They had had her for more than a week.

Two waiters brought two carts of food to the room on the other side of the hallway. The fare included a bottle of bourbon, since we thought the one we had might not be enough. The waiters must have thought we were having a party. Yeah, not a wedding celebration.

Vera looked to be recovering rather quickly after food with a glass of bourbon to wash it down. The way she handled it, I could tell she was no stranger to alcohol.

Other than a *thank you* several times after her rescue, Vera asked, "May I have a cigarette?"

Earl gave her a cigarette and lit it with his metal lighter. She seemed to savor the smoke, telling us she was a smoker and they had deprived her of tobacco. Another form of torture as far as I was concerned.

She asked, "Who are you? Obviously not cops."

Earl answered, "We're the partners of Joey A and Gus Reese."

"Oh," she said with concern. "And the woman?"

When I quickly said, "She's my partner," I used my peripheral vision to see a slight smile cross Addie's face.

"So, I'm still a prisoner."

"Yes. We're going to handcuff you to a bed, though nothing more than that," Earl said. "Why didn't you tell them what they wanted to know?"

"You've figured this out."

"Some of it," Earl said to her.

"I was told they murdered Gus Reese. I'm guessing that was true."

Earl nodded. "Were you carrying on with Joey?"

"Yes. I was in love with him. That's how this whole thing started."

"You lied to the police about how Joey got it."

"I don't trust cops. I can see you don't, either, because I'm here and they're not. My life was threatened, if I didn't tell that story."

I needed to know. "Was it a small guy with a New York accent?"

"Yes. Well, Joey and Noah. I don't know about Gus."

"Besides the books, how much money?"

"Sixty-five grand. I told Joey it was enough, even with Gus getting a third. Joey wanted more."

Earl asked, "What went wrong?"

"Noah discovered what was missing a day too soon. He told Tony and they killed him for it. I guess they thought having me was enough to get it back." Her face didn't break, but tears broke from her eyes. "Tony was once in love with me, in his way. I thought he would believe me and not…"

Though Addie was supposed to leave the questioning to Earl and me, as the professionals, she asked, "Were you in love with your husband?"

"In a way. I didn't have to work after I married him."

Addie wasn't satisfied. "While you were married, did you also see Tony Bacca, Jr.?"

"Yes."

"And Joey. You were in love with him, too?"

"Yes."

Addie's next question showed astonishment. "How many men can you love at one time?"

"More than one. Though, not in the same hour."

Yeah, she was a tough dame, a wrong dame. She could make a man a fool. I felt less sorry for what they did to her. I was over the idea of plugging the two guards; what I had done was enough.

Backing off the love angle, Earl said, "You gave them Gus Reese."

"I was afraid. I saw Joey and Noah murdered. Anyone would have given up their mother."

"But you didn't give up the books and money? Did you think they would kill you after you did?"

"Earl, right? I wished I was dead a couple of dozen times. I don't know where Joey and Gus hid the stuff. Maybe only Joey knew. They didn't give him a chance to tell them. It happened so fast. I told them about Gus, but I also said I wasn't sure if he knew. I'm sorry he's dead. I'm sorry about everything," she said with tears rolling down her cheeks.

The air seemed to go out of the room. I believed her about Gus. They had taken their time torturing him. Once they believed he didn't know, he was murdered, putting her back on the hot seat.

Her head and whole body seemed to straighten up. "Tony believes they may have told their partners. You two. Or maybe you know enough to lead them to the books and money. You don't know or you would have cut a deal by now. Tony is not to be trusted. He'll make a deal and never forget to kill you. We're in this together."

She was tough. She was a wrong dame and right about everything she said.

"You don't have to handcuff me to the bed. My best chance to get out of this alive is to work with you."

Addie surprised me. "We don't know how many more lovers you have walking around alive, who would do most anything for you."

If Addie felt sorry for her, it had disappeared like the air from a pricked balloon.

Vera had a way about her, especially with men. She could tell a sap the moon and sun switched positions and he'd believe her. I could tell Addie felt it from her female perspective. I always believed women knew other women better than men knew those other women.

Yet, despite what I knew and believed, there was sexual magnetism about Vera. I was in love with Addie, yet I felt its pull. A guy at a bar once said about a dame's sexy allure, "You can't put your finger on it, but you want to put your dipstick in it."

I took her into what had been, and still might be, Earl's bedroom in the suite. Like an obedient dog, she went along.

"This is for your own safety."

When she said, "I understand," I knew she understood more than what she simply said.

Vera sat on the edge of the bed, leaning forward with her elbows on her legs short of her knees, while I looked for a portion of the headboard to place a handcuff.

Maybe a half dozen or a few more times in my life had a woman unintentionally given me a generous look at an exposed breast. They were accidents of positioning and loose blouses. Though I had seen Vera naked in the Terminal Tower bedroom, her leaning forward offered me a sneaky peek. Vera's blouse was loose on her. For whatever reason, she wasn't wearing anything under the blouse. I wondered how sneaky and accidental the view was. The view was more titillating than seeing her naked. I suspected she knew it. Such a seductive ploy wasn't meant for here and now. It was meant for further down the line, when Addie and Earl were out of the suite. I could be wrong about it, but thinking I was right about it was for my own safety.

Pulling my eyes away from her, I changed my mind about handcuffing one of her wrists to the headboard and chose a post at the foot of the bed and her right ankle.

"If you need anything, call out and Addie will help you."

"She's your girl. You wished she wore the wedding dress for real."

Her perceptive ability had me at a disadvantage. I didn't quite know how to answer her, so I didn't. "Just call for Addie."

I closed the bedroom door as I left. Her look told me I could have stayed with her as long as I wanted.

As I rejoined Earl and Addie in the living room, I was certain she would try to seduce Earl, with me as the backup sap if that didn't work. She was the kind of dame who wouldn't respect another woman's claim on a man. I barely knew her, yet from everything that I knew about her, I was safer to doubt everything she might say or do.

We talked low, expecting she couldn't hear through the bedroom door, though it might not have made a difference if she did.

"We're back to square one, if we believe her." After a short silence, Earl said, "If we don't and they couldn't get her to talk…"

Addie showed her improved detective skills every time she spoke. "I don't believe she doesn't know. Playing devil's advocate," she harrumphed saying it, "if only Joey knew and didn't have time to tell Gus and was killed before he could give up the information, where would he hide it?"

After I shrugged and said, "Who knows? It could be anywhere. A key could be taped under a tabletop at Mo's bar. Who knows?"

Earl said, "It would be like looking for a needle in a haystack that isn't a haystack in the first place. Good ole Joey only wanted to cut Gus in, so they didn't tell us anything. But he would want us in it, if trouble happened. How would that work?"

As if she had been nurturing an idea all along and was only waiting for us to say what we did, Addie said, "You worship Sam Spade, the detective in *The Maltese Falcon*. I liked the movie, but not like you guys did. I'm probably wrong about this, but what did he do in the movie with the falcon?"

"We saw it together, Earl. Before we enlisted. We double dated. You were with Betty and I was with that nurse. Hell, it made us want to become private eyes."

Playfully, Addie asked, "What nurse?"

Equally playfully, I retorted, "She was teaching me about mouth to mouth resuscitation. I'm a slow learner."

"Enough yapping. I don't get it, Addie. Say what you're thinking," Earl said, tired of our repartee.

"He mailed the falcon to himself or something like that. Don't you remember? They had to wait at his place for morning, when his secretary received the falcon in the mail at his office."

I said, "So, Joey mailed the books and money to the office?"

Because Addie loved me didn't mean she couldn't look at me like I was a moron. "No. Maybe he mailed the key to a locker."

Earl asked Addie, "Is the mail opened, if it's marked *personal*?"

"No," Addie said. "He could have mailed it to himself at the office, figuring someone would eventually open it, especially if something happened to him. He wouldn't mail it to his place or Gus's house. If something bad happened, he would want you two to have the key and do something about it."

Earl continued her line of thinking. "If he's in trouble, he would assume Gus would be in trouble. Vera knew about Gus. If he's not in trouble, the key is safe in the US Mail until he picks it up at the office. We're only cut in on the deal if he's in trouble."

"Bastard," I said meaning part of it.

Earl qualified my word. "Smart bastard. Christ, it's possible. Much of what we think and how we act comes from the movies."

Addie's eyes shined as she said, "The mail is shoved under the door if it is locked. The last time we were at the office was Saturday, after Joey's funeral reception. We found it ransacked. An envelope addressed to Joey and marked *personal* could be lying on the floor inside the office door."

Earl said, "It almost makes too much sense. Let's add another possibility, our lawyer, Paul Burston. I might mail a key to him with instructions to give it to my partners if something happened to me."

I wanted to participate. I was feeling less than smart. "Burston's afraid of his shadow. Since he hasn't been able to get ahold of us, since we've gone into hiding, he would hang on to the envelope. I wonder if he would have the courage to give it to the cops, since Joey and Gus are dead and we're missing."

"The cops could figure out what the key was for, right?" asked Addie.

"Yeah, same as we could," Earl said. "If the cops have the books and money, would they let us hang in the wind like dead meat?"

I said, "Maybe. It's kind of what Matthews suggested to me at Vera's house. We're bait. They want more than the dope business; they want murder charges to stick on Tony Bacca, Jr. and his mob."

Earl summed it up. "If we don't want to be the bait, we need to become the hunter."

Chapter 27.

Earl slept on the couch, with Vera handcuffed in the second bedroom. Addie was as restless as I was. I must have checked on Vera four times, meaning I had to fall back to sleep four times.

At three in the morning, Addie and I were awake again and looking at each other from our pillows, about six inches apart. Something hung over us to keep us from starting anything close to lovemaking.

I whispered, “How come, the more we know, the less we know, and the more we guess? I hope your mail theory pans out. If not… I’m worried about Earl, because Vera is short on men she can use. She’s as dangerous as an ice pick in the heart.”

After keeping her laugh low and quiet, Addie asked, “Did you learn to talk like that at private detective school or at the movies?”

Morning came as it always does. Once it didn’t, it wouldn’t come again. That was my mood, tired from too little sustained sleep and worried leaving Earl and Vera alone would turn out wrong.

The room service carts carried four breakfasts, up from two, up from three. Our numbers continued to increase. Did the room service workers gossip about who spent the night with Mr. & Mrs. Spencer Washington and what may have happened overnight?

Vera was friendly, as if we had been friends for years. It was more than just having the handcuffs off. She was recovering quickly from whatever she had been put through at the Terminal Tower apartment. Even her appearance had improved.

Addie and I left, taking the Chevy. Earl would tell her what we were doing, as if we believed everything she told us and she was a full-fledged member of the team. As if we were all in this together. Left alone, how much together Vera and Earl would be might answer a few questions.

I needed to shake off the rotten idea we could return to find Earl dead and Vera gone. I saw Vera as capable of anything. We had rescued her from Tony Bacca, Jr., yet she was capable of going back to him with a new story, saying we might know where the books and money were. I hoped she wouldn't think of doing that, because it would be so unexpected that Bacca might just believe her. Then, Addie and I would find the torpedo from New York and several other goons waiting for us at our hotel hideout.

I was in a deep dark hole, thinking I would someday have to kill Vera, kill Bacca, kill the guy from New York, kill all of them, if the worst happened and I survived. Lately, wanting to kill people seemed to be my answer for everything. The Jekyll and Hyde in me were trying to kill each other. Maybe spending the day with Addie, away from the hideout and all the wrong possibilities, would get me back to being a human being who didn't want to kill anybody. Wasn't that what love was supposed to do, make a person a better person, like less of a killer?

Addie purchased a black hat with a black veil, like a woman would wear to a funeral. I wore a dark suit with a black necktie, like I was accompanying her to a funeral. If the veil with the wedding dress was a good disguise, so were mourners' rags. On the downside, I missed seeing her face clearly.

I wore my hat pulled low, barely allowing me to see. I was growing accustomed to fake facial hair. My growing beard itching less meant I was growing accustomed to that, too.

I parked two blocks from the law office of Paul Burston, our agency's lawyer. He wasn't the best shyster in town. He was relatively inexpensive. Most of our legal needs were simple. If something serious came along, we would pay more for a better shyster.

While I went to check for surveillance on Burston, I left Addie in the Chevy. I didn't like leaving her alone. But she was safer in the car than with me. If I was caught by surveillance, I wanted the getaway car outside the vision of the surveillance.

After a dozen or so minutes of not spotting anything suspicious, I went back to the car for Addie. We walked the two blocks like she was a recent widow and I was her older brother visiting an attorney for a will reading. A story and an attitude made disguises more believable.

The two-story office building of inexpensive professional types could have been built before I was born. Decades of dirt and soot gave it a dark grey yet brownish look. Like Civil War photos I had seen in a book.

I steered Addie past the door with Burston's name on it. We turned a corner and I stopped at an unmarked door. I said, "Wait out here and try to listen." I knocked once, then twice, then three quick knocks. The private door was for clients who didn't want to be seen.

When the door opened, Burston looked surprised and mystified, until I raised my hat and he could see my face above the facial hair. I said, "Yeah, it's me. No need to blurt out my name."

Burston was a nervous type to begin with, as if he wasn't sure of the legal advice he spouted. His nervousness was abnormally increased. But he let me in.

I used the sneer of a Bogart private eye with my lips tight across my teeth. Maintaining the look when I spoke caused my voice to sound sinister. "Anyone been here looking for Earl or me? Sit down, you won't shake so much."

"A couple of police detectives. I told them I didn't know anything."

"One of them named Matthews?"

"Yeah, maybe. Yeah."

"Anyone else?"

"Three hoods. Again, I knew nothing."

"Was one of them a smaller sleight guy wearing a too-big overcoat with a New York accent?"

"The description is right. He didn't speak."

"Joey or Gus leave you anything for Earl or me?"

"Like what?'

"Like, in case something happened to them. Maybe something arrived in the mail."

"No. Please, I don't want to be involved."

"If I find out you've lied to me, I'll come back and break your fingers and thumbs, one at a time."

If Burston hadn't soiled himself up to now, he might have after my threat.

"I wasn't here," I ordered.

"Of course, yes."

When I came out of the office with the same sneering grin I had entering the office, Addie said, after I closed the door, "Do you practice that look in front of a mirror?"

"I don't anymore. I have it down pat."

During the ride to the offices of Diamond Detective Agency, our abandoned place of business, Addie said, "I want to stop sometime today and buy a few clothes for Vera. I don't like her wearing my clothes. I don't want her to rub off on me."

Using the same process as I did with the lawyer, I found no one watching the building, though I was ready for anything in case I missed something.

From the outside everything looked normal, while inside was the same mess we saw over a week ago. Part of Addie and Carla's jobs was to clean the place. It filled up their time and they didn't seem to mind. Neither had snotty airs. So, the place was like we left it.

Searching for something didn't mean you had to destroy a place unless you were sending a message that you intended to do worse than toss around office furniture and file folders.

Inside the door on the floor was a wide spread of mail. I said, "Let's grab the mail and hightail it."

Like she had previously thought about it, Addie found a framed photo on the floor. She shook lose the broken glass. It didn't take a smart detective to guess the family in the picture was her family; a mother, a father, three sisters and a brother. I wondered if I would end up seeing her family on holidays, birthdays, and anniversaries.

She cradled the picture and the mail she'd gathered in her arms, while I gripped more mail with my left hand in case I needed to go for my gun with my right. We left, expecting never to return.

Back inside the car, Addie lifted the widow's veil and brushed a few tears from her face. As I drove, Addie opened the mail.

Nothing in the mail mattered. The bills didn't matter, unless by some miracle everything could go back to how it had been. Fat chance of that happening. Was a skinny chance more possible than a fat chance? I decided a fat chance made no sense.

Addie started, "So much for Sam Spade and my bright idea. Any place left to check?"

"No. I can't see Joey being too clever about it. He wouldn't send it to his Aunt Minnie. If he was in trouble, he would send it to someone who would get it to Earl and me."

"How about to where someone else working at the agency lives?"

With a pocketful of coins and Addie's good memory, I phoned Carla, Tommy, and the other three ops. They were worried, though happy I was alive. When they indicated they didn't know anything, I begged-off those calls as quickly as possible. They seemed to care about my wellbeing, though they seemed to care more about not being involved, except for Tommy. I promised to call him if he was needed.

Checking for surveillance was slow and tedious at Addie's apartment, Earl's place, and at my Colton Arms rooms. Addie didn't want to see her place in case it was ransacked. It was. And so were mine and Earl's. No mail matched what we were looking for. The mail angle had been played out.

She was disappointed. She went to a conclusion. "Eliminating the possibilities means Vera is lying. It's what she does."

"Very good, precious."

"Okay, Harry. Enough Sam Spade. Don't call me precious or sweetheart or angel."

"How about *doll*?"

"No. Just Addie. Maybe Mrs. Hamm, sometime in the future."

"It could be worse. It could be Mrs. Pork."

I'd made her laugh. She needed to laugh.

I drove into the suburbs and found a hand-me-down clothes store. Spending too much time downtown didn't seem like a good idea.

Addie took off the veil saying, "A widow wouldn't be clothes shopping."

After she picked out two simple outfits and two sets of undergarments for Vera, we were back in the Chevy. Addie commented, "She'd look good in anything. Or out of anything."

We ate at a family style restaurant in the suburbs, taking a back booth where I could see everyone in the place.

While we were eating, Addie said, "Wonder what Earl is doing right now? Don't you think Vera would move fast to get her claws into him? Do you think Bacca and his hoods knew that most of what they did to her was something she was accustomed to?"

Spinning spaghetti with a fork on top of a spoon, I said, "So far, her fast recovery has been…surprising."

Addie cut right to it before I could take another mouthful. "Was it rape if she enjoyed it?"

Chapter 28.

Around five, I parked a short distance from Mo's Bar, the place I often had drinks at after work. Perhaps Joey had given a casual drinking friend something to give to Earl or me? It was the longest of long shots, a last-ditch effort.

While I watched the joint for a half-hour, Addie tried to talk me out of going inside. I took off the fake beard. For someone to give me something, they had to see my face, even if I looked like an unshaven mug hiding out from the cops. She thought it was too risky. My name and picture were plastered over the news as missing and wanted by the police for questioning.

Once, at the track, I'd accidently bet on the wrong horse. Liquor had been a factor. The wrong bet won the race. At 35 to 1, two bucks paid $70 bucks. Accidents happen and long shots do pay off.

Addie didn't buy my logic. Once is once and doesn't mean twice could happen.

She'd learn I would do things she didn't want me to do. As long as another dame wasn't involved, she'd learn to accept it. Then again, if anyone could talk me out of doing something, it would be Addie or Earl. Over the last several days, she had reached that status in my mind. But this time – I wasn't changing my mind.

"Keep the car running, precious."

"Damn you, Harry!" she said as I left the car.

Unlike every time before, no one called out my name as I entered. Everyone who knew me looked surprised. As If I didn't have a care in the world, I walked to a position at the bar where I could see the pay phone, the phone behind the bar, and the front and back doors. I found the only space at the bar to see everything I needed to see. If I moved two feet, I would be out of position.

"Mo. Boilermaker. Make it the good bourbon."

Customers began talking in hushed voices, unlike the normal volume of Mo's. I nodded toward a few guys I knew and waited for someone to approach me.

When Mo placed the shot of bourbon and glass of beer on the bar in front of me, he said, almost apologetically, "How's it going Harry?"

"Aces. Nothing but aces, Mo."

Billy Kutler, the telephone line repairman, came to stand next to me, carrying his beer with him. I nodded and told myself not to stare him in the face for too long. My eyes needed to watch what they needed to watch.

"Harry, should you be in here like this?"

"Probably not, but here I am. Do you have anything for me?"

"You need money? I can spot you a double sawbuck."

"Nah, I'm good. Did Joey or maybe Gus give you anything for me or Earl?"

"No. Too bad about Joey and Gus. Are you going to be okay?"

Billy Kutler was okay; he seemed to care like a friend should. I responded, "I'll let you know the next time I'm in here."

I downed the bourbon, tapped my beer glass against Billy's beer, and chugged half the beer. It went down so fast I barely tasted it. What I tasted, tasted good. There was something about danger that made anything alcoholic taste better.

After waving Mo over, I tossed a fin on the bar and said, "Give Billy a shot and a beer on me. Keep the change." I chugged what was left in my glass, then I held out my hand to Billy, who shook it. "See you around, Billy."

"Yeah, hope so. Thanks Harry."

I walked quickly though smoothly through the bar, nodding and smiling at guys I knew. As I went out the door, I faintly heard a voice I didn't recognize say, "Good luck, Harry."

Seeing the car parked across from where I left it, repositioned to go in the direction we would be leaving Mo's, I once again noticed Addie's smarts. I hopped onto the passenger seat and said, "Drive away at a normal speed."

Ten seconds down the street Addie asked, "Anything?"

"No. Only good bourbon and beer."

Addie drove back to the hotel following my directions as I kept my eyes peeled for anyone who might be tailing us, while I stuck the fake beard back on my face. The double-sided tape had lost some adhesiveness but the phony beard looked okay for going into the service entrance of the hotel. For a split second, I caught a glimpse of Woody Blanton peeking at us from around a corner. He seemed to be keeping an eye on us, making me think we needed a new hideout.

The house dick bugged me. I stopped Addie in the hallway by taking hold of her free arm. Vera's new used clothes occupied her other hand and arm. I turned her to me. I think she thought I was going to kiss her – not a bad idea – but I had something important to say.

"If something happens and we get separated, find your way to Uncle Josef and Aunt Babs, the Polinski's. They aren't really my uncle and aunt, and no one, not even Earl knows about them. They have a farm outside of Tiffin, Ohio. They're in the book. Tell them how you know me. They'll take care of you. He's a retired doctor and an outspoken socialist. Everyone leaves them alone."

"What are you saying, Harry? You're scaring me."

"Wait a month for me to show up. It will be okay with them. If I don't…"

"I'm on my own."

After I simply nodded, I said, "Repeat it back to me."

"Josef and Babs Polinski. A farm outside of Tiffin."

"Good," I said and kissed her.

We took the stairs instead of the elevator. "Wait here," I said. Seeing her hand shaking, I took hold of it and kissed her palm. "I love you."

Her voice cracked as she said, "I love you, Harry."

I turned, not wanting to see any more of her fear and trembling. I walked to the hideout door pointing the Browning to the carpeted floor, knocked, said, "It's Harry," and quickly backed off to the side five feet from the door. I raised the gun and waited. I wasn't going to use my key and enter into a trap. If everything was okay, Earl would understand, open the door, and stick his head out. His face would tell me everything I needed to know.

Odd thoughts come at the worst time. Earl had said that private eyes think too much about too little. Not this time.

I heard the door opening. My finger was tight against the trigger. Earl stepped into the hallway, quickly looking from his right to his left, where he saw I was pointing my gun at him.

His smile told me two things: the hideout was safe and he'd had sex with Vera. A best friend knows a look like that.

Was Vera a fast worker because she knew Joey never had a key, because Joey never touched the books or money?

Chapter 29.

Before Addie took Vera into the bedroom to show her the new used clothes, I tried to read Vera's face to confirm what I read in Earl's face, looking for something like a cat who ate a lovebird and didn't want anyone to know. Her face gave nothing away.

Earl and I didn't have long to secretly talk. I rushed through telling Earl how everything came up empty. I asked, "Anything on your end?"

He nodded without a smile. "If she was a horse, she'd win the Kentucky Derby. Harry, she's a thoroughbred."

"Everything?"

Again he nodded. "She wants to work with us, share everything. She has the books and money in a safe place. Had them all along. She wouldn't tell me where. She wants us to go to Miami Beach. I believe somehow someone there has the goods. She thinks we're smart enough to blackmail Tony Bacca, Jr. and get away with it."

"Wish she would have said something before Addie and I went on a wild goose chase today."

"Ready for this? She said she can tell if she can trust a guy from sleeping with him." Earl shook his head and shrugged as if he believed and didn't believe her at the same time. "We should go along with her, until we can figure out something better."

"Yeah. Did she say the same thing to Joey? Listen, Earl, I caught Blanton spying on Addie and me as we came in. He's getting awfully curious. It's a good time to leave."

"How does after breakfast tomorrow sound?" After I nodded, he continued, "Have you ever been to Miami Beach?"

"No. That's right, you took a vacation there a few months ago. Did Jeannie the travel agent book it?"

"Yeah. We went together. It might be too warm for you, since you think San Francisco is your kind of weather."

Considering everything that had recently happened, it was the strangest night, as if we were two couples and good friends. After a room service dinner, Vera told a couple of stories about when she was a teenager – funny, endearing stuff. She was a charmer. Earl and I talked about the war. Nothing was said about the diamonds or my experiences on the farm with the mother and daughter. If the stories sounded like the war was fun and games, there were four hundred stories we didn't tell that were completely the opposite.

Vera stood and held out her hand for Earl's hand. They went into Earl's bedroom as if it was the most natural and accepted thing that ever happened.

Inside our bedroom, Addie's incredulous look was followed by her whispering, "Do you believe her? Earl is only playing along, right?"

"That's what he told me."

"I hope he knows what he's doing."

I smirked. "He knows. By the way, we're leaving for Miami Beach tomorrow morning after breakfast," and then I whispered everything Earl and I had said privately.

"She's been here a little over a day and she's getting her way," Addie said.

Though I heard nothing through the wall between the two bedrooms, I had a strong premonition that what we did was what Earl and Vera did. For Addie and me, after what we did, sleep and then morning seemed to come quickly.

Everyone agreed to clean up and pack before we ate breakfast, before we left for Miami Beach. Earl and I flipped coins. Addie and I would go in the Chevy, while Vera and Earl would take the Packard. We split up the unused stolen license plates and the cash we had left.

Done packing sooner than everyone except Vera, who had only what Addie had bought her, I took two suitcases to the Chevy. I didn't see anyone, but I sensed Woody Blanton was watching. I shrugged it off as the jitters, since Blanton didn't start his hotel cop job until two.

As I entered our hideout suite, Earl placed two suitcases by the door. I noticed the Remington shotgun leaning against the wall by the door. "Who's taking the sawed-off?"

"Why don't you take it? I've never shot the damn thing."

Ten minutes later, with the breakfast orders in his hand, Earl was about to open the door and cross the hall to place the order, when I said, "Take your gun. Wear your coat. Remember, it's the little things."

“Yeah, okay. Want to come help me mess up the place one last time?”

Smartass, I said, “Nah, everything is messed up enough already.”

“Ha-ha,” Earl spoke the laugh.

In three days, at noon, we were to meet at the bar in the Saxony Hotel on Collins Avenue in Miami Beach. We would have a few drinks before we looked for a less expensive place to stay. Each couple would decide the route they would take to arrive at the rendezvous. Simple yet smart enough, though the continual use of the word *couple* sounded too sudden and too presumptuous.

We wouldn’t see Earl and Vera for three days. Sure, it sounded great for Addie and me to be on our own, but I wouldn’t be able to judge the effect Vera was having on Earl. Vera could double-cross Earl. She might never show at the Saxony and Earl might be dead. He was a grownup man who packed two guns. So was Joey, though Earl was smarter and well-aware of what being with Vera meant.

If they didn’t show at the Saxony, Addie and I would have to disappear for life. If they did show, the possibility existed we would end up blackmailing Tony Bacca, Jr., doing exactly what Vera wanted us to do. I wondered how agreeable Vera would be splitting the money four ways or by couple. Again, the word *couple* stuck in my craw. A lifetime on the run from a mob was not the future I hoped for with Addie.

Turning the books, the money, and Vera over to Tony Bacca, Jr. might be our only way out. Even that was risky. It seemed mob hoods didn’t trust each other, let alone outsiders, if you believe the papers. If Vera were murdered, it was no skin off my nose. If they sent the rest of us for the long sleep, my nose wouldn’t matter.

No sir, I didn’t like any of the possibilities. So maybe Addie and I wouldn’t show up at the Saxony, we’d go to Uncle Josef and Aunt Babs’ farm outside of Tiffin and live our lives as farmers with new names and never bother anyone about anything.

Addie and I would talk about the possibilities for three days before we decided. I would have told Earl about the farm, but he might say something about it to Vera. He probably wouldn’t. I couldn’t take the chance, despite how much I always trusted him. Joey brought Gus into Vera’s web and look at what happened to both of them.

I was as nervous as a cat during a thunderstorm filled with lightning. Everything was taking too long, from the packing to waiting for room service. So, I looked through the peephole toward the room across the hall.

I saw four hoods, one of them the New York torpedo, and a waiter with a cart piled high with breakfast food. As I grabbed the shotgun two steps away, I immediately jumped to the conclusion that the hotel dick had betrayed us. He must have seen me with the suitcases and figured it was his last chance to cash-in by fingering us to Tony Bacca. Jr.

Quickly back at the peephole, I saw two hoods were positioned on each side of the doorjamb. Earl wouldn't be able to see them. I thought I could see the waiter's knees knocking together.

In case Addie or Vera saw me at the door holding a shotgun, I held up a hand behind me hoping for quiet while I couldn't stop staring through the peephole.

With hardly the time to think it, I thought Eddie Dorn had never told Woody Blanton about the room across the hall or the killers would be outside the door in front of me.

I saw the waiter knock, then heard him say in a vibrating voice, "Room service. I need you to sign the bill." The waiter's inside left pant leg ran wet.

The hoods were poised with their guns and staring at the door. I made my move, flinging the door open and fired one shotgun blast toward the torpedo and the hood on my left and the second barrel at the two hoods on my right. The waiter caught some of the second blast and fell to the floor.

Earl's shots came through the right wall next to the doorjamb, finishing the job my second shotgun blast started. The four hoods and the waiter were on the ground, dead or dying. The New York torpedo shot at me from the floor. I felt the impact in my left chest where my heart might be. I went down, dropping the shotgun as I did.

The torpedo hobbled down the hallway, bleeding as he went. Earl was in the open doorway plugging the other fallen hood on my left, leaving no doubt about his death.

With my left hand on my left chest trying to slow down the bleeding, I was on my feet running after the torpedo with my Browning in my right hand. I hoped the footsteps I heard behind me were Earl's.

The torpedo was slowed from the shotgun wound. I was about ten feet from him when he reached the elevator. I shot three times. Bang. Bang. Bang. The first two shots knocked him down and killed him. The third shot would have hit him if he hadn't gone down. It went into the wall.

Though the burning pain of being shot nearly overtook the shock, I walked and stood over the New York torpedo. I wanted to see the dead look on his face. I looked over to see the elevator doors being held open by Woody Blanton. His free hand had his gun leveled at me. In a fraction of a moment, I heard a gunshot and knew I was being shot again. I heard and saw the hotel dick take a slug that splattered his face before I went down and everything went black.

I gained consciousness for several seconds. Addie was driving and I was bleeding. I felt too weak to stay conscious. The pain and loss of blood sent me back to nothingness.

Chapter 30.

Uncle Josef stood next to the bed looking down at me. He said, “You’re lucky. One bullet missed your heart by a sixteenth of an inch. Sorry, but I had to remove one of your kidneys because of the second bullet.” He wiggled the fingers on his hands, “I guess there’s still magic in these old digits.”

Addie’s fingers and lips were all over my face. I had a strong reason to stay alive.

Over the next couple of days, my weakness kept me in and out of consciousness. I didn’t have the strength to even speak.

The sun was shining through the window. It could have been morning. I pulled myself into a seated position. My whole torso seemed to be one dull ache.

Addie sat on the bed touching my face and kissing me.

I was strong enough to speak. “You know I’m not in any condition to…”

“You will be. Uncle Josef said you’re going to be fine. It’s going to take some time.”

“I guess I’m down one kidney. Probably have to cut my booze intake in half.”

After a full on-the-mouth kiss, Addie said, “You’re being a wiseacre. Now I know you’ll be fine.”

“How long has it been?”

“It’ll be a week in a couple of hours. I wanted to call an ambulance. Earl said that your life wouldn’t be worth a plugged nickel if you went to a hospital. Bacca would get to you and finish you off. Driving here was my only option to keep you alive. I went crazy thinking you would die while I drove. I would have never forgiven myself.”

“Earl was right about a hospital. Does Earl know where we are?”

“No. I wouldn’t tell him. I told him he should leave with Vera. I don’t know where they are. They don’t know where we are. Earl chose her and not us. He fell hard for her. She must have a magic pussy.”

The moment I laughed I had to stop. Laughing hurt. “So the house dick put one in me.”

"Earl shot him in the face. Killed him. Earl thought the house detective went to Bacca for more money than we paid him. Earl said to tell you he didn't think the hotel manager was in on it, or they wouldn't have gone to the wrong door. Earl had a look on his face and in his eyes – he didn't believe you would live."

I barely nodded because somehow my head was connected to my torso pain.

"Earl and Vera helped me get you into the Chevy. It's hidden in the barn. Earl said, in front of Vera, to tell him where I was taking you. He wanted to send money. I told him *no* again. Yeah, Vera was as wrong a dame as you always thought. I don't care about money, only you."

"Was the shooting in the papers?"

"Big story over several days. You and Earl are wanted in connection with the death of six people. The waiter died. The three hoods were suspected of working for Tony Bacca, Jr. The guy by the elevator was wanted for murder in New York. They guessed the hotel detective was trying to be a hero, since he was a former cop. How ridiculous is that? Earl and you left fingerprints in the empty suite across the hall. There was no mention of Vera or me. I don't think the cops know anything about where we were actually staying. What dirt do you have on the hotel manager?"

"He fornicated with a sixteen-year old who looked and acted like she was thirty. The agency acted as a middleman, paying off the family of the girl. We let him think we kept evidence. We lied. Remind me to send him a Christmas card in about ten years."

Addie was smiling, though it seemed for a different reason. "He's lucky he didn't get her pregnant. You weren't as lucky, Harry."

I hoped she saw in my face that I considered her being pregnant with my child was the next best news to my being alive.

Healing was slow. I spent many days watching winter arrive and bring snow. Addie was beginning to show the baby we'd made. Uncle Josef explained the difference between communism and socialism dozens of times. Aunt Babs taught Addie to be a better cook. I finished growing a real beard and let it continue to grow.

The mailbox was a quarter of a mile down a bumpy rutted road. No one visited. I don't believe anyone knew we were living with Uncle Josef and Aunt Babs.

Uncle Josef had been a boyhood friend of my father, like an uncle to me, though not related. My father and Josef argued about politics whenever they saw each other. They disowned each other after an argument ended in a fist fight. I was a teenager and broke up the fight before any real damage was done.

Though they weren't actually my uncle and aunt, I always called them that. They were united on what they believed. They didn't want to bring a child of theirs into an insane world. Dr. Josef Polinski delivered many babies and helped countless sick people, yet the good doctor and Aunt Babs were shunned for their political beliefs.

I remembered Uncle Josef saying, "Why should one man have one million dollars, when twenty men could have fifty thousand each? Did that one man work harder than the others? Did that one man inherit wealth or was he lucky? It doesn't make sense that one man should be more than happy, when twenty men could simply be happy."

It made sense to me. I was never all about money, as most everyone I knew was. No matter how much money Earl and Vera had or would get, I had a strong hunch I would end up happier than they were.

Uncle Josef and Aunt Babs had always treated me like the son they never had. When I was a man, I visited them on the farm a couple of times a year, except during the war. I could never tell my family or any relatives that I continued to visit them. There was never a reason to tell Earl, Joey or Gus.

Addie told them the whole story of what led to the two slugs in my body. They said we could live with them for as long as we wanted. When they both died, I would inherit the farm. The gunshot wounds must have softened me, for I cried when they told me that I was their sole heir.

By March, the winter broke and it rained rather than snowed. I was walking around and exercising like I did at boot camp. Addie was five months pregnant and getting bigger each day, or so it seemed.

We were in the barn, when Uncle Josef stopped talking about the spring planting and began talking about new identities. It had something to do with birth certificates, him having been a doctor, and two babies who'd died young. Would I mind being William Becker? Would Addie mind being Mildred Blonsky? We could be Will and Milly. We could legally get married before the baby was born. They would change their wills to show the new heirs were William and Mildred Becker.

Chapter 31.

On July 23rd a baby boy was born to William and Mildred Becker, delivered by retired Dr. Josef Polinski. I wanted to name him Harold Robert, reprising the name I had given up. I thought better of it. Small details might or might not get you killed. We named him Oliver after Addie's father, whom I most likely would never meet, with the middle name of Josef. Ollie sounded like a good nickname.

We used our new names as often as possible, though during private moments we often reverted to our real ones.

The closest town was Corkton, off Highway 224, eight miles from the farm with another seven miles to Tiffin, the big-time burg of the area. Whatever you needed to farm you could find in Corkton, though going to a movie meant driving to Tiffin. The only bar in Corkton was Jim's Wayside, where you could buy gasoline and drink alcohol.

On a farm, weekends were the same as weekdays. Many in the farming community took a half day off from farming on Sunday to attend church and have a family meal. Uncle Josef and Aunt Babs were socialists and didn't believe in religion. Addie, I mean Milly, suggested we attend Sunday church to get out of doing chores. She also thought our son would need some religion when he was old enough. When he was a man, it would help him decide what he believed. I didn't mind going to Sunday church and thought it would help people get to know us as Milly and Will Becker with a child called Ollie.

I was occasionally cornered by a few men who wanted to talk politics after church. They wanted to know if I was a communist like Josef and his wife. I assured them I was an American capitalist. We were distant relatives and working at the farm, hoping to own it someday. I agreed Josef was a crazy old man, though a harmless socialist, not communist, and not likely to start a revolution.

Besides learning about farming, I looked like a farmer, what with my blue dungarees, work shirts, work boots, and most often a green John Deere baseball cap. When my hair or beard became too long, Aunt Babs would "trim me up."

Chores around the farm meant all of the work around a farm. There was always something to tend or fix. Mostly I did the chores and Uncle Josef watched and criticized.

I told Addie about the farm in England, leaving out the bedding of the mother and daughter. It wasn't that I was worried what she might think of me. It bothered me. Perhaps Sunday sermons were sinking into my war-hardened heart.

Uncle Josef said we were using five times more of his land, thanks to me. Except for a few things from the Corkton general store, we ate what we grew, including farm animals. Tough guy that I had been, I couldn't watch Uncle Josef killing and butchering an animal. He said I would have to learn sooner or later. I chose much later or never.

Producing more on the farm, thanks to my hard work, meant more money earned. Uncle Josef shared it with me. More the second year than the first.

For a change, I had nothing to do on a rainy Saturday. Mr. Whitney had phoned to say the part for the John Deere tractor had arrived. Of course, Uncle Josef was frustrated because I was a slow learner when it came to fixing farm equipment.

I had taken to chewing tobacco and smoking fewer cigarettes. Once I recovered from the gunshot wounds and started doing farm chores, Uncle Josef complained how often I would take a cigarette break. It was inefficient and dragged my chores on for longer than they should take. He suggested chewing tobacco.

Once I got used to the awful taste, it became a habit just like cigarettes. My wife hated the spitting. If I wanted to kiss her, I had to brush my teeth and use mouthwash.

After a hard day of chores and eating a meal mostly produced on the farm, I would sit on a porch rocking chair, stare out at the night, and smoke a few cigarettes, since I wasn't doing chores. So Uncle Josef didn't complain.

Less and less I thought about Earl and Vera or how I had gone from a city slick private eye to a farmer wearing dungarees and chewing tobacco while I worked. It wasn't a life I would had chosen.

Milly, when she was being more Addie, would ask me about the future. Though I never expressed it, I thought someday when Uncle Josef and Aunt Babs passed away we would own the farm, meaning we could sell the farm and move back to city life, maybe own a business, though I wasn't going back to being a private eye, and we would never go back to Cleveland. We were both sad about the prospect of never seeing our families again. "Maybe in thirty or forty years" sounded like never. I would say something about the future taking care of itself. Not certain what I meant by it. Maybe we would buy more farm land and hire men to work it, so I could be a lazy boss.

I looked like a farmer. I talked like a farmer. Tough talk and sneering looks had no place on the farm, at church, or in Corkton. The best part of living on a farm and being a farmer was Addie and my son were safe.

As I sat on the porch in a rocking chair watching the rain and staring at the land and sky, Uncle Josef reminded me for the third time, "Did you forget about picking up that part for the John Deere?"

"No, I'll get to it."

"If I'd known you'd wait so long, I would have gone for the part early this morning. I could be half done with fixing the tractor."

I responded, "Relax. It's supposed to rain right through tomorrow. Plenty of time to fix the tractor by Monday."

"Who died and left you the boss? Why put off to tomorrow what you can get done now?"

I decided to tell him the truth. "I'm waiting for the bar to open at Jim's Wayside."

"At least you have a reason. We have beer."

"It's not the same. I want to sit at a bar, smoke cigarettes, and drink a few beers."

Uncle Josef recoiled. "How many beers? When will you be back? I'm going to lose the whole day."

Tilting my head, I said, "And what's wrong with losing a day?"

"You and Milly going to church tomorrow?"

"Probably."

"Well, horse manure. I'll be working on the John Deere myself until you get back. You have to learn this stuff, son. Looks like I haven't worked the city out of you yet."

I laughed. “You’ve certainly tried. Why don’t you come with me, Uncle Josef?”

“I couldn’t do that. Babs would be angry with me.”

“What, is she going to divorce you?”

“Why would you jump to that conclusion?” He sat on the swing and said, “I used to have a few beers now and then. Once I came home with a broken nose.”

“Arguing politics?”

“Yep. Actually, I felt good standing up and being knocked down for what I believe.”

“Come on, Uncle Josef, we’ll have a few beers and maybe get into a fistfight. I may not be able to fix a tractor, but I can carry my weight class.”

“Huh?”

“A boxing reference,” I explained.

“Do you miss city life, son?”

“Sometimes. Mostly, I never knew what was going to happen next in the city. Around here, I always know what’s going to happen next – you tell me.”

He bent forward, looked down, and then up at me from under his bushy eyebrows. “You know that you can take your family and leave whenever you want. Babs would miss all of you very much.” He paused as if he wasn’t going to say it. “I would miss you, too, son. I don’t mean for the hard work you do around here. It’s good to have another man to talk to, even if we don’t much speak the same language. It’s good to have another woman around for Babs’ sake. The sounds of a baby are especially good.”

“We’re not going anywhere. You’ve been better to me than anyone has ever been. I’ll never forget it.”

His moist eyes seemed to affect his voice. “You take the day for yourself and go into town. The tractor can wait.” The sound of his voice sparked, “But don’t forget to pick up the part.”

Chapter 32.

When I parked the '41 Chevy pickup outside of Whitney's Farm Supplies, it was slightly past 1:00 p.m. I paid the forty dollars plus change for the part. In the bed of the truck, I covered it with a tarp.

At the general store, I picked up a few things Aunt Babs needed, along with a list of child things Addie had given me.

At the counter, I asked Annie, a freckled teenager, "Did your father save me the Sunday newspapers from Cleveland?"

"Let me go look, Mr. Becker." She returned shortly saying, "Looks like four Sunday papers, a month's worth I guess."

I paid for everything and put the bags on the passenger seat of the pickup along with the newspapers. I drove to Jim's Wayside and parked by a gas pump. I told the middle-aged attendant to fill the truck up, park it over by the bar, and come inside for payment. Unlike living in the city, I knew nothing would be missing from the truck.

I hustled from the truck to the bar door, trying not to get too wet from the rain. "Good afternoon, Alma," I said as I took the barstool closest to the door.

"Hiya, Will. Miller in a bottle? It went up to 60 cents."

"That's fine, thank you. No glass."

"I remembered," she said and placed the beer in front of me. "If you're having more than one, I'll run you a tab."

"Yes, thank you." The cold bottle felt good in my hand, like one was created to be held by the other. As I took a long swig, I was thinking of bourbon, though I had no intention of having bourbon. Going into town for a few beers was one thing. Coming home drunk was another. No one would be happy with me and everyone would give me a difficult time the next time I wanted to go to town for a beer. It was funny how I would never consider those kinds of thoughts before the farm, a wife, and a son.

When I lit a cigarette, Alma lit a cigarette. Since I was the only customer, she leaned back against a beer cooler and said, "It's going to rain all day today and tomorrow. It will be good for the fall crops."

I smiled. "And my back."

"You're originally a city guy, right?"

"Detroit," I lied because everything about me was a lie. "I would have weekends off in Detroit. If it wasn't for the rain, I'd be working on something at the farm."

"Farming is a hard life. I went to Columbus for a few years when I was younger. It was a fast life. One thing I learned was city men lie to women. Not saying you're a liar, Will. Maybe you were, but I don't think you are now."

"No reason to lie when you're a farmer," I said and noticed I was emptying the beer bottle quickly.

"Nope. Only good ole honest folks. How is your little one?"

"Good. He's growing fast."

Alma went into a story. "I was engaged to this feller in Columbus. Don't think he ever intended to marry me. He got what he wanted and broke the engagement. I came home, but the pickins' have been slim. All the good ones are already married."

Thankfully, two other men entered and Alma went to serve them. Otherwise, I thought she might be flirting with me. Not that Alma was bad on the eyes, but she was right – we weren't in the city.

The gas jockey came into the bar and handed me the keys saying, "Two seventy-five, Will."

I paid him the exact amount, since I always carried coins.

Into my second beer, I began to think about Earl and Vera. I thought maybe someday I would read something in the saved newspapers about them. Realistically, I assumed they would never set foot in Ohio again and never make it into a Cleveland newspaper. I wondered if they were still together or if one had killed the other. As smart as I knew Earl to be, I guessed she had him wrapped around her little finger until she was done with him.

On rare occasions, the papers would mention Tony Bacca, Jr. and his father as suspected of something, though they seemed to get away with whatever they were doing.

With my third beer, I fired up my third smoke. Addie and I had left everything behind: family, friends, and things. My rooms, her apartment, and the offices. What happened to those things? I guessed our families had something to do with their disposal.

Everyone had to believe we were dead and our bodies would never be found. How forgotten were we?

I could tell Addie was homesick at times. I was at times. But if we made any contact with anyone from our previous lives, we would put ourselves, and maybe them, in danger. Once, I had the idea of driving for a couple of days and phoning from wherever I was to tell our families we were alive, though we would never see them again. That's what it was, never again. What good would it do? They had already mourned us. Why put them through knowing we were alive? It was too dangerous to have any kind of relationship with them.

What we had done grew harder when I thought about it. Day by day, it didn't seem hard. The whole picture, the whole story, though, that was hard. I was lucky to be alive. If I had died by the elevator, what would have happened to Addie? And she was pregnant with my son at the time. Would Earl and Vera have helped her or left her to fend for herself? I didn't want to think about what they might have done to her.

If I had died during the car ride to the farm, I believe Uncle Josef and Aunt Babs would have taken care of Addie and my son. Would Addie have taken our son, left the farm, and tried to disappear on her own?

My hands rubbed my face and ran over my beard. Would Addie be married to someone else by now, if I had died?

The way it happened was the best that could happen, given what had happened. Still, I had deep anger. Joey and Vera started everything. Addie and I weren't dead like so many were. We didn't deserve to have our lives uprooted and become new people without families and the life we would have chosen. Yeah, I was good and angry inside of me.

Finishing my third beer, I noticed I couldn't hear the rain outside. It would be a good time to leave, especially since I was confused, thinking what I was thinking. Would a fourth beer help put my mind to thinking about the tractor repair and church the next day? I didn't want to return home to the farm with *what-ifs* colliding in my brain. The past couldn't exist, didn't exist, for Will and Milly Becker and their son Ollie.

I realized what I knew. Another beer or another bourbon, though I hadn't drunk any, never solved anything. So, I placed two dollars and fifty cents on the bar and said, as I rose, "See ya, Alma. Keep the change."

After she acknowledged me by saying, "Take care, Will," I remembered I'd never carried coins in my pocket as a private dick; they could make noise. As Farmer Will, I always had coins clinking in my dungarees.

Since the rain had stopped, I was in no rush to get inside the truck.

From behind me I heard, "Hello, Harry."

Before I could turn, hands were holding my arms, while another set of hands forced me to breathe into a cloth with a pungent odor.

Chapter 33.

Ammonia. I was groggy and disoriented. More ammonia.

I heard, "Keep at it until he's fully awake."

Consciousness came in stages and not without pain in my head. Nausea crawled up the back of my throat. Images of the people I loved were on shards of mirrors and confused by a hot ice fog. I sensed moisture on my skin, not from sweat but from being near water.

Finally, though I had no concept of when it finally came to me, I could see my surroundings. A room with a bed, though not a bedroom. No light came through what looked to be portholes in one wall. The dim lighting made the air in the room look soft. I could be on a boat, in a cabin, though I didn't feel a sway from the waves. No waves?

Two men watched me. One applied smelling salts. I flailed my arms and hands to prevent another dose of ammonia.

As if slowly turning a corner to see what was around the corner, the broken mirrors in my mind assembled to resemble thoughts. My best guesses might not be right guesses. I guessed I had been chloroformed and abducted by thugs. The room suggested something more about having sex than having sleep. My two plus two could equal three or five, but the four might be a back room at Captain Nero's, adjacent to Lake Erie. The four also could be Tony Bacca, Jr. abducting me over something to do with Earl and Vera.

The food they brought would have looked and tasted good if it weren't for the lingering nausea. I told myself to eat – I would need my strength. I nibbled at the pasta dish, making an effort to keep the food down. My thirst caused me to drink half glasses of ice water at a time, though I had to fight against vomiting.

When he entered, I recognized him. Tony Bacca, Jr. was tall, around my age, with a hint of dark Italian skin and black greasy hair combed away from his face. If I had to guess what dames might think, they would think he was handsome and dangerous.

"Harry, what are you, a hillbilly?"

"My name is William Becker. We've never met. You've taken the wrong man."

"By the looks of you, you might be right, but you're not. Your mother was befriended over a substantial length of time. In case you care, her mind is slowing down. She mourns you. While mentioning what else she mourned, and regretted, came the names of the people you call Uncle Josef and Aunt Babs. It was worth looking into. Mind you, this has taken a long time."

"What do you want?"

"Good. We're over the part where you claim not to be who you are. You have a wife and a son."

"If anything happens to them…" I left the word *murder* off the end of my voice.

"Of course, I would expect no less of you. They'll be fine as long as you cooperate. Someone spoke to your wife over the phone. She's smart and quickly picked up on what happened. She also made a threat. And yes, she picked up the truck you left outside Jim's Wayside."

"Cooperate? Are Earl Griggs and Vera Jameson still alive? I don't know that. I don't know anything."

Tony Bacca Jr acknowledged, "I believe you. You wouldn't be hiding out and living like a hillbilly."

"I'm a farmer." Once I said it, it sounded almost foolish.

"You were involved with that bloody business a couple of years ago. I'm sure Earl Griggs wasn't alone in killing some of my crew."

"Did Woody Blanton give us up?"

"Yes. It's always about money, isn't it?"

"Not always. Sometimes it's about what's right and sometimes about revenge."

"Aw, good. You're beginning to sound like your reputation. If Griggs and you had come to me, we could have worked something out. Why would you take sides with that bitch, Vera? I'm surprised your partner hasn't been thrown over or murdered by now."

"You sound like a guy who used to be in love with someone."

"Love?"

"She knew you would kill her after she gave up the books and money."

Tony Jr. moved around, used his hands and arms to gesture as he talked. "Yes, that. Noah was intelligent and weak. I think most smart people are weak."

"But not you," I said with growing confidence, though I didn't know what I had to be confident about. "Finding me was a waste of time. I took two slugs. Want to see the scars? Addie and I split from them. End of story of what I know."

Smiling, he said, "I thought you would bounce back to your old self quickly. I want you to find them."

I used the Bogart sneer and smile. "What? That's crazy. If you haven't by now… Are they blackmailing you?"

"Yes. In the scheme of things, it's not much money. It's about the principle of it."

"And maybe those books could send you to jail, or more importantly, put you in Dutch with your father."

Tony Bacca, Jr. responded, "Only because you need to know, my father has come around to my way of thinking. My lawyers assure me the *books* would only be an expensive nuisance."

"Then why all of this? You had Joey and Gus murdered. I buttoned a couple of your guys. You and I are even. Let's call it a day."

"Actually, I agree with you. I don't want to harm you or any of your family. In some ways, I admire much of what you did back then. Under different circumstances, we could be friends, and you could certainly work for me."

"Great. We're pals. I should be getting home."

"Honest, Harry, I would like nothing better, but there's the little problem of your partner and the bitch. Maybe I should say 'former partner'? Find them and you have nothing to fear from me. I'll even sweeten the deal with ten grand."

I was feeling more like my old self. Being chummy felt right. "Tony, may I call you Tony? I would like nothing better than to help you out. They didn't share any of the money with me. My former partner betrayed me. He put me in a car bleeding to death and told my wife I wouldn't be safe in a hospital. I'm sure he thinks I died. But I got lucky and lived."

"Because old Uncle Josef is a retired doctor."

"Yes. I drew two cards and made an inside straight. Lucky. Up to now."

"Stay lucky, Harry. Help me find them. Don't make me do things I don't want to do. Who would know better how Griggs thinks than his old war buddy and former partner?"

"He was always smarter than me. I was a two-bit gumshoe. Small potatoes. Now I'm a farmer."

Opening his arms with a pretense of understanding, Tony Bacca, Jr. said, "That's probably true. The fact remains that you know him better than anyone."

"Didn't think I could talk my way out of this." I paused to think, and he kept quiet. Even if, somewhere along the line, I thought I had a way to get away, I had two old people, a wife, and a son who would need to safely disappear. There wasn't one card in any deck anywhere that could make that a winning hand. "Okay. What if I do my best, better than my best, but I can't finger them for you? Is there a way out for me?"

"Perhaps."

I was adamant. "I need a way out. I need your word. Or kill me now. So my family dies – everybody dies sooner or later. If you kill them, you better kill me first."

"Good. That's what I wanted to hear from you. You have my word. If I believe you did your best and I couldn't ask for one more drop of your sweat, I will let you and your family go free without any fear from me." He gave a gangster smile, something I recognized. "You're back, Harry. We need to get you to a barber. Get you some real clothes and a gun or two." His smile broadened. "Don't consider putting a hole in me. My men, my father, they would kill your family, even your mother and father and brother and sister. We wouldn't kill your wife. We would do what we did to Vera, then make a dope fiend and whore out of her."

He didn't need to say that! Whatever I owed him for Joey and Gus, I owed him a million times more for what he'd just said. What was that saying about *sticks and stones can break my bones, but words can never hurt me*? Bullshit!

Tony Bacca, Jr. may have sensed he went too far, because he softened. "We never need to go that far again. You have my word on everything. Do I have yours?"

"Yes. I will do everything I possibly can to get you Earl and Vera. I won't take any action to break my word on that." It was half true and half lies. Sometimes words meant nothing. Sometimes words meant everything.

Chapter 34.

Dressed like the old Harry, looking like the old Harry without a beard, and mostly feeling like the old Harry, three days later I asked Sal Vittali, my assigned keeper, if I could call my wife from a public phone. Several hours later, he said I could.

I picked a phone booth on a street with minimal traffic noise. I needed to say her real name. "Addie, it's me." Her silence told me she was too relieved to speak. "Everything will be okay. I know you were called. Once I find Vera, everything goes back to normal for us. I needed to hear your voice."

Her voice was soft. "I love you. I'm coming to help you."

"No," I firmly said, though I knew she was capable of doing what she had done before, when Earl and I kept her with us for her safety. Actually, she was smart and would improve the odds. Before our son, I worried about her safety when we worked together. "No. Not yet. Trust me, if I need your help…"

"Give me your word on that, Harry."

"You got it." Everyone seemed to want my word on this or that. Didn't they know, my words were only words and not sticks or stones? "Did Uncle Josef get the tractor working?"

"Really, Harry, that's what you want to talk about?"

For the first time since we became a couple, we had little to say to each other. The silence was awkward. Hearing each other breathe through the phone was enough.

I needed a place to live when I wasn't chasing Earl and Vera around the country. The Vincent House fit the bill before, so why not? I figured the damage had been repaired and the blood cleaned up. Besides, I could trust Eddie Dorn; it was the hotel dick who had betrayed us, and Earl had shot away his face. The sex with a minor would always make Dorn a trusted ally.

Sal Vitelli was only half as dumb as Tony Jr.'s other hoods. He also didn't seem to drink too much. Both were good reasons why Tony Jr. picked him to keep an eye on me. Sal paid for everything with Tony Jr.'s cash, so I ate and drank whatever I wanted. Might as well, while I could.

Crown Investigation was at my disposal, whatever I needed. It must have ruffled their feathers that Tony thought I could do what they couldn't – find Vera.

The two whose legs I broke in the room above the pizza parlor weren't working for Crown any longer.

I ran across the two phony cops who had guarded Vera. They gave me hard looks, although said nothing. Their ribs had healed, but being hog-tied and left with their dicks exposed was something they would never live down. If I ever used the ops of Crown, those two would not be involved.

I learned Earl and Vera were still a couple. Earl must have devised the blackmail cash payment method. It was simple and clever. They would phone Captain Nero's with the amount of the payment. It was never bigger than what Western Union could wire and pay out. They would call back and give a Western Union office too far away for anyone to get there before Earl took payment. Even if they could, Earl picked up the cash, leaving Vera to follow through on the threat of turning over the books to the authorities. No one believed Vera would do it. She would find another sap to play Earl's role in the blackmail. If they managed to catch Earl, he put it out to them that he wouldn't know where Vera was until he safely made the cash pickup. Torturing or killing Earl almost meant nothing to Tony Jr. He wanted Vera, preferably alive.

Western Union offices are all around the country. The pickups were relatively small amounts, like paying rent, but they added up. If it weren't for Tony Jr.'s need for revenge, it could simply have been a minor expense to the lucrative drug business.

I had a sense Tony Jr. was still in love with her, a bad love with the wrong dame, but love nonetheless.

If the Feds had been involved, since the crime crossed state lines, they would have staked out every Western Union office in the country, and utilized intricate methods to follow Earl to Vera. I always thought the Feds spent too much to catch too little. Of course, no Feds or cops could be involved. Even for Tony Jr., the potential cost of finding them would be greater than the blackmail amount.

I'm sure Earl realized Tony Jr. would do anything, pay anyone, to get his hands on Vera. If I had been Earl, I would make a deal for my life and some money and turn her over. But Earl was in love with her, just as Tony Jr. was in love with her. Didn't Vera say something about being able to love more than one man? How many? Six?

Something in my gut told me Tony Jr. wouldn't kill her. He would keep her locked up for his own amusement. On the flip side, he'd allowed, maybe encouraged, his men to do things to her when he had her stashed at the Terminal Tower apartment. By anyone's standards, what was in Tony Jr.'s mind was perverted and sick. Earl was simply lovesick.

I needed to get out of town. Nearly two years had passed, but I was still considered missing and wanted in connection to the killings at the Vincent House. It had been self-defense, but the cops would want someone to fry for it.

Most likely Sal was ordered to make friends with me. It wasn't a bad idea from my angle, either. Making friends with Sal and his boss might help me out further down the line. I asked Sal to ask Tony Jr. to come over to the Vincent House that night and bring me a bottle of bourbon and whatever they were drinking. I needed to talk.

The three of us sat around, drinking hooch, with me doing most of the yapping. I started with the whole true story. Both acted impressed. Since Addie was already in danger, leaving her out of the story would only make them wonder if I was telling the truth.

It was probably the booze, but in another life we could have been drinking pals. It wasn't another life, where no one had killed or tortured anyone, but the make-believe part of it gave me hope of returning to the farm.

Tony Jr. thanked me for killing the New York torpedo. He owed him money a dead man could never collect. When I asked him to share a part of it with me, he laughed and said *che palle!* Sal told me it meant *what balls!*

When I took the liberty of calling Tony Bacca, Jr. simply *Tony*, he didn't voice an objection. "So, Tony, it was Vera's idea that we meet in Miami Beach. Maybe it was a dodge to get away from Addie and me, though maybe it wasn't. Do you know if she was ever in Miami Beach?"

Drinking hooch either made people think in fast bursts or slow like a turtle who never won a race. I waited.

Finally, he said, "No. I don't know. I never took her there and she never mentioned the place."

"What if Miami Beach was on the level? I'll bet they think I died from the gunshot wounds. Nothing was ever in the papers about Addie or me. They may think Addie was smart enough to disappear. It's been a couple of years and no one has come after them. None of the Western Union offices they used are in Florida."

Sal offered, "So, this Earl drives hundreds and hundreds of miles to pick up the cash from Western Union, while she sits pretty in Miami Beach. What's her pussy made of…honey?"

It was similar to what Addie had said about her.

Tony began to laugh before he scolded Sal. "You're supposed to stick your dick in it, not eat it."

We laughed, although my laugh was forced. If Tony had his way a couple of years ago, Earl, Addie, and I would be dead. Joey and Gus were dead. I had to keep that thought under the surface and be friends with this sick killer, who only cared about his life and money.

Tony ordered, "Not tomorrow, but the day after tomorrow's hangover, Sal, you and Harry are driving to Miami Beach. I'll pay for everything. Take your Ford Crestline, Sal. Take guns. Flying with guns is too risky. You'll need wheels down there anyway. Now Sal, this isn't carte blanche. You know what that means, right?"

"Yeah, boss, cheaper hookers and wine."

Tony laughed, "Yeah that's right. Harry, maybe you could use some strange stuff since you been living on a farm for two years."

Though I promised myself more than I promised Addie that I would never cheat on her, I went along to get along with these hoods. "Yeah, maybe."

Sal said, "I love Miami Beach. French-Canadian dames on vacation seem to be everywhere. The less English they speak the better. And I know this place, the Suez Motor Lodge. It's right on Collins Avenue. A pool and then the beach. There's an outside hut bar. It's reasonably priced and swell."

"Sal, you'll be there to do a job. If you come back with too dark a suntan and no results, I'll cut off your dick myself."

These were my new drinking buddies. I preferred the boys back at Mo's.

The next day, when the hangover only ached in my brain but didn't impair my thinking, I made a decision. If Earl got in my way, I would kill him. I wouldn't think twice about it or even once about it. I had decided. I would try to turn Vera over to Tony Jr. I didn't care what happened to her. If she had to die, she had to die. Tony could cook her and eat her like a cannibal. I didn't care. Earl and Vera were nothing to me compared to those back at the farm.

Having made life and death decisions, all I had to do was to find them. Good luck with that, Harry.

Chapter 35.

During the two-and-a-half-day car trip, with motel stops, from Cleveland to Miami Beach, I learned about Sal Vittali. He talked, he whistled tunes, and he sang along with songs on the radio. His voice sounded professional. Someone, not Gus, made a crack that Italians were good at either being criminals or singers or being in concrete, the business or their feet.

Sal was a half-dozen years younger than me. He served during the war protecting Texas from Mexico. Who would have thought a war with Mexico was possible? He didn't see combat and didn't receive overseas pay. Lucky him.

Could a current mobster and a former private eye become friends driving together from Cleveland to Miami Beach in a Ford Crestline with a maroon body and white hardtop? He was assigned to befriend, watch, and help me find Vera. If I went wrong, he'd rat on me to his boss and then be told to kill me. Could a guy trying to keep his family from harm by finding a couple of blackmailers become friends with such a personable hood? To my chagrin, the answer was *yes*. We were a team matched somewhere closer to hell than heaven, yet we got along better than any reasonable person might expect.

We checked into a smallish, by Miami Beach standards, motor lodge. The rooms at the Suez were undersized and efficient. The motel offered an inside cocktail lounge, an outside bamboo hut bar, a concrete freshwater swimming pool, and yards of sandy white beach against sparkling blue saltwater. Reasonably priced for Miami Beach, it was a swell place, where I would love to spend a week with Addie. Instead, I had the room adjacent to my new friend, mobster Sal. Hopefully the day or night would not come when one of us had no choice but to kill the other.

Our M.O. was me looking like me and Sal keeping his distance to back me up. We would canvas the hotels, bars, restaurants, night spots, and swimming pools. If I couldn't recognize Earl or Vera, I wanted them to recognize me. Sal would be watching to see if anyone tipped their hand by the mere sight of me.

Yeah, it was tougher than guessing how many jelly beans were in a fifty gallon drum, but I had nothing else to go on.

The promise of a sawbuck or maybe a double sawbuck caused three false alarms in three weeks. Sal would be a distance away as I showed a valet parking attendant, hotel bartender, front desk clerk, or hotel maid glossy photos of Earl and Vera. I handed out wallet-sized photos of them with my name and the Suez's phone number on the back of Vera's photo.

Someone might think they would cash in more by telling Earl and Vera about me than the other way around. A reasonable description of me would surprise them that I was alive. After that shock wore off, they would wonder why I was looking for them. Vera would think I wanted money, while Earl would wonder if there was more to it. As long as mobster Sal wasn't spotted watching over me, how could they possibly consider I was working for Tony Bacca, Jr.? If I didn't find them, they might be curious enough to find me.

Sal came back from the saltwater-free swimming pool, toweled himself off, and took a seat on the reclining padded chair next to mine. We were in the shade, agreeing Tony Jr. might not want to see us with deep tans, since he was picking up the tab.

Two margaritas in the late afternoon had become a habit. Sal suggested the tangy citrus drinks with tequila and salted glass rims. They packed a sneaky punch. Later we would be canvassing more bars and restaurants. Late afternoon at the pool was our work break.

"Harry, I don't get it. I love it, but I don't get it."

"What's that, Sal?"

"Women normally hide so much, yet they show almost everything in a bikini."

"I've gotten to know you, Sal. You don't seem like one of Tony Jr.'s normal *guidos*. You seem smart, sane, and have a good sense of humor."

"Tony wanted someone who could better work with you. Someone who would understand not to push you around and make decisions for you. I'm only supposed to kill you if you try to run off with them. Why would you? Your wife and kid – you have too much to lose." He changed his patter a moment later, probably not wanting to think too much about what he said, "I'm meeting this Canadian dame, who only speaks French, at the cocktail lounge at midnight. Okay?"

"Okay. When is your boss going to grow tired of what we're doing here?"

"I don't know. He'll spend anything to get his hands on that Vera broad."

Too much salt was too much salt. I picked a section of rim where I had already consumed the salt and took a sip. "When Vera was at the apartment in the Terminal Tower, were you one of the guys…?"

"No. I don't want a broad who doesn't want me.'

"You told Tony that?"

"Yeah. I'm a first cousin on his mother's side. He can be reasonable."

"Do reasonable people have other people murdered?"

"First, I'm not going to say anything bad about Tony. Working for him puts bread on my table. Remember, she stole from him and they're now blackmailing him."

Though I liked Sal, I wouldn't hesitate to plug him if he got in the way of my family's safety.

Three days later, around ten in the evening, a heavier middle-aged guy, who ran the parking concession at the Algiers Hotel on Collins Avenue, said, "That's definitely them. Her hair is different, short almost like a guy's, and she's dark-haired. If anyone was wearing a wig, he was."

As I slid him a sawbuck, I asked, "When was the last time you saw them? What were they driving? Were they staying here?"

"That's three extra questions." After I passed him two more sawbucks, he said, "Two weeks ago. Maybe a day less. They drove a Chevy sedan, black hardtop with light blue body. Nice car. They were here for a dinner and a show. What did they do?"

"They have insurance money coming from a distant aunt."

"Heard that before. You a private dick?"

"Yeah."

"For a C-note, I can probably get the name from restaurant reservations. I heard her say his first name. It wasn't a normal first name. It will take me maybe 15 minutes inside to figure it out."

"Go. A C-note will be with me waiting for you."

Fifty feet away, Sal was lifting his head and craning his neck. He could probably tell I was about to jump out of my skin.

I stared at the name *Mr. and Mrs. Everett Burke,* written on a slip of paper exchanged for one hundred dollars. Earl thought about everything; he had often said *too much thinking about too little*. At the Vincent House he registered the empty room as Mr. & Mrs. Spencer Washington, telling me he didn't have an underlying reason for picking the name.

Driving back to our hotel, Sal said, "Son of a bitch, you were right. I didn't think we had a snowball's chance in hell."

"Easy. That guy could have seen easy money and made the name up."

"Harry, I wouldn't mess with you. You must know, you're one tough-looking *hombre*."

"*Hombre*?"

"Lot of wetbacks in Miami Beach. Hard not to pick up a few words. Do you know what *la chupada* means in Mexican?"

"What?"

"It's a dame with a welcoming mouth."

"Like I've said before, you're smarter than most *dagos*."

"I think I should be offended, but it's been a good night."

I wanted to call Addie and tell her the good news, though it was only a lead and might not turn into anything. Every time I phoned she wanted to join me, if I would only tell her where I was. I missed sleeping with her and everything that came with it. While Sal was having a swell time with women, I was only thinking about Addie, my son, Uncle Josef, and Aunt Babs.

Not being able to sleep, I focused on where Sal and I would start the next day. One of my guesses was that they would move from hotel to hotel. Hotel rooms in Miami Beach were expensive. Earl wouldn't want to blow the blackmail money as fast as it came in. They did have the stolen drug money to start. Still, Earl would want to save for a rainy day, like Addie used to tell us to do at the agency. It rarely rained in Miami Beach. When it did, it was sudden and over quickly. Everything dried so fast, it was hard to believe it rained, ever. My arrival wasn't their rainy day, yet.

If I knew Earl, he would have a cash goal. Once the starting cash and continual blackmail cash reached that goal, he would stop and disappear more thoroughly than he already had. I could see Earl running out on Vera and taking the cash. He might be lovesick, but he wasn't stupid. He might end up in Brazil or something. He would leave Vera with the books. She would recruit another sap, who probably wouldn't be as smart as Earl.

What would I do, if I were Earl? I would rent an apartment and build up to my cash goal quicker than living high and fancy.

As I laid in bed unable to sleep, I wondered if the Earl I knew had changed. If Vera changed him, I wouldn't know who he was or what he would do. I wasn't thinking too much about too little. I wasn't thinking enough about a lot.

Did the noise seeping through the wall, from Sal's room next door, involve a French-Canadian dame doing something that would cause a Mexican to call her *la chupada*?

Chapter 36.

Everyone was right: I had the mug of a thug. Sal, on the other hand, could pass for a lawyer's investigator looking for Everett Burke, who inherited money from a distant aunt. We started with apartments on the coastline and gradually worked our way north.

After three days without any luck, I sat in the car while Sal entered yet another apartment building. I wasn't discouraged. I had learned the detective business was about patience. You don't give up on an idea until it is completely played out.

Unfortunately, my growing friendship with Sal might get in the way of what I might have to do. More and more, an idea was brewing in my head. If I had the drug business books hidden away, I could blackmail Tony Jr. to leave me and my family alone. That's all it would cost Tony Jr. I wasn't after money, only safety. Tony Jr. had almost casually mentioned the books would only cause him inconvenience and cost him lawyer fees and bribes. Still, my offer would be a good deal. What would he gain from harming my family and me? If anyone stood in my way like Earl, Vera, or Sal, too bad for them.

Sal came back to the car and brought my train of thought to a dead stop when he said, "I almost pissed my pants. They're here at the El Condor Apartments. Number 301."

Needing to rebound from being shocked and keeping control of what would happen, I said, "Let's wait until we have them before we tell Tony. I've seen sure bets go wrong."

Convincing Sal was important. I didn't want Tony Jr. to send thugs to take over. Of course, Sal wanted to barge in and get it over with. I told him we would stake out the apartment. I made up what I said. "Rule number five of being a private detective is to watch and wait before you make a move."

It must have made sense, because Sal said, "It makes sense."

Thinking about it, it did make sense. I kept my straight mug on, though I found it humorous wondering what lies I could make up for rules one through four, if Sal asked.

The first time I spotted Earl, I was alone, parked on the street, where I could see the exit door leading to the parking lot. Seeing Earl was like seeing a ghost. He'd think the same about seeing me.

After two years, he looked different, though mostly the same. His hairline had receded, leaving a widow's peak, and what remained was blonde instead of gingerbread brown. When an easy wind pressed the loose floral shirt against his body, I could see he was thinner. His wide walk was different from the way he always stood as tall as he could be and walked with a marcher's gait. I always believed his ideas came from above him, so he held his head high to capture them. In less than the ten seconds it took for him to walk to a black and light blue Chevy, I read him as unhappy, maybe depressed.

From a safe distance, whether it was Sal or me, we watched Earl leave early in the morning and return late in the afternoon, as if he was working a day shift job. Earl having a job sounded stupid, but sometimes stupid turns out to be smart.

We didn't tail Earl, because he was a professional and would spot a tail before he drove two blocks. Besides, Vera was the primary objective.

After three days, we still had not seen her.

Sal made a joke. "Maybe she's staying inside because she has the flu. They say a warm weather flu is the worst."

What began to make more sense was Earl going out to look for her. Maybe she'd skipped out on him before he did the same to her. Or he might have a job because she'd left with the books and the money.

I decided we would take him as he went to his car in the morning. He would take us back to their apartment, as if he had forgotten something. Once we were inside the door, we would either have both of them or know she was gone.

My gut told me Earl's days were numbered. I had four reasons living on a farm for why I shouldn't care, but I did. We had been buddies before and during the war. We were buddies and partners after the war. He had saved my life during the gun battle at the Vincent House. These acts mattered.

Sal and I approached him from both sides. He didn't resist and wasn't armed. He looked at me like I was a ghost. His words meant one thing, while his face meant the opposite. "I'm happy to see you alive, Harry." Reality returned. "I have both my guns in the car."

When he nodded toward Sal, I said, "One of Tony Jr.'s guys. I'm working for Tony Jr. Let's go up and get her."

He showed sadness and maybe shyness about being a fool. "She's gone. She took the books and most of the money. She played me for a sap. I've been out looking for her. How long have you been watching me? I didn't spot you. I guess she left me not as good as I used to be."

Two days later, Sal, Earl, and I entered Tony Jr.'s suite of rooms at the Miami Beach Saxony Hotel. Tony had brought the three thugs who had abducted me.

I guessed Tony Jr. had been fuming since we told him the news of having Earl but not Vera, because his anger fully overtook him, when he spoke to Earl. "Did you have a good time on my dime? Fucking my whore for two years? When you kissed her, did you taste my jism?"

Earl knew better than to say anything.

Tony Jr turned to one of his guys and said, "Find a place and cut him up in little pieces. Better yet, make him suck you off and shoot him in an eyeball, so he can see the slug coming."

"Easy, Tony, let's talk about this," I said, knowing I was taking a risk.

His anger turned on me. "And you. You spent a lot of my money to find this piece of dog shit. Where's the dame? Where are my books, let alone the cash? Now that you've found him, why do I need you? What special knowledge do you have about her?"

"Whatever I know or don't know, Earl has known her for the last two years."

"So I should switch you for him?"

"You gave me your word. I'm not done. I need Earl. Together we can find her."

He pointed his finger like it was a weapon. "You know what I'll do if you don't, farmer." His anger decreased. "What do you think, Sal?"

"Harry was right about Miami Beach."

Tony Jr. paced the room, thinking. He poured himself a drink without offering anyone else a drink. He lit a cigar. He paced more. Finally, he said, "Sal, you stay with them." He pointed at Earl and me. "If anything happens to Sal, you'll wish you were never born. Remember what I said before to you, Harry."

To my surprise, Earl spoke. "Is there any way I can get out of this alive?" He had become bold to a degree beyond fear and approaching foolishly heroic. "If I don't have a chance, might as well do what you said and then cut me up and feed me to the fishes."

"What balls you private dicks have."

Earl said, "We didn't start this. You trusted the accountant and her. We've only been trying to stay alive."

I loved Earl like a brother again, like a stupid brother who would probably get us both killed.

"*Che palle*? Get the dame, the books, and whatever money is left…we'll see. I'm not making any more promises." His voice soared, "I want this done!"

After the highly charged meeting with Tony Jr. at the Saxony, Earl and I sat in the shade at the Suez hut bar, while Sal cavorted on the beach with two nubile young women. We drank highballs, whiskey and ginger ale, not in the mood for anything with rum or fruit.

"You're my responsibility," I stated to Earl. "Will you promise not to run and disappear?"

"I'm tired, Harry. Vera ditching me was both the best and worst thing to ever happen to me. If heaven and hell can be wrapped up in one dame, it's her. How dangerous is Sal?"

"I don't know. He seems to be a brain or two above a normal mob thug. He might be smiling and friendly when he puts a hole in you."

"I would have sent money, if I knew where Addie took you. I told her that they would finish you off if she took you to a hospital. I didn't betray you, Harry. I thought you had bought the farm. So, Bacca called you a farmer?"

Involuntarily I laughed. "I'm not going to tell you where we went. I would have trusted you before that dame got her hooks in you. I'm not convinced you won't try to get back with her. You need to know, I'll put a slug in you if you try that. Addie and I are married with a kid. Tony Jr. found us. I either deliver Vera to him or else. Cards on the table."

"Couldn't we use the books to make it work out?"

"Tony Jr. said that his father has joined him in the dope business. If the authorities got the books, it would be a nuisance and cost him legal fees and bribes, but he's not that concerned. I believe him."

Earl said, "Why did he continue to pay the blackmail money?"

"In the scheme of things, it wasn't that much money. He hoped you would slip up. He wants the dame."

"So he found you, and you thought the Miami Beach play was still good because we believed you were dead."

"The rest was shoe leather and showing photos. I may be a farmer now, but I'm still a shamus. Was she worth it?"

He signaled the bartender in a flowery shirt for two more drinks, before he said, "It started as *yes*. It became like the war, you survive each day, but when it's over you wonder how and why you went through it in the first place. Then you remember, it was what you chose."

We nodded our fresh drinks toward each other, before taking sips. It seemed like we talked as we always had, but everything was as different as black from white. We could be partners and even buddies until we came to the end and her name was Vera.

"Sal and I watched you for days, like you were going to a job. Do you have a clue to where she is?"

When Earl stopped talking, I knew he had a lead on her. He was deciding whether to be with me or against me. Maybe he thought he could get away from Sal and me. Maybe he was thinking he could get back with her. Maybe he wanted to die for her, like I would die for Addie and my family. Maybe we could never be friends or buddies again. Maybe Sal and I would have to try to beat it out of him or kill him in the process. Earl's next words might be the last wrong decision he would make.

"Am I taking too long to answer?"

"Yes." I knew he knew what I was thinking.

"Ten days ago, she took a rented boat to Cuba with three Cuban guys. That information cost me half a grand. I was trying to confirm the information when you found me. I wasn't sure if I would go to Cuba after her. I'd be alone and she would have allies."

"What made you think of a boat to Cuba as a possibility?"

"I'm going to have to prove myself every step of the way?" he asked more than stated. I stared at him until he continued. "She mentioned wanting to go to Cuba for fun and then stopped talking about it. She lives every moment like it's her last. She wasn't born the way she is. This isn't going to make much sense, but what happened to her a couple years ago, especially in the Terminal Tower, left her dead, yet more alive, like living on borrowed time."

"And you thought your love could save her. She was Tony Jr.'s girl, then the accountant's wife, and then there was Joey. She could have walked away from all of it, before they tortured and abused her. You helped her by continuing the blackmail. Maybe if you would have returned the money and books, then disappeared with her, it wouldn't have come to where we are now. I nearly died. And now I have a wife and a kid to protect. You were too smart. Thought you had it sized up. Thought she could be someone she could never be again."

"You're right, Harry. If you can't do it, you should have Sal put me out of my misery."

"You won't do it yourself, because somehow, some way, you think you're going to end up with her."

"When did a guy with a mug like yours become so smart?"

"I'm not smart. I have too much to lose to be stupid."

Earl signaled for two more highballs. "Let's get drunk again for old time's sake. If we didn't get lucky and find those diamonds, would everything have turned out different?"

After I shrugged, I said, "If she would never have been born, a number of guys would still be alive and a number of other guys wouldn't be facing possible death."

His smile was odd. "Hell, Harry, we should have died in the war. Everybody is on borrowed time."

Chapter 37.

Earl should have told Tony Jr. at the Saxony about Vera and the three Cubans going to Cuba. He was making a deal to save his life and he left out that tidbit of information.

If Earl thought I would ditch Sal and go off to Cuba to find Vera, only him and me, he was crazy. Did Earl think he could find her and put what he had with her back together? Would I be along to prove to her she needed him? After the hut bar conversation, he must have known I would never join him in continuing to blackmail Tony Jr. I would never choose them over my family. It led me to one conclusion. He would kill me to prove to Vera how much she needed him. If he couldn't personally do it, her Cubans would.

Most of what Earl said about being able to trust him was bunk. He should have told Tony Jr. about Cuba. Clearly, either Sal or I would have to watch Earl every second of every day.

With the door to my Suez room open, Sal and I could see Earl sitting on a chair and staring out at nothing, though his mind wouldn't be on nothing – it would be on Vera.

We could see Earl, but he couldn't hear what we said. I told Sal about Vera and Cuba. I wanted him to tell Tony Jr. I wanted to prove to Tony Jr. that I worked for him, but I didn't want to tell him face to face. I had vouched for Earl and now Tony Jr. needed to know Earl couldn't be trusted.

Sal went off to tell Tony Jr. the news. I worked for Tony Jr. Whatever he wanted me to do, I would do.

With Sal gone, Earl wanted more alcohol. I nixed the idea and suggested he watch television while I laid on the bed with a .38 lying on my chest. I wished it was my Browning, but it was in the Polinski barn in the trunk of the Chevy, the vehicle I received from Honest John in return for my Buick. Everything that had seemed so long ago seemed like it just happened.

When Earl left me in the Chevy with Addie and went off with Vera, he signed his death certificate, with the date and time of death left blank. When Joey and Gus died, many death certificates followed theirs. More were likely to follow. Some sooner. Some later. Later might happen sooner. I hoped none of them were mine or a family member.

I wanted to say 'My ass!' to Earl's assertion that he didn't betray me. Only my tough skin kept my anger from Earl. He had put me in a car with Addie, for her to drive me to my death. Even if he were certain I would die, he should have been with me doing everything he could to save me. He went off with Vera instead, unlucky that my death certificate wasn't yet signed.

When Sal returned from seeing Tony Jr., we stood outside my open door, while Earl watched television.

Sal said, "If you think we don't need Earl, I'm to kill him. Tony said it's your decision. You scored points, Harry, by having me tell him about Cuba. He only wished you would have told him yourself."

"I'm afraid of him, Sal."

"Tony said that, like it was the way he wanted you. You're to meet him for breakfast, at nine, in his suite." He put his hand on my shoulder, like a friend, and said, "I'll watch Earl tonight. Get some sleep, Harry."

Stepping off the elevator and turning to walk down the hallway toward Tony Jr.'s suite the next morning at the Saxony, I saw a beautiful dame, dressed to the nines, walking toward me. She had the look of an expensive call girl who had spent the night with a john. Odds were reasonably good the john was Tony Jr. I hoped she left him in a good mood.

As I passed her, I smiled and went to tip my hat, only I wasn't wearing a hat. I had been in Miami Beach long enough to know wearing a hat and suit in the sunshine and heat would make me look like a gumshoe from up north. A loose tan shirt outside of loose tan pants meant I packed a .38 in a waistband holster.

Her eyes shifted left for a look at me. Her eyes left me as quickly as they landed. I knew my mug didn't frighten her. A true pro skirt never cared what a john looked like as long as he had a stack of green. More likely, in that moment, she sized me up as not having the money to afford her, like she was better than me. Under different circumstances I might have said something wise like "have a nice lay." But my mind was too busy to give her one tenth of another thought.

Tony Jr. answered my knock wearing a white robe with the hotel insignia where a left breast pocket would go. Smiling, he said, "Harry, good morning.

You must have walked past that dish in the hallway? Everyone is wrong about mixing pleasure with business. I love Miami Beach."

As I looked around, I said, "Where are your guys?"

The door was closed and we faced each other, when he gestured by opening his arms and said, "I gave my boys the night off, so they could have some fun. If you want, you have about an hour to rub me out. Now's your chance."

His good mood told me the pro skirt had been worth every dollar.

He ordered two breakfasts from room service without asking my opinion. He sat in a plush chair with his legs crossed at the knees, showing his bare hairy legs, as if he owned the world. Well, he owned me.

"Sit down, Harry. Relax." When he looked at his expensive gold watch, I noticed he wore a ruby and gold pinkie ring. I couldn't imagine the ruby not being real. "We are going to give room service twenty minutes. If the waiter brings the food after that, I want you to shoot him."

"What?"

"Ha-ha. Just joking with you, Harry. Is Earl Griggs alive or dead?"

"He's alive. I may need him to help me find her."

"Okay. It's your decision, your responsibility. Whether you find her or not, I want him to die in Cuba. Got that?'

"Yes."

While we waited for breakfast to arrive, he talked about Havana with enthusiasm and wished the Bacca family had a mere slice of any hotel and casino there. Havana was better than Las Vegas, because the police were corrupt and everything was for sale.

"I'll set the three of you up at the Montmartre. Don't take any hardware. I'll have weapons waiting for you. I have connections. It's not that you can't pack them in a suitcase, but you might get checked, and paying off the cops would be expensive."

"Should we rent a boat or fly? I know nothing about Cuba."

"You could drive to the end of the Keys, nearly a couple of hundred miles, and take a 90 mile boat ride. But it's better to take a plane from Miami. It's about an hour and a half or so."

"You seem to know a lot about it. How long would it take a boat to go from Miami Beach to Havana?"

"The best part of a day, depending on the speed of the boat. Remember why you're there, Harry. Havana can be very distracting. You'll have to bring her back by boat. I'll arrange something once you have her." Like it was a minor afterthought, he said, "Keep playing it smart, Harry. You're almost off the hook."

When the knock on the door and the words "room service" came through it, my heart beat faster as if I was back at the Vincent House unloading both barrels of the shotgun.

Checking his wristwatch, Tony Jr. said, "Don't shoot him, Harry. Give him a tip. I seem to be temporarily out of cash. Ha-ha."

During breakfast, he continued talking about Havana. At any moment, I thought he was going to say he was taking his hoods to Cuba with Sal, Earl, and me. I wasn't sure if that would be helpful or gum up the works. Regardless, I would be agreeable with whatever he wanted to do. I worked for him.

"I'm going to stay a few days in Miami Beach. Life should be enjoyed or what good is money? If you need us, my boys and I can be there in a couple of hours."

Another knock on the door didn't surprise him. When he looked at his wristwatch, the ruby ring on his pinkie finger stared at me. "Let my boys in." He laughed. "You lost your chance, Harry."

Chapter 38.

Sal let me into his room after I knocked. While I was having breakfast and getting my marching orders from the boss, he had been guarding Earl.

Leaving out the part about Earl never leaving the island alive, I explained to both of them the plan to go to Havana and find Vera. I wondered if Earl made something of the fact that my direct looks at him were short.

When I told Sal we would be leaving our guns in the parked car at the airport and would be supplied, once we checked into the Montmartre, I saw a flinch in Earl's left eyelid. If I was him, I would find an airport cop and turn myself in and take my chances with the law. But I could tell that he wanted to find Vera, see her again, and be with her again. He had to know she would be the death of him, though he wasn't dead yet. He sure was lovesick.

After Sal and I were done packing, Earl wanted to go back to his apartment, take a shower, put on fresh clothes, and pack a bag. If I didn't agree, he would absolutely know what was to happen to him in Cuba.

The last thing I wanted to do was to be alone with Earl in his apartment. I had nothing left to say to him. I didn't want to hear what he had to say to me. So, I told Sal to go up with him. I made an excuse about having to fill up the car with gas. Miami International Airport was about a half hour away. Why I would want to park with a near full tank wasn't questioned.

When I returned from the gas station, I parked on the street near the front door to Earl's apartment building. The warm breeze through the open driver's window had a hint of salt water to it. I lit a cigarette, thinking it would be at least another half hour until Earl and Sal came down to the car.

I hadn't told Sal he would be killing Earl in Cuba. Although I could do it, I figured it might give me haunted moments later. Despite everything that had happened over the last two years, Earl was Earl, my best friend for most of my life.

A second thought made me wonder if Earl would be able to kill me if it meant he would get away with Vera. Would he do for her what I would do for Addie, Ollie, Uncle Josef, and Aunt Babs? In any reasonable person's mind, saving someone like Vera was not close to comparable to the people I wanted to save. It seemed to me love could bring good or bad. Fairness often played no part when it came to love.

When I lit a second cigarette, I saw something strange. Three men, who looked like they could be Cubans, came out the front door of the apartment building and walked down the street away from where I was parked. I had no experience distinguishing between Hispanic people. Wasn't it odd? Three men, who might be Cubans, casually dressed, not like workers, came out of the apartment building in the later part of the morning. It came to me too easily that Vera might have sent them to finish off Earl.

They walked casually, as if they didn't have a care in the world. I was confident I was wrong, but if my wild imagination were right, then Earl and Sal were dead and I couldn't do anything for them. I decided to follow the Cubans, not on foot but by car.

For over an hour, I followed them, moving up and then lagging back, only to move up again. I was fairly certain they didn't spot me. I had time for plenty of crazy ideas of who they were and what they did.

Using my binoculars, I watched them board a cabin cruiser, maybe a twelve-footer. I easily spotted the writing on the hull. It read, "El Gato Verde – Havana."

"Coincidences do happen," I told myself, but didn't believe it.

Most of me expected Earl and Sal to be waiting outside the apartment building wondering where the hell I'd been and saying we would have to hurry to make our flight.

Back at the El Condor Apartments, everything was quiet, as if it was any minute of any ordinary day. Earl and Sal were nowhere in sight. If something happened, it happened quietly or there would have been cops everywhere. I remembered I had heard nothing out of the ordinary after I returned from filling up with gasoline. Quiet was good during war. I wasn't sure quiet was good now.

I stared at the doorknob to Earl's apartment. I leaned forward almost touching my ear to the door. I heard nothing. I took a handkerchief from my back pocket to use on the doorknob, not wanting to leave fingerprints in case I found what I expected. When the doorknob turned, meaning the door wasn't locked, I expected the worst.

Through the open doorway, I saw Sal face up about five feet inside. His throat was slit, almost ear to ear. Blood soaked the carpet under his head, neck, and around part of his torso.

The drapes were closed, leaving the living room in shadowy darkness. Wearing a blue bathrobe, Earl was face down and unmoving. I guessed blood surrounded him like it did Sal, but the blood was hidden in the darkness. If I could make out a fraction of a movement, I would go to help Earl. He was dead as a doornail, an odd expression. Why was a doornail any deader than any other nail? Maybe standing outside the open door triggered the thought.

I wasn't going into the room. I had seen enough. I didn't want to chance leaving evidence of my presence. I quietly closed the door and left.

I drove away as casually as the three alleged Cubans had walked away. Inside, my nerves were crashing against each other. I may have looked calm, but I was frightened and nauseous. I knew I was in the kind of shock that allowed people to act normally and do normal things, like drive a car. It was that numb protective shock making me think what happened hadn't happened. It was that way in the war. Seeing others die or become maimed didn't paralyze me, when by all rights it should have. I went about doing what I had to do to stay alive.

I found a bar and chugged a double bourbon and drank most of a bottle of beer. Immediately afterwards, I ordered another setup.

I wanted to be on the farm listening to Uncle Josef explain something I didn't understand. I wanted to hold my son. I wanted to give Aunt Babs a kiss on the cheek. I wanted to make love with my wife.

It dawned on me. If I had gone up to Earl's apartment instead of Sal, I would be dead. Even if the three of us went up together, we would be dead, though maybe one of them might be dead.

My hands began to shake. I had to drink the next bourbon using both hands. Shock became reality. Earl was dead. Gone forever. Sal, who had been okay, was dead. Gone forever.

A clock on the wall, above the shelved liquor bottles behind the bar, showed me the plane to Cuba had taken off without three passengers. Tony Jr. would be thinking we were on our way to Havana to find Vera.

I took a cocktail napkin with the bar's name, address, and phone number on it to the phone booth inside the joint. I put in a nickel and dialed the operator, then asked her to put my call through to the Saxony Hotel. I hoped my eyes could focus enough to read the cocktail napkin. Looking up a phone number in a phone book had to be beyond what I was capable of doing.

For all I knew, someone could to be listening to Tony Jr.'s phone calls. I was surprised I was able to consider the possibility.

Although I knew Tony Jr.'s room number by heart, my heart was busy with the revulsion of Earl and Sal's brutal murders, so I asked the hotel operator to connect me to Tony Bacca's room.

I'm guessing one of his guys answered, because I didn't recognize the voice. I kept it simple and said, "It's Harry. Come and get me," and then I read the name of the bar and the address off the cocktail napkin.

When I returned to my beer on the bar, I was only certain of one thing; I wasn't going to Havana alone. I thought better of ordering another bourbon. Getting drunk never solved anything. It might postpone or worsen something, but it never solved anything.

With a cocktail napkin, I wiped the moisture that had collected at the bottom of my eyes. The best friend I ever had, despite the last two years, was dead. Sal, an okay standup guy, was dead. Too many had died over the wrong dame. I was lucky not to be one of them.

Chapter 39.

After telling me not to drink anything alcoholic, Tony Bacca left his Saxony suite to make calls on a pay phone, in case someone was listening in on his room's phone. Mobsters didn't want their business conversations recorded. I slouched in an overstuffed chair, exhausted from what I had witnessed and what the shock took out of me.

He came back into the suite with a determined energy. Tony Bacca, Jr., his three men, and I were flying to Havana to intercept the arrival of the boat with the three Cubans who'd murdered Sal and Earl. Associates in Havana would arm us. By the time we arrived, the associates would know where the boat normally docked.

Bacca's plan was to take the three Cubans, torture them, perhaps murder one or two, to get one to talk about where Vera was.

I thought better than to offer the option of following them, after I also wondered how we would accomplish that if the Cubans split up and went in different directions. Five against three sounded better than one or two following one. What if they were met by others, perhaps Vera herself?

Earl made his bed when he first climbed into bed with Vera. Avenging his murder, when he set himself up to be murdered, wasn't my responsibility. Being one of Tony's men was. I had no choice but to follow orders. Same as the war.

"Tony, what if there is more opposition waiting there for them?" I asked.

"What? Do you think she hired an army?"

"We don't want to be outgunned. This isn't what I signed up for."

Bacca's response was quick. "You didn't sign up, you were drafted. Remember your family on the farm. But, you make a good point about the enemy."

He left the room and returned shortly to say, "The timing will work out. Three more of my guys are coming from back home."

Compared to flying, a boat trip from Miami Beach to Havana was like a slow boat to China. We could get there with plenty of time to spare.

Each of us took a suitcase. We might have to change clothes because of perspiration, blood splatter, or both.

We were the quiet ones on the flight. Everyone else seemed to be going to enjoy what Havana had to offer, which was just about everything, maybe something you couldn't get at home.

I hadn't bothered to call Addie. What would I say? I'm going to Havana where there might be gunplay, torture, and murder?

During the many weeks since I was abducted and taken to Tony Bacca, I knew that Addie, Uncle Josef, and Aunt Babs had had too much time to think. I could only imagine what about. My thoughts went back further to the murders of Joey and Gus, then to taking Vera from Tony Bacca at the Terminal Tower, to the gun battle where I took two bullets and nearly died, and to the peaceful life on the farm and the birth of my son.

Before I knew it, we arrived and were met by another Italian looking hood named Jimmy Gratta, a Havana associate of the Baccanelli family, whatever that meant.

Havana was warmer than Miami Beach, with so much moisture in the air I could taste the salt from the sea. The milling people and cooking smells gave it a close human odor. Even the street noise sounded different – more spirited and louder than anything I had ever experienced.

The colors of the people, tourists and natives, ran the gamut from white to tan to brown to black. Their garb mimicked the buildings; both were in bright, loud colors. The living conditions appeared meager, yet the people seemed happy. I wondered if it was a sham to get money from the tourists for whatever was being sold.

The Capri Hotel was a different world from the streets of Havana. Everything was clean and opulent. One of Bacca's men said it reminded him of Las Vegas. I wasn't a gambler, so I had never been to Las Vegas. Another hood mentioned the actor George Raft owned a piece of the Capri.

It would be several hours until the additional men were expected, and a couple of hours after that before the *El Gato Verde* could possibly arrive from Miami Beach. After we inspected the impressive array of weapons left for us in one of the suites, Tony Bacca, Jr. warned us against drinking too much. He told us not to leave the hotel. We could gamble or rest or find a prostitute. I had the same feeling as before going into a battle during the war, though such lavish surroundings and opportunities didn't exist in the war.

When I found a bed, I hoped I wasn't so tired I couldn't sleep. So much had happened today, and it wasn't dark yet, though the room was dark and what I saw when I closed my eyes was as dark as seeing Sal dead by the door, looking up at me, and Earl face down in a blue bathrobe on the living room carpet.

I must have fallen asleep, because I was awakened and told to eat before we left. Food had been brought in. The sleep didn't feel restful and I wasn't hungry. I thought it best to eat something, though, not knowing what might happen over the coming hours.

The other three men had arrived, so the meal in the main room of Tony Jr.'s suite was a buffet laid out on several tables. His hired guns seemed to eat like it was their last supper, yet they joked around as if they were going to a party. Maybe that was what made a criminal a criminal, enjoying the excitement of something dangerous about to happen.

Jimmy Gratta was in the lead car, guiding the three-car convoy to the pier where the boat was expected to arrive. I was in the backseat of the last car with Tony Jr., while two of his mob were in the front seat.

Darkness had finally filled the skies, but it didn't seep into the lights and noise in the streets. The cars moved slowly, since the streets were more like sidewalks to the tourists and locals.

Once we left the city, the car headlamps cut through the heavy darkness and lit what would be called a backroad in the States.

The pier stretched for several hundred yards with minimal lighting. It looked like a place for simple fishing boats. After the loud sounds of the city, this was quiet and uninhabited, as if the work of the fishing boats was done for the day.

We spread out on a perimeter covering the only two open piers where the boat could possibly tie up. It wasn't like docking spaces were assigned and organized, since the pier and boats had a haphazard appearance.

My position was only a few feet inside a line of palm trees. Vegetation between the trees rubbed against my knees. A steady wind came across the water, across the pier, and across thirty feet of sand until it stirred the palms and vegetation.

Looking to my left, then my right, I could see the amber pinpoints of light from guys smoking a cigarette with one hand, while like me, they probably had a gun in their other hand or a machine gun or shotgun in the crook of an arm. My hand on a .45 was sweaty from the humidity and fear of what would soon happen.

After standing with my back against a palm tree and staring out at the black water for a half hour, I closed my eyes trying to imagine I wasn't where I was.

The word passed from man to man, down the perimeter line, of a boat's lights out on the water. Also passed was, 'No more smoking.' It made sense. I wouldn't dock if I saw several pinpoints of light along the shore in the trees. Not giving your position away was no different than during the war.

It seemed like the boat was taking forever to get closer to the raggedy pier. It was the slow boat to China thing, again.

The three Cubans would never have expected me to be sitting in a car in front of Earl's apartment and curious enough to follow them. They would be completely surprised by the unwelcoming committee waiting for them.

A thought struck me as odd. Earl said the captain of a rental boat told him that he took Vera and three Cubans to Havana. Why would they rent a boat, if they had the *El Gato Verde*? I could understand why Vera would not want to fly to Havana. Moving anything between Havana and the States was more secretive by boat than flying. Smuggling by boat was legendary for the waters between Cuba and Florida.

Perhaps Vera met the Cubans in Miami Beach. Once they were in Cuba, the *El Gato Verde* could have been rented.

From behind, a hand covered my mouth as I felt something hard against my spine. A voice, Earl's voice, said, "Don't move a muscle, Harry, if you want to live." Earl's voice!

A few guttural grunts, not much more, added to the sounds of palms and vegetation rustling. A strong feeling told me throats were being slit, blood was flowing, and Tony Jr.'s men were dying.

My gun was taken. My hands were tied. I was blindfolded and gagged.

We had walked into a trap. The face-down body wearing a blue bathrobe was God only knew who. For anyone looking for it, my parked position outside the apartment building would have been easy to spot – I had no reason to be careful about it. The three Cubans made it easy for me to follow them and see the name of the boat. Earl had played me like a pawn. He knew Tony Bacca, Jr. would do exactly what he did and come to Cuba with gunmen. I expected Vera was somewhere on the island waiting.

Manhandled, I was thrown into the trunk of a car and driven away. I wondered if I was the only one left alive, and if it was because Earl and I had been friends. That was good and bad. My mind and my heart went to hell in a hand basket. What would happen to my family on the farm after what had happened in Cuba? I didn't want to live if Fat Tony Bacca took revenge on my family.

Chapter 40.

With no concept of time, I only felt the road under the vehicle becoming bumpier and more rutted, like a road worse than the one leading from Uncle Josef and Aunt Babs' farmhouse to their mailbox. Since I wasn't dead, yet, I needed to block the farm, Addie, and my son from my mind and focus on staying alive.

I was hauled out of the car by strong hands and taken into a room with a wooden floor. Being inside the car left me soaking with sweat and needing more air to breathe than there seemed to be inside the trunk. The heat inside the room wasn't much better. The air felt moist and sticky. Breathing the air was like breathing melted saltwater taffy.

They laid me down on something similar to an army cot, because I remembered the feel of it from the army. If they placed me in a prone position, thinking I might be able to sleep… How could I, when I was feeling like I was being cooked in my own juices, like a stupid turkey, who had been led into a trap and ambush? If I was being softened up for whatever was coming next, I was already wet, basted, and roasted.

Finally, after I don't know how long, I was raised by strong hands into a seated position on the cot. I felt dizzy from being yanked up so suddenly.

The blindfold was removed. My eyes adjusted quickly, since the room was lit only by candles. Vera stood in front of me with her hands on her hips. She looked as warm and sweaty as I felt. She wore a khaki shirt and trousers, as if dressed for a safari. Her hair was as short as a man's. The candlelight caught dark red in her black hair, like the color of black cherries. Yet she looked beautiful and seductive, like you would expect the devil's temptress to look.

"Harry, I'm going to take off the gag. No one who could rescue you can hear you. You're smart enough to know that."

She removed the gag and began to wipe my face with a wet cool washcloth. Several times she rinsed the cloth in a bucket of water and brought the cool relief to my head and neck.

With a soft reassuring voice, she said, "Everything is going to be okay," and then took me by complete surprise when she kissed me fully and forcefully on my mouth. "I've wanted to do that since you rescued me. Thank you, Harry."

Though I was awake and aware, my senses were confused. I was thinking crazy thoughts. From that one kiss, I felt like I was in love and wanting sex with Vera. It only took a few seconds. I could only imagine what happened to make Earl turn into what he had become.

"If I untie your hands, will you promise not to do anything foolish? You see the men behind me?"

I hadn't seen the two strong Cubans with the knives in their belts until she spoke of them. I had a couple of dozen important, life-and-death questions, but my voice wasn't working. I nodded to her.

Vera leaned into me to reach behind my back to untie my hands. Her breasts through her shirt against my chest felt too good. She couldn't seem to untie my hands. I realized she was doing it on purpose. She was seducing me for something.

She gave up and said something in Spanish to the men. They helped me to my feet and untied my hands. She took my hand in hers and said, "Let's go see that prick, Tony Bacca."

Like a sheep, I let her lead me out of what I now saw as a mere shack toward a bigger shack, maybe thirty yards away. I almost felt like a schoolboy with my first crush on a girl. Everything in my brain was crashing into everything else. I kept telling myself I was in love with Addie, yet I wanted Vera as badly as I had ever wanted any dame. My emotions were topsy-turvy and inside-out. No wonder so many men had been taken in by her allure. Yet, Bacca's men weren't seduced into setting her free from the Terminal Tower apartment. I knew why. They were having everything they wanted from her.

Earl smiled at me, as if I now knew why he did what he did. Was he planning on sharing Vera with me? I forced Addie's face into my mind's view to fight the spell eating at my heart with lust.

Then I saw Tony Bacca, Jr., naked and tied to a chair. He was beaten black and blue and looked to have burn marks on his body. Maybe on his genitals, though I didn't want to look below the waist. Most of all I saw the round whites of his eyes inside the bruising of his eye sockets. His pupils were coal black and large, as if fear had frozen his pupils wide open.

"What's killing him going to solve?" I said.

Earl answered, "We're not going to kill him. That would be too easy. I told him you were duped into leading him into our trap. Let's go talk, Harry."

I followed Earl through the room and down a short hallway into another room with a small square table and two chairs. On the table was a large clay pitcher, two glasses, and a bottle of bourbon.

"Vera's not joining us?" I asked like a schoolboy with a crush. I regretted my question, which let Earl know I was falling under her seductive spell.

"No. Sit down, Harry. There's cool water in the pitcher. We don't have ice out here. Drink as much as you want. I can get more."

The water was more important than the booze or what Earl was going to explain. Dying of thirst took preference. I drank two full glasses.

"We're tired of this penny ante game of blackmail. We're only punishing Bacca for what was done to Vera. We're going to ransom him back to his father. You're going to be the go-between."

Not seeing Vera decreased the fever I had for her, like the first feelings of getting over the flu. "She's driven you crazy, Earl. You're going to end up dead like Joey and Gus. And maybe get me killed in the process. I want no part of this," I said, as if what I said might matter.

"Bacca is a weak coward. He told us about the farm where your family lives. So, the Bacca family knows and now we know. That puts you dead in the middle. Maybe dead wasn't the right word. Don't glare at me so hard, Harry. I'm going to prove to you we're still best friends."

"That's going to take some doing."

"You're going to take his ruby pinkie ring, pinky included, back to his father. We want $250,000. You'll get $25,000. You bring back the money to me. I won't know where Vera has him. She'll call me. If I feel safe, she'll tell me where to find him and I'll tell you. You take him and the books back home."

"What if Fat Tony doesn't think his son is worth the money?"

"He'll get his son back, piece by piece."

"They will hunt you down. If I'm extremely lucky, I'll be hired to hunt you down."

Earl poured bourbon in both glasses. "It's a big world. It's not like we're broke and desperate. We have enough money to disappear. That's where crooks make their biggest mistake, they spend themselves broke. We'll take our chances."

"Two hundred and fifty grand?"

"The Bacca family is fully in the powder business. It's a few months' profit. Like I said, 'Bacca is weak.' I haven't heard or seen so much begging and crying, since... Well, never."

"You're not the guy I knew in the war."

"We risked our lives for what? Democracy? The war would have been won whether we lived or died."

"So, you're risking your life for money and the dame."

"Most people die for a lot less. When you think about it, you'll know it's a good plan."

"What happened to the other men on the beach?"

"They're chum for the fish. These Cubans are very efficient with knives and machetes. They're communists, willing to do anything to pay for a revolution. Who knows, maybe they'll succeed."

"They're going to overthrow the government, the military, and the mobsters? I doubt it."

"The Cubans will take you back to Miami Beach by boat. It's probably a good idea to keep the finger in ice. Rest up a day or two and drive back to Cleveland. Make the ransom demand. It may take them a few days to get the cash together. Drive back to Miami Beach and stay at the same place. Another couple of days for me to make sure they don't have eyes on you. I'll pick up the money from you. After a couple more days, when I know I'm safe, Vera will call me and tell me where she has him. I'll call and tell you. You pick him up and drive him home."

"You can't trust her. Look at what happened to Joey and Gus. Sooner or later she'll throw you over for some other lovesick fool."

"Maybe. Or maybe, I'll do it to her," he said and laughed toward something behind me.

I turned to see Vera was behind me smiling at what Earl had said.

Chapter 41.

The boat ride with the Cubans and Tony Bacca, Jr.'s finger and ring in an ice chest took forever. They barely spoke English, so I had plenty of time to think.

If Fat Tony was willing to pay the money, the plan would work. If he wasn't, I figured I would end up dead. Six of his son's men, associate Jimmy Gratta, his nephew Sal, and some other unlucky sap had also been killed. I remained alive. How could he overlook those facts? He might believe Earl and Vera were going to kill his son anyway. Vera had her grievances against Tony Jr. In a way, it was hard to blame her. But she had started it all by stealing the books and money in the first place. Maybe money was more important to Fat Tony than his son. Earl was right; I was dead in the middle. I hoped it didn't mean what it sounded like.

Once alone in my room at the Suez, I blasted the air conditioning and slept in only my boxers on top of the sheets. I awoke chilled and took a long hot shower that may have run the place out of hot water.

Going out to eat was an eerie feeling. I was alone, though people were walking, talking, and eating. They went about their business of living, not knowing what the tough lug who looked like a prizefighter had lived through. I envied each and every one them. The world went on. I hoped I would.

As I drove back to Cleveland in Sal's Ford Crestline with the maroon body and white hardtop, I used every trick I knew to make certain no one was following me.

Every time I stopped for fresh ice for Tony Jr.'s finger, I filled up with gas. I stopped to eat whether I could stomach food or not. My strength returned; it was the best thing I had going for me. Earl always said I should have been a prizefighter instead of a private dick. No one ever said I would make a good farmer. Judging by his criticism, Uncle Josef seemed to agree with that assessment.

Halfway through North Carolina, I rented a motel room. With everything going through my mind, I didn't think I could sleep, but I did, for seven hours. So long that the ice melted and the finger was turning more yellowish brown. Fresh ice seemed to bring it back, but only as far as a slight color improvement. I cleaned up, ate, and was back on the road.

When I entered Ohio, it hit me that I wasn't in a race. There was no timetable. I needed to see Addie and my family. Maybe it would be for the last time. I hadn't called Addie since before I went to Cuba. I didn't know what I was going to say.

Before I returned to the farm I needed to find out if anyone, whether Bacca's people or Earl and Vera's, were keeping tabs on the farm.

People in town had questions about my sudden disappearance. I shrugged it off saying a sudden well-paying temporary job opportunity came up. I was only visiting before I went back to that job. Country people act like they believe something, though they leave plenty of room for doubt, especially when I asked about strangers who might be interested in me or the farm. I made it sound like some folks were interested in buying the farm. Only I understood the irony of it.

Days ago, I was told, a few city strangers had a meal and drinks, but none mentioned or asked anything about the Polinski farm.

I didn't think Earl and Vera would send a Cuban to watch my family. I doubted whether Tony Bacca had enough men left to keep constant surveillance on the farm. Threats to my family were real, unless they left the farm and disappeared.

Leaving the paved road, I drove up the bumpy, rutted drive leading to the farmhouse. Every bump and rut in the road felt good, unlike the ride in the car trunk to see Vera, Earl, and a physically abused Tony Bacca, Jr.

I left the finger and ice chest in the trunk of the car, knowing every several hours I would have to take fresh ice to it. I wasn't about to visit my family carrying an ice chest with a finger in it.

Addie answered my knock on the door. To say it might have been the greatest moment of my life so far would be an understatement. We hadn't seen each other since Bacca abducted me.

Seeing and hugging my son…

Finally, after the tears, kisses, and hugs, I sat down with Addie, Uncle Josef, and Aunt Babs to tell them everything, including about the finger. They needed to know how much in jeopardy their lives were. Their calm surprised me. Maybe they had enough time after I was abducted to realize what might happen.

With a twinkle in his eye, Uncle Josef said the whole thing was a way for me to get out of helping him fix the tractor.

Lusting for Vera now felt like temporary insanity. Maybe it was Cuba and the heat. Maybe it was wondering how long I had left to live. Seeing Addie was what I needed. Later, we made love as if for the last time. It was different than how comfortable we had become with each other. It was rushed, dramatic, almost fearful.

Maybe it was the birds chirping or the first light of dawn, but I awoke and found myself alone in bed. I made my way into the kitchen to find Addie drinking coffee at the table.

"I'll get you coffee," she said as if it was any old morning on any old day on the farm.

After sitting and lighting a cigarette, I said, "You lost some weight. I'm not sure I like it."

Her smile lasted only a few seconds. "From what you said, maybe it's a good time for us to leave the farm and get out of harm's way. If no one is currently watching us… You can follow and make sure. You said you weren't on a specific timetable. If you knew we were safe, it would give you more freedom to deal with everything. I have a few ideas."

"Let's have them, precious."

Her smile returned. "Okay, you can call me that for now." Seriousness returned as she spread her hands out on the table and stared at her wedding band. "Listen, Harry, I want to help you. After you first called after you were taken, and I knew you were alive, I began practicing with the small Smith & Wesson. The Browning is too much for me."

"We're not going to rob banks like… What were their names?"

"Bonnie and Clyde. No. But I can back you up."

"Huh?"

"Let's assume the father gives you the ransom money. Let's say we've moved to a hotel in Columbus. It's on your way back to Florida. You stop at the Columbus hotel and give $25,000 to Josef, Babs, and our son. It's your payment from Earl and Vera, right? You and I drive different cars to Miami Beach. Earl will be watching to see if any mob guys are watching you."

"He knows what you look like."

"We'll have to make sure he doesn't see me. If he's as smart as we know he is, he'll expect that you left your cut of the ransom money with your family. He won't expect a woman with a gun. I don't trust him. Do you?"

Though I didn't like the idea of Addie backing me up with a gun, it made sense.

"I don't want to live without you," Addie said defiantly.

"For our son?"

"I trust Josef and Babs to raise Ollie. I mean it. I don't want to live without you. As I see it, the only chance we have is for Tony Bacca to be returned to his father alive. Vera wants the money and him dead. I can't say I blame her. Earl will do what she wants. Hasn't he so far? They won't leave you alive, Harry. You found them in Miami Beach. No one knows Earl better than you do. The father would want revenge for the death of his son. He'll use you and end up killing you, whether you find Earl and Vera for him or not. Isn't it the way those mob guys operate?"

"I don't like the sound of any of this."

"Would you die to save me?"

"Yes."

"The same for me. It's love, Harry."

"I always heard that love is the most dangerous thing in the world."

"And the best. Anyway, you need to change the rules of the game. Earl expects you to hand over the money, then he'll tell you where Tony Bacca is. Tell him that the only way he gets the money is a face-to-face exchange, Bacca for the money."

"And if he's already dead, they'll set a trap for me, where they will kill me and take the money."

"Unless we kill them first. It won't be murder, Harry, it will be self-defense. We take their bodies and the money back to Bacca's father and tell him his son is dead. We would give back the $25,000 – all of the ransom money. I'm not him, but I would let us live after that."

"I knew I married you for more than your looks and to have a child."

"Children, Harry. We're having more than one."

I wished I had her optimism. She hadn't lived through and seen what I had seen. I wanted her just like she was.

"You said I'd make a good private eye."

"How good with my gun have you become?"

"Depends on how close I am. Didn't you tell me Gus said, 'If you can't hit what you're aiming at, move closer'? I miss Gus and Joey. I miss Earl."

Though I didn't like it, she made sense. "Once I know Fat Tony is going to pay the ransom, I'll phone you, if I can. It may take him time to get the cash together. You head down to Miami. The Aztec is next door and west of the Suez. Take a room on the bottom floor. Take binoculars."

"I'll buy walkie-talkies in Columbus. Pick one up when you drop off the $25,000. I'll drive the other one down to Miami Beach."

"Beauty and brains. How'd I get so lucky? Take my Browning to Columbus, so I can pick it up after I have the ransom money. I don't want to be packing iron when I meet up with Fat Tony."

Her tongue wet her lips before she said, "Most wives would think browning had something to do with a roast, and iron about doing laundry. But I'm the wife of a private dick. You're never going to be a farmer, Harry."

"Yeah, I'm not a farmer, but if we survive this, I don't want to be a private dick anymore. We'll think of something else."

"I can think of something for a private dick to do right now."

"You're too clever for me, precious, but I like the way you think."

Chapter 42.

After Addie and I left bed for the second time that morning, we found Aunt Babs fixing breakfast, while Uncle Josef minded little Ollie's running around and almost falling. Once kids learn to walk, they want to run. They teeter and run with little balance, though rarely fall. I had been away too long and missed too many new things my son had done.

At first, Uncle Josef balked at the idea of leaving the farm. He never ran away from a fight, being a socialist and all that.

Aunt Babs seemed to understand better, though she was fretfully worried about both of us. "If the worst happens to both of you, we can raise Ollie. I don't see why we couldn't go back to the farm. Why would anyone want to harm two old people and a little boy, after Addie and you are dead?" Her question was so honest, so direct, that tears came to her eyes, evoking tears in all of us.

Dropping his head, Uncle Josef looked like he shouldered the weight of his despair. For a man who always had strong opinions about everything, at that moment he had nothing to say.

Aunt Babs wiped her tears on her dress sleeve, held her head up, and remarkably said, "But that won't happen. I know Addie and Harry will come back to us. God is on our side."

With a raised, cocked head, Uncle Josef said, "I'm a socialist. I don't believe in God."

To his surprise, Aunt Babs said, "I do. I never bothered to tell you. Everyone knows I'm more sensible than you, Josef."

Over the next several hours, time and time again I repeated that they were packing for a vacation, not for forever. Regardless, Aunt Babs was taking three photo albums, end of discussion.

We mapped the route to the Columbus hotel where Addie had temporarily stayed a couple of years ago, before she boldly forced Earl and me to take her back to the Vincent House hideout. Addie would drive the Chevy we arrived in when I was wounded, while I drove Sal's Ford Crestline.

During the drive, I would fall back a quarter of a mile, then catch up, paying attention to every car I saw and what the drivers looked like. We planned for three unnecessary turns and one double back.

I felt tense the whole drive and kept my mind off of Addie's plan. Staying focused on the drive was the most important thing in the world to me. Once, I thought about the ice chest and Tony Jr's finger. I decided it didn't matter whether it looked kind of flesh-colored or black and rotting.

When I arrived, certain they had not been followed, Addie was checking into the hotel. We made ourselves busy carrying in bags and three photo albums and getting the family situated.

I wanted my leaving to be less traumatic than my arriving at the farm. Without hugging or kissing anyone like it might be the last time, I acted like I was going to work and would be back after work. I couldn't look anyone in the eye, as I cavalierly said, "See you in a few days," and walked out.

Fifteen minutes up the road toward Cleveland and Captain Nero's, I stopped on a berm and cried. Big tough Harry Hamm cried like a baby. I didn't know if I would survive Fat Tony and come back to them in a few days. Maybe I had seen my family for the last time. Maybe I had looked at my ugly mug in a mirror for the last time.

When I was done with the crying jag, I was done. It was time to force my tough mug back onto my face before facing Fat Tony.

What was the fat man thinking? The story was he had agreed to go into the drug business with his son. That's what Tony Jr. had told me. Was it true? Fat Tony must have known Sal was in Miami Beach, then his son with three thugs, and then three more thugs. Did he know they went to Havana? He knew he hadn't heard from any of them in several days. Maybe he sent more thugs to Miami Beach and Havana to look for them. Maybe a Havana associate had told him Jimmy Gratta and the others from his mob were missing.

Mostly I wondered how much he loved his son. From hearsay and reading newspapers, a mob family was like a religion worthy of violent retaliation toward anyone disrupting or even slighting the family. Money can change all of that, whether a mob family or an ordinary family. Was Tony Bacca, Jr.'s life worth $250,000 to Fat Tony Bacca? If it wasn't, how much was my life worth? Less than a plugged nickel? Two cents, tops.

It was fully dark when I parked at the wood pier where customers parked to eat at Captain Nero's. I felt naked without a gun, but a weapon might send the message I wasn't on the Bacca team. That was it – my attitude would be as a member of the gang. Tony Bacca, Jr. had made me one of his guys, meaning I was one of Fat Tony's guys. Sure, it was only for the Vera business, but still, I was now a member of the family.

For half of a half hour, I watched Captain Nero's and set my mind to what I had to do and how I had to act. The restaurant and bar were busy. What day of the week was it? I had lost track of the days of the week. Maybe it was Friday or Saturday, logically busier nights than the others. It didn't matter.

I had personally experienced the back room where sex, torture, or murder could occur. Tony Bacca. Jr.'s men were chum for the fishes off the coast of Cuba. Whenever I died – a good question – I didn't want to be fish food.

I remembered what Earl and I talked about when we joined the Army. In a plane you could be shot in the sky and then crash, possibly dying twice. Same with the Navy, you could be bombed and then drown, dying twice. As an infantryman, it seemed you died only once. The somewhat moronic conversation was not worth remembering. Certainly we'd had our share of hooch when we discussed it. But the memory existed. I didn't want to be murdered and then fed to the fish in Lake Erie, dying in several ways.

I made the walk to the entrance without the finger in the ice chest. It didn't seem right to walk into a restaurant with it like I was selling a set of encyclopedias. The proof of my story would be in the Ford, when his father wanted to see it.

The walk on the pier to the front door of Captain Nero's was too short. I needed more time to work up my courage. Of course, a long walk on a short pier, as the saying went, was a bad thing to do. During a less-than-serious argument at Mo's Bar, Gus Reese had said to Earl, "Aw, go take a long walk on a short pier." If Earl had taken Gus's advice seriously, I wouldn't be taking a short walk on a pier to Captain Nero's.

Chapter 43.

An attractive hostess with an ample bosom greeted me. She either seated people in the dining area or sent drinkers to the bar. She asked, "May I help you?"

"I'm Harry, Harry Hamm. I need to see Mr. Baccanelli about his son. Hope he's here tonight."

"I'll be right back."

I watched her sashay to the bar, where she whispered in the ear of a mob guy, who followed her back. He had extra pounds under his natty suit with a bulge under his left arm and curly hair in shiny swirls.

He gave me a nod and sneer. "Who are you?"

"I'm Harry Hamm. I was in Miami Beach with Tony, Jr." With that, he knew who I was. "If he's not here, I can wait at the bar. Can I get food at the bar?" I preferred not to be stuck waiting in the back private room, where they had me after they took me.

He eyed me.

As I half-raised my arms, I said, "I'm not packing iron. You can frisk me."

He took my word for it; he wouldn't want any diners to see him pat me down.

"Tell the bartender I said *okay*. My name is Romano, like the cheese," he said, like he said it every time he introduced himself. He didn't offer a handshake.

I spotted the bar to my right and said, "Okay, Romano, I'll be at the bar."

With my walk to the bar, I was attempting to show confidence without being cocky. At the bar, I took a seat next to another mob-looking guy drinking with a dame, who looked like she could handle her booze and whatever the guy eventually wanted from her.

The barstool to my right was empty. I ordered a beer, though I wanted a bourbon. A bourbon might settle my nerves, while too much might soften my brain.

When I asked the vested bartender to see a menu, he said, "We don't serve food at the bar."

When I said, "Romano said it would be okay," a menu was produced. I assumed, whatever the rules were, they didn't apply to the mob members. Members, brotherhood, or family, whatever they called themselves, I was acting like one of them.

What I knew about Anthony Baccanelli, Sr., aka Fat Tony, I knew from newspapers or hearsay. I had seen enough of his pictures in the newspaper to recognize him, though newspapers always made people look worse than they actually are. Vera's picture had not done her justice. My newspaper photo, on the other hand, showed more what I looked like.

To the best of my limited understanding, no one called the boss Fat Tony to his face. Only close associates called him Big Tony. Big had several meanings. He was fat and the head of an Italian crime family. He was old school, meaning gambling, prostitution, loan sharking, labor unions, and robbery. His son was new school, meaning the drug trade. Tony Jr. had told me his father had come around to his way of thinking about dope.

My stomach was tied into too many knots for me to be hungry, though I hadn't eaten since before I followed my family to the Columbus hotel. Maybe food would untie a few of the knots. Besides, I didn't know when I might have an opportunity to eat next, or if ever again.

I ordered a veal parmesan sandwich with French fries.

The food went down well with the beer, or so it seemed. I waited, felt a gurgling in my stomach, and then it went away.

The whole time my back was toward the entrance door. I wasn't about to turn around in the chair and anxiously watch for Fat Tony. I figured the sound level in the joint would tell me when he entered, unless he entered through a less public door.

When Romano came to get me, I was at the end of my second beer. I followed him toward the private back room. We were met in a hallway by two thugs. One of them frisked me professionally, like a cop would.

When I entered the back room, Fat Tony was seated at an oblong table for six. He was fat with a round head and neck folds. He opened a hand to the seat across from him. As I walked closer, I observed the same dark eyes his son had. His elbows rested on the arms of the chair with his hands joined in an attempt to intertwine his fingers. His fingers were fat, so he only made it to his second finger joints.

On the table was a thin bottle of something dark, either a wine or liquor. Two glasses were filled two fingers high with a brown looking liquid.

Once I nodded in reverence to him, I sat and he said, “Talk.”

This was it. Do or die. “We were ambushed in Havana by Vera Jameson, Earl Griggs, and a group of mercenary Cubans. Tony is alive and being held by them.”

“The others.”

“All dead.”

His head dipped with sadness for a moment, before rising again to stare at me. “Sal Vittali?”

“He got it in Miami Beach. Cubans slit his throat.”

Again his head dipped. He knew the men who were killed. Sal being Tony Bacca, Jr.’s first cousin meant Big Tony was his uncle. He said, “All dead, except Tony…and you.”

“Yes. You probably know Earl Griggs and I used to be private dicks together. We were friends a long time. We served in the war together. We were friends until that Vera dame came along. I was their choice to bring you a ransom demand.”

“Ransom?”

“Yeah, $250,000. Tony is alive, but he’s taken quite a beating, as of a few days ago. You know what he had done to Vera in the Terminal Tower apartment.”

With a head nod toward Romano, he said, “Take him out in the hall.”

In the hallway, I wondered what was being discussed in the room. I wonder what Fat Tony knew and what he was learning for the first time from the other thugs.

To be friendly, like a member of the gang, I struck up a conversation with Romano. I kept my voice soft and friendly. “Geez, I don’t know what to do. I have Tony’s pinky ring and pinkie finger on ice in my car. I couldn’t see walking in with it. What do you think I should do, Romano?”

My consulting tone and openness surprised him. He said, “I don’t know. It’s a tough thing.”

“Did you know the dame, Vera?”

"I knew she was Tony's dame for a while. I heard chatter about what was done to her. I had nothing to do with it. Were you the one who sprung her?"

"Yeah, me and Griggs." Whatever I said to Romano would be repeated to Fat Tony, so I was careful. "Two of our partners were murdered. She was the key to it. Griggs fell for her hard. I ended up with two bullets and nearly died. Tony hired me to find Griggs and the dame. I did, in Miami Beach."

"You're the guy from the farm."

"Yeah."

He was nodding as he said, "Your family still on the farm?"

"I moved them for their safety." Why lie, when they could find out easy enough. "Not sure how this is going to turn out."

"Wait here," he said, knocked on the door, and entered before the knock was acknowledged. Within seconds one of the other goons was standing with me in the hallway. Romano was telling Fat Tony everything I said, exactly as I expected.

I saw no reason to say anything to the new thug watching me. I had said what I wanted.

The minutes waiting added up to nearly a half hour before I was brought back into the room and sat facing Fat Tony again.

"Drink with me," he said.

We tipped glasses of the brown liquid in each other's direction. The brown liquid was strong and went down hard like a knockdown punch to the gut.

"Grappa. Homemade," Fat Tony said. "Why should I trust you? You might take my money and get away with your family."

"Two elderly people, a woman, and a kid. I'll lay odds I wouldn't be hard to find." I took a chance, thinking honesty would go a long way with Fat Tony. "They promised me twenty-five grand if I bring the ransom to them."

"Of my money?"

"Yes, of the ransom money. I didn't ask for it. I'm not as crooked as they think. I only want to get out of this alive. And I want to get Tony back alive. I'm on his team, and now your team."

"Would sending any of my boys with you and the money have a better chance of getting my boy back?"

His words were music to my ears. Not the part about sending the guys, but considering to pay the ransom.

"I wouldn't try it. Griggs is a smart gumshoe. He'd spot them. He'll contact me at the Suez Motel in Miami Beach, when he thinks he's safe. The dame will have Tony somewhere even he won't know about, in case someone tries to strong-arm him. Once he has the money and she contacts him for an okay, she tells him and he tells me where to find Tony."

"Alive?"

"A coin toss at best. She has grievances against your son. She hasn't had a problem with guys being murdered before."

"They hold all the cards. What if I assume they'll kill him, so I don't pay them?"

"One hundred percent they kill him."

Fat Tony poured two more Grappa's and we drank the awful homemade hooch that tasted like medicine. "What happens to you?"

"I go back to the farm with my family and grow corn and turnips. I'll feel real bad about Tony. We got along. I'll hope you find them and they get what they deserve."

"What if I want you to find them and kill them? For twenty-five grand."

"I'm not in the killing business."

"Tony told me he trusted you. He said you were a right guy."

"I'll take the money to them if you want. If Tony is dead, I suspect they will want me dead after they get the money. If you give me the ransom money, I'm going to give $25,000 to my family, like its death insurance money. I'm to drive back alone. If you have me followed, the deal is off. Maybe things will work out or maybe not."

"Where are you staying?"

"I just got into town."

"I'll have a couple of my boys stay with you at a nice place. I need a few days to decide. Do you want a woman?"

"No. I'm married, with a son. And faithful."

He seemed to respect my fidelity to my wife, probably unusual for the guys he knew. "Where's your car parked?"

"It's Sal's Ford Crestline, maroon with a white hardtop. It's parked on the pier."

Chapter 44.

Before taking the ice chest with the finger and ring to Fat Tony, two of his guys searched the car. They found no weapons or anything to discredit my story.

I never saw Fat Tony's reaction to his son's finger and ruby ring. I'm certain he wanted it that way.

I was under house arrest with one guy always with me. Most of the time food was brought to the swell Terminal Tower apartment where I was kept. It wasn't the same one where Vera had been held captive. The only place I ate out was at Captain Nero's. They brought me a bottle of bourbon. I was treated like a right guy.

I tried not to replay and second guess what I said or didn't say to Fat Tony. No details were asked about the ambush. If I had stepped into the room to look closer at Earl's facedown body, I would have known it was some sap in Earl's bathrobe and suspected something sinister was going to happen. Earl had me figured for what I wouldn't do, making me an alive sap.

Though I wanted to phone Addie to tell her I was still alive, I didn't take the chance. I didn't know if the apartment phone was tapped, and a guard would be there listening to me. If I convinced the guard I needed to use a public phone, it would get back to Fat Tony and might seem secretive and tip the scales against me. His guy might see and remember the number I dialed. It was too much of a risk.

On the third day, at ten in the morning, Romano showed up with two briefcases. One briefcase held one big bundle of packets of cash for the ransom and a smaller bundle for me. I was asked to count and verify the amounts. It took time.

The other briefcase held two Smith & Wesson Model 10s with shorter and longer barrels, like what Gus Reese carried until he was murdered and stripped. I wondered if they could be his. An adjustable shoulder holster, a belt holster, and four boxes of ammo were also in the briefcase.

After I inspected everything, Romano said, "He wants something back, either his son alive, the money, or them. Or don't come back."

Simply-phrased threats are the most dangerous.

After several driving maneuvers to verify I wasn't being tailed, I was twenty miles south of Cleveland when I stopped and phoned Addie. It was like a business call and we were back at the Diamond Detective Agency.

After telling Addie a half-dozen times to be careful, she left for her drive to Florida. I would plan it so I was at least one day behind her. Earl might not expect someone watching me to be there a day earlier than I was.

In the Columbus hotel room, after hugs and kisses all around, Ollie was tottering around the hotel suite as I gave the twenty-five grand to Uncle Josef and Aunt Babs. The money sparked a fire in Josef's eyes. Some socialist. I said, "Give us two weeks. If you haven't heard from Addie or me, leave for Iowa or Idaho, wherever you want. Do not go back to the farm."

Aunt Babs said forlornly, "I knew I should have brought more photos."

Uncle Josef asked, "What about Kansas?"

"Sure. Wherever you think. Create new identities, like you did for Addie and me."

Maybe Aunt Babs read it in my face, because she said, "We don't regret for one second taking in Addie and you." To which Uncle Josef nodded.

Mostly I watched and played with my son. I had barely learned how to be a father. Now I was leaving and might not be back. I guessed that's why people had kids, to leave something of themselves behind.

If the boys at Mo's Bar could only see me with my son, they wouldn't believe it. A pug like me, quick with his fists, booze, and dames, being so sentimental and watery-eyed.

Though I was never religious, I had prayed often during the war. Maybe it worked. I prayed once again, hoping I would see my son, Uncle Josef, and Aunt Babs again.

Taking my trusty 15-round Browning gave me a cache of firearms. As I instructed, Addie purchased the Motorola SCR-536 handheld walkie-talkies. Several times I had used one during the war. Bulky and weighing five pounds each, their range depended on terrain and obstacles, from a few hundred feet to a mile. Until we were both in our adjacent motels, we wouldn't be able to use them.

Wanting to give Addie the day's head start, I took my time during the drive to Miami Beach, like I was a tourist stopping to see the sights along the way. The buildings, houses, and people seemed mostly the same everywhere I stopped. The big difference was the gradual change in accent from Midwestern to Southern. Why did geography cause people's accents to change? I'm sure some egghead would be able to tell me why, though I didn't care that much to find one and ask.

The driving was like a slow wait, driving me a little nutty. It wasn't like waiting for a battle to start during the war. Nothing compared to that. It was more like waiting for the Friday night high school football game to begin.

Reasonably big and tough, I had played offensive guard and end on defensive line for the high school football team. I enjoyed the brutishness of the game and physically going against strangers. There was a tough guy manliness about it. A fist fight would get you into trouble, but a forearm shiver and bumping helmets like fighting rams was okay, because it was a high school game.

You weren't in a foxhole or a burned-out building, you were walking the school halls with your game jersey on and flirting with the teenage girls. You were riding in a car singing a popular song or having a soda at the malt shop. The waiting time moved so slowly. Suddenly, it was game time with winning or losing coming at you like a tornado.

Romano's instructions from Fat Tony repeated in my head. "He wants something back, either his son alive, the money, or them. Or don't come back."

'Don't came back' made me think we should have run and disappeared when I brought the $250,000, all the ransom money, to the Columbus hotel. Addie could have waited there, and we could have left with our son, Uncle Josef, and Aunt Babs for Kansas or wherever.

"Or don't come back." It echoed loud and clear.

Addie and I were going up against and trying to outsmart Earl, Vera, and whoever else they paid to help them. The odds were against us. I was risking the life of the woman I loved, who had given me a son I loved. And the promise of more, if we lived.

I didn't want any part of it. Not the money. Not satisfying big fat Tony. Not for the revenge of Joey, Gus, Sal, or a bunch of hoodlums on a Cuban beach. Not for Tony Bacca, Jr.'s life. Vera shouldn't have tried to blackmail

Tony Bacca, Jr. He shouldn't have had her abused in the Terminal Tower apartment. They were enemies for life until death do them part.

I had too much time to think stupid things as I drove to Miami Beach.

That son-of-a-bitch Earl, my buddy, my wartime pal, my partner in the sleuth business, and my best friend gave it all up for the wrong dame. What did she have, or do, that was so special? Maybe it was love, the most dangerous emotion of all. Good love with the right dame was what I had with Addie. Bad love with the wrong dame, like Vera, was whatever it was, until others were harmed or killed because of it. Wish we had never rescued her, no matter what Bacca's boys had done to her. She made her bed and should have suffered in it.

If I didn't get my mind under control before I arrived in Miami Beach, I would be ready for the looney bin and my own personal headshrinker.

When I accepted the $25,000, I had shot the works and over-played my hand. I was in it up to my eyeballs and accepted my wife being a part of my play. Was there a bigger fool than a not-dumb but not-too-smart fool?

"He wants something back, either his son alive, the money, or them. Or don't come back."

I told myself, "Stop thinking about what you should have done. Don't fuck up more what is already a fucked-up situation."

Chapter 45.

By the time I arrived at the Suez motel, my head was almost screwed on correctly. The warmth, the smell and taste of salt water in the air made me wonder if rigor mortis was slower or faster in Miami Beach.

The front desk clerk, a seriously over-tanned twist, who would have caught more than my attention before I was married, mentioned I had received a few phone calls, but no one left messages. A man's voice. She was happy to see me and to see another room rented. I told her I might stay a week or two. I asked for a ground-level room on the east side of the motel. It was not a problem to accommodate me.

On my first trip to the room, I brought the briefcase full of cash and the other briefcase full of guns, ammo, and holsters.

As I opened the door, I wondered if Addie was watching me from the Aztec motel, no more than forty yards to the west. The forty yards might as well be four hundred miles. I purposefully didn't glance at the Aztec, to not give the slightest thing away, in case someone other than Addie was also watching me.

Though I was only going to the car, I locked the room's door and even went back, after five steps, to make sure it was locked. The last thing I needed was an impulsively lucky burglar to steal the cash and guns.

On second thought, it wasn't a good idea. If Earl or someone half as smart was watching, it would tell them something valuable, like a briefcase of cash, was in the room. Perhaps a quick break-in or getting the drop on me, since I was foolishly not packing iron, would have ended my play before it started.

The Ford wasn't far away, though I continually looked back over my shoulder. If I hadn't given too much away already, I certainly was now. If Addie was watching, she'd see and might think I was a lousy gumshoe.

Walking fast, like one of those Olympic race walkers, I was back in the room with my two suitcases. No sooner had I opened them, I heard the gurgle of the walkie-talkie and Addie's voice. "I watched you. I'm two doors down from straight across, to the north. I love you. Over."

I engaged the button. "Could you tell what a dope I was bringing the money in, precious? Over."

"Stop that. Yes, though I thought you might want them to know, though it didn't make much sense to me. Over."

She didn't know, and I wasn't about to tell her, the screw needed two more turns for my head to be solidly on my shoulders. "Any sign of the opposition? Anyone give you the eyeball? Over."

"A guy looked at me when I checked-in, the way you used to before we were in love. Other than that, I haven't seen any opposition. Am I saying *love* too often? Over."

"I don't need reminding, but I like it. The folks back home are primed to do what they may need to do. I wasn't followed and haven't seen anything so far to clue me into anyone interested in me. I'll be moving in and out of the room and going to the outdoor hut bar to see if I can spot anyone. Over."

"And I have to stay cooped up here. Can I come over at about three a.m., or do you want to come over here? Over."

"No. Don't tempt me. I'm signing off for now. Talking to you makes me feel like a priest looking at a naked dame. Over and out."

After unpacking, I went to the hut bar for a couple of stiff bourbons with ice water on the side. I wore a jacket with my Browning in a shoulder holster. I carried the briefcase of cash with me. Hearing enough from the pool and seeing enough of their young bodies, I knew Sal would have liked the two French-Canadian girls cooling off in the pool.

Too tired for a third drink, I went back to the room and laid down hoping to catch some shut-eye. Too much driving had worn me out. I never was nutty about driving a car like many guys were. Driving to get to work or a bar or a dame's flat was okay, but a slow drive from Cleveland to Miami Beach was too much.

I awoke with a start, as if I heard an unexpected sound. The walkie-talkie and phone were quiet. I could see it was dark outside through the center join in the window curtains. Maybe the sound was in a dream I wasn't remembering.

I lit the nightstand lamp and looked at my wristwatch. It was quarter past two in the morning.

I splashed water on my face and especially my eyes. Sleep has a way of leaving something foggy on your eyes. On second thought, why wake up more than I was?

It struck me that Addie hadn't called on the walkie-talkie to check-in or chat – she must have been bored just waiting. I wanted to know she was okay, though I didn't want to wake her if she was asleep.

Sitting on the edge of the bed, fully awake, I wondered what to do next, as if there was anything to do alone in a rented room so early in the morning. Looking up, I saw the briefcase of cash. As I stared at it, it seemed to tell me it was in the wrong place, too accessible to Earl with a gun and Cubans with knives.

Having a plan is okay until a plan isn't as good as it could be. I should have had Addie wait in Columbus and drive the cash to Miami Beach and keep it with her. Considering the play I would make to Earl, it was better if the cash wasn't sitting in my room.

I spoke quietly, above a whisper, saying her name several times before saying *over* and releasing the talk button.

Her voice sounded mostly asleep and quickly moved to awake and fearful. "Harry, what time…? Are you in trouble?" She forgot to say *over*, though I could tell by the lack of sound she had released the button.

"I shouldn't have the money here. I'm coming over to you. Give me fifteen minutes, maybe more, I'll be careful. Over."

"Is that smart? Over."

"Smarter than me having the money here. Over."

After a bit of silence, as she considered what I'd said, she said, "Okay. I understand. Be careful. Over."

"Over and out," I responded.

Carrying a briefcase at that hour of the morning would look curious. I needed to move around outside, circle the motel, double back, find shadows, and make certain I wasn't being watched. Anything out of the ordinary, like a guy standing and doing nothing but smoking or something like the glint of eyeballs looking out a widow of a parked car were the types of slightly off things I would be looking for.

Before I slid on the sport coat to hide the gun under my arm, I stuffed packets of money in the waistband of my pants. It took shifting around before I tightened my belt to ensure the money wouldn't slip out onto the ground.

Enough of the day's heat was left after so much of night's darkness. The wind had picked up enough to jostle my hair, making me wish I had worn a hat.

I circled the motel to my right, stopping to peek back around corners. Anyone seeing me would think I was a thief looking for a score.

Around the back, the hut bar was shuttered and closed for the night. I went to the back of the Aztec motel and circled around with as much care as I went around the Suez. Passing one outside door to a room, I heard a couple *going to town* with each other. I suspected it would be Addie and me doing the same thing before too long.

Addie was smart enough to turn off the lights so no light filtered out of the room. After a short light tap, the door opened. I slipped inside the dark room and closed the door softly behind me. She was in my arms and I was kissing her.

"I can tell you're happy to see me, but have you gained a lot of weight since I saw you several days ago?"

"Yeah. Too much rich *dago* food. It's the cash."

We arrived at *going to town* with each other sooner than usual.

I turned on a small table lamp. We didn't bother to put clothes on, because we knew we would only be taking them back off in a short time.

Seeing two loaves of bread, a jar of pickles, mustard, and a dozen bottles of soda pop on the dresser next to an ice chest told me what she was eating. I walked to the ice chest and lifted the lid, knowing I would see something other than a finger and ruby ring. I saw ice, wax paper-wrapped packages, likely cold cuts, and a cheese or two. Two bottles of soda pop, one grape and one cola stood face up in the ice against one side. Addie thought it up on her own. I hated her being involved, but she upped the IQ of our team.

From behind me, I heard her say, "I miss coffee. How long can you stay?"

"I think dawn is the same down here, so an hour before that."

"What if Earl phones you at, say, four in the morning? Do they let calls go through at that hour?"

"Good question, precious."

"Christ, Harry. Stop calling me that."

"If he should ask, whenever I see him, why I wasn't in my room at four in the morning, I'll say I was cheating on you."

"Cheating on me, with me. I like the sound of that. So, I get to keep the money?"

"You get to hold onto it. Don't get too fond of it."

Chapter 46.

Since I'd had plenty of sleep earlier, the hours with my wife were well-spent, with only some talking and no sleeping.

I could have dashed over to her room in the darkness, but Earl had always warned me not to take shortcuts. My days of believing everything he had to say were long gone, though I remembered the wise things before that.

As careful as I was going over to Addie's room, I was as careful going back to my room. I swore to myself not to visit Addie's room again until this business was over. Swearing can go several wrong ways, one of them being a waste of breath. I hoped I would heed what was best for the situation and not for me.

I was hungry enough for breakfast, but Addie left me needing sleep. My schedule was off-kilter on this trip to Miami Beach.

Two days later, my sleeping and waking schedule were normalized, thanks to no more early morning visits to Addie. Poor Addie, she stayed in her room eating sandwiches with pickles and drinking soda pop, while I moved around as if I was on vacation. Going out to eat or drinking at the hut bar gave me an opportunity to spot whether I was being followed.

At the hut bar, drinking bourbon, neat with an ice water back, I was casually dressed in a straw hat shaped like a fedora, a slightly too large colorful shirt hiding the short barrel Smith & Wesson in a holster clipped to my belt, and loose lightweight trousers. The two French-Canadian twists were going from the pool to the beach and ocean, playing around with two young guys with southern accents. They offered an amusing distraction. I was bored, though not bored, knowing anything could happen at any time. I felt like I'd felt when I was a private eye.

Mostly through my third bourbon and I don't know how many ice waters, a voice I knew to be Earl's turned my head. "Hello, Harry." He took the wicker barstool next to me and ordered from the Oriental-looking bartender. "I'll have what he's having. And freshen his."

"What took you so long?" I asked.

"I needed a couple of days to watch you."

"I didn't spot you, so you must be better than me. Where are the Cubans?"

"Paid off. We trusted them long enough. They're on a crusade to get cash – something about a revolution."

"The mobsters and corrupt government won't allow that to happen."

"I suppose."

"Where's Vera?"

The drinks arrived and we clinked glasses like we were still friends, swallowed some bourbon, and took a mouthful of ice water to wash it down, before he said, "I don't know, so I can't tell anyone if things go wrong for me."

"You were always the smart one, Earl. Is Bacca alive?"

"I don't know that either. Vera promised he would be, but I'm not sure she wasn't lying and crossing her fingers behind her back."

I earnestly said, "Maybe you can get out of this. How much do you love her?"

"Too much. It's funny. I know she's a wrong dame, but I can't get away from her."

"She's going to break with you, maybe in a hard way. You know, like on the wrong side of grass. She'll want all the money after having enough of you."

"Maybe I'm smarter than her."

"Maybe you haven't been smart at all. Maybe she's more committed to how she wants this to end."

Earl pointedly said, "Do you have the money? Did you take your cut like I expected?"

"*Yes* to both questions."

"Let's say I had a gun pointed at you below bar level."

I laughed. "You'd have to make a move and take it out first. Think you can outdraw and outshoot me?"

"No. I was only asking. Let's have another or two, then you can give me the money. The sooner I'm safely away, the sooner I can answer a prearranged phone call. She can tell me, so I can tell you, where to find Tony Bacca."

"It could play out that way, but it won't," I said looking into his face as it turned downward.

"Harry, she won't go for any other way."

"Screw her, and not like you have been. Joey and Gus are dead. I'm lucky to be alive. That doesn't even count Bacca's guys."

"You'll be signing Bacca's death warrant," Earl said, anxious and despondent at the same time.

"Unless she's already punched his ticket. I have the money in a safe place, in case you're thinking I haven't thought this through. All the driving, all the waiting, plenty of time to think. Fat Tony Bacca wants his son alive or the money back." I didn't tell Earl the last part of my orders about Vera and him.

"How do you see it going down?"

"Face-to-face exchange. Somewhere where I can spot a double-cross."

He was silent and went at the bourbon till the glass was empty and didn't bother with ice water. He signaled for another for only him, since he saw my latest was barely sipped.

"You're wondering if she'll kill him and leave without you. Who has the cash you have left from the blackmailing and what she originally stole?"

"She has most of it."

"Earl, don't tell me you didn't expect something like this and what she would do. Being in love with someone stinks if the other person doesn't feel the same way."

"Addie has made you smarter."

Our prior friendship tugged at me from the past. "Let's take her down, whether Tony Bacca is alive or not. We turn her over to Fat Tony with the money and the books. If he lets me keep the twenty-five grand, I'll split it with you. You were just another sap in her long line of saps. Fat Tony impressed me as a straight guy, if the other guy is straight."

"You can't split money with a dead man. If we did take her and Tony Bacca is alive, then I'm a dead man. Maybe not right then, but soon. I did too much. We'd have to kill Tony Jr. ourselves and take both of them back in body bags for me to stand a chance. A chance – like a snowball in hell."

It took a second to sink in before I uttered, "What?"

"Why should you have any loyalty to Tony Jr.? You said it. He had Joey and Gus killed. His thugs tortured and repeatedly raped Vera. He threatened Addie and your family. You took two bullets and nearly died. You should kill him yourself, if he's still alive."

Now it was my turn to chug bourbon. "You're right as rain, Earl. Listen, let's work together, like partners, like the best friends we are, like when we killed Nazis to stay alive. Let's double-cross her and I'll kill Bacca."

"We don't go back. We split the money. I'll bet your family has disappeared with the $25,000. You know where. With everything going on and Bacca losing so many guys, they stopped watching the farm, didn't they?"

"Yeah. They're safe for now."

"Harry, you'll have to be the one to kill Vera. I can't do it and I can't watch it happen." He was down and feeling lousy; his whole body seemed to droop. "I know she's a wrong dame. I've always known it. How could I know it was all wrong and would end up wrong for me, yet I did everything she wanted me to do? If that's not straightjacket crazy, I don't know what is."

"I believe you. I don't believe you could lie to me about this."

"You have my word, Harry. I need a couple of days. I'll figure this out to work for both of us."

Chapter 47.

The rest of the day and most of the night, I wondered if Earl's words were worth anything. I wanted to visit Addie that night, early in the morning, and tell her everything, but I didn't want to tell her the part about me killing Tony Bacca, Jr. and Vera. What would she think of me for killing two people in cold blood, even if they both deserved it many times over? Something told me I could do it, like I killed in the war without remorse or regret. This wasn't that kind of war. What would I do when it was time to stop thinking about it and act?

From her room's vantage point, she wouldn't have seen me at the hut bar with Earl. She would only know what I told her. I didn't want to tell her any of it.

The walls were closing in on me; I needed to go out and drive around. To where? I didn't know.

Sal and I had lost money at the dog track. People down here seemed to enjoy it as much as betting on horse races. Sal told me that if a dog caught the mechanical rabbit, it would be useless to race again and be put to sleep. I wondered if my memory was giving me advice. Did it mean the prize was not a prize and ended with my death? It seemed to fit and yet not fit. It wasn't an answer. It was a memory of a night in Miami Beach with someone whose throat was slit.

Continuing on Collins Avenue, I drove past the Saxony Hotel, where Tony Bacca, Jr. had stayed before the ambush in Cuba. I made a couple of turns looking for a small bar or restaurant, though unsure whether I wanted booze, food, or both.

When I became lost, I asked for directions back to Collins Avenue. Maybe that meant something, because I was feeling lost, not knowing what Earl might be planning.

The car drive ended up doing nothing for me.

Addie must have watched me return to my room, because I heard her say over the walkie-talkie, "Where did you go? Can you hear me? Over."

I held down the send button. "For a ride." What should I say? I said, "This waiting around has me restless. Over."

"You're lying to me, Harry. You better sneak over. I saw you with Earl at the outside bar. Over."

"How could you see me from your room?"

"You forgot to say *over*. I left the room for a short time to watch where you were going. I was going stir crazy. I'm coming to you or you're coming over to me. Over."

"Okay. I'll come over. Over and out."

Though it had only been dark for a few hours and people were moving around, coming and going from both motels, I did my best to blend in and not look wary, cautious, or simply crazy. If Earl was having me watched, I was being stupid to visit Addie. Maybe he would expect me to expect him to be watching, so I wasn't being watched.

Wearing a sport coat, I carried both guns, one under my arm and one in the belt holster. I went to the Ford Crestline and drove away. After several turns, stopping, doubling back, and more turns, I was certain about not being followed. I parked a quarter of a mile away, changed into a windbreaker and put on a baseball cap I had in the car. I casually walked to Addie's room.

"Where the hell have you been?" she asked as a greeting.

I told her everything. The truth. I added my impressions and side comments. Although I was as exhausted as any dog who had ever run for the rabbit at a dog track, I was thirsty and hungry. Unburdening my brain and soul to the woman I loved set me free to feel normal human needs.

She made me a sandwich, gave me a pickle and a soda pop. I expected her to start talking about what I had told her, but she was silent. I knew her well enough to know she would think before she spoke.

The sandwich bread was a day or so older than fresh. The ham, cheese, and mustard were okay. The pickle was warm and soft, so I said, "You should have kept the pickles in the ice chest."

"Really, Harry, that's what you want to talk about?"

"I don't hear you talking," I said and took a swig of grape soda pop.

"So, we really don't know what is going to happen and how this will turn out. It's up to Earl."

I swallowed a half mouthful of sandwich before saying, "In a way. He may think one thing and we may do something in another way."

"If we don't get murdered, we might be running and hiding out with Josef, Babs, and Ollie all of our lives, but with enough money to maybe get away with it. Maybe you commit two murders to make that happen."

"It's possible."

"Or you double-cross Earl, who may be double-crossing you, and we end up taking something back to Fat Tony, though we're not sure if it's his son, maybe dead, maybe alive, or the money, or them both probably dead."

"It's all possible."

"And maybe Fat Tony lied and you die, maybe me, maybe our family."

"Another possibility."

"Or maybe Earl leads you into a trap like he did in Cuba."

"Also possible."

I was finished eating and drinking when I said, "We both know you're smarter than I am. What do you want to do?"

"I want to hold my child in my arms again and maybe make love to you. The second thing is somewhat up for discussion."

Suddenly I stood up and went to peek out of the curtains.

Addie said, "I thought you were amazingly careful."

"I was. It doesn't hurt to take a look."

Her breath escaped her mouth like she was blowing out a candle on a birthday cake, before she said, "The only thing we may have going for us is that Earl doesn't know I'm here. You don't think that he might think someone is here with you and holding the money, do you?"

"Maybe. More like I have it in a locker at the bus depot."

"Why not the airport?"

"The bus depot would be easier access and less traffic."

"Did you two use it before, when you were on a case for the agency?"

"Yes. That wouldn't rule it out for this."

"Unless he was watching the bus depot waiting for you to arrive."

"I didn't think of that. He seemed upset when I told him I had the money in a safe place."

Addie started pacing the room as if walking pumped more blood into her brain.

"I'd like to spend some time here with you. That thing you said earlier about making love to me…"

"Not thinking about this might help when I start thinking about it again. I'm not sure I can stop thinking about this, no matter what we are doing."

"We could try."

Slowly a smile filled her face, "It's always the best alternative for a man, isn't it?"

"Yeah."

It seemed like she forgot what we were talking about, because she said, "Let's listen to Earl's plan first. I wish we had alcohol to drink. Even a cup of coffee would be great."

Chapter 48.

A day and a half passed before I heard a knock on my door at ten in the morning. I peeked through the curtains. It was Earl. I let him in.

He went right to the point. "She's in Belle Glade, Florida, about 90 miles north, just south of Lake Okeechobee. I told her I'll get the money from you in two hours. It was her scheduled phone call to me. It gives us extra time. She claims Bacca is still alive. I didn't ask to speak to him. She would take the request wrong."

"Never heard of Belle Glade. Why there? Does she know someone there?"

Earl sat on the edge of the bed like he was tired at ten in the morning. "I don't know. She never once said anything about the place to me. She was born and raised in Cleveland – she said. I'm to bring the money to an abandoned warehouse. How would she find such a place? Unless she has a new boyfriend to take my place, from Belle Glade?"

"I was thinking that might be the case. Someone younger, prettier, and not so smart. So, your plan is…?"

"We drive there separately. You never know when you might need an extra car. We meet up and check out the place and the opposition together. We go from there. If it's only one guy, I go in with the money and you save me."

"Where are you supposedly going to hide out with her?" It was a good question and important.

Earl answered it with something sounding truthful and planned. "South Africa. Her idea."

I said, "I would never have thought of that in a million years."

He produced two road maps, like you might find at a gasoline service station. "Let's pick a place to meet. If we're not there by, say, three or four, she might get suspicious."

"She must think you're in love with her to trust you not to run off with the money and turn coppers onto her location."

"I am. I always will be, no matter how this turns out."

His response made more sense than if he said he suddenly didn't love her anymore.

Like when we were private eye partners, we hashed out a plan. We would drive separately and meet a quarter of a mile away. He needed to know I would be there to jump into the mix at the right time. He wondered if she would wait until she had the money to say where Bacca was, if he wasn't inside the warehouse. Or even, if he was dead or alive. Putting a gun to her head wouldn't make her talk. She had taken much worse from Bacca's men and hadn't talked.

"Once her or her boyfriend have the drop on me, you come in and get the drop on them. If you kill the boyfriend, I would consider it a favor," Earl said casually, as if we were going to Mo's for drinks after work.

I walked him to his car, saying I might be a half hour or so behind him. I needed to pack my suitcases. We shook hands. The flesh on my friend's hand felt no different, even if the friendship was different.

As I watched the back end of his car going down Collins Avenue away from me, I also looked around to see if I could spot any eyes on me. There was the possibility someone would follow me to the money and rob me, if Earl was thinking in that direction.

Positive Earl was too far down the street to suddenly double back, I ran to Addie's room.

Neither of us liked the idea of handing over the money to Earl before he entered the warehouse, but his plan would stop there if I didn't fork over the cash.

Though it sounded simple that Addie would get the drop on whoever might get the drop on me after Vera or her new boyfriend got the drop on Earl, the logistics were complicated. Vera could have a team of mercenaries inside and outside the abandoned warehouse. I told Addie the key word was *abandoned.* If there appeared to be a bum or two hanging around the building, it would probably be a bigger trap than Earl suspected.

We were running out of time and had to leave soon. We needed to pack up everything. If we ever returned to Miami Beach it would be on a vacation. Nothing sounded better to me.

Addie said with complete confidence, “Harry, if you see the slightest thing wrong, you don’t go in. Your life is more important than anything to do with these greedy degenerates.”

She had it right. I agreed.

We set a meeting place near the meeting place set by Earl. Nothing would happen until Addie and I were together again one more time. She’d give me the money there. Why take any chance on me being robbed before that? Neither of us commented, though I could tell we were praying that it wouldn’t be the last time we would meet anywhere this side of above-ground.

She wouldn’t be driving so close behind me the walkie-talkies would work. The longest part of the drive was on US 27 North. Earl knew the maroon and white Ford I’d be driving. If he was double-crossing me, someone might pick up my tail. It couldn’t appear Addie was following. She might need to save me.

About a half hour or so outside of Belle Glade, I stopped at a gasoline service station. A full tank sounded like a good idea. If Addie passed me, it would only mean she arrived first at our meeting spot. Besides, stopping was a good way to glom whether someone was tailing me.

As I stood watching the traffic, I told the attendant to fill it up. Sure no one was following me, I entered the service station building.

At a stand-up desk, a man in a white shirt with the name patch reading “Al” was studying a racing form. Since the attendant wore a blue work shirt, I guessed Al was the boss.

Al was my age, give or take a few years. He smoked a cigar and wore reading glasses perched down on his nose. When he looked over at me, I saw the cutlet-sized scar on his neck. I could tell his left eye was glass, because it didn’t move in tandem with his other eye. We probably had the war in common, but might not want to jaw about it.

“How are you doing, Al? I don’t mean to disturb you.”

“That’s okay. What can I do for you?”

“I’m headed to Belle Glade.”

“Muck City. Stay on this road. Maybe a half hour.”

“Thanks. Why Muck City?”

“Sugar cane grows in muck.”

"Huh. I'm scouting locations for a farm equipment store."

After a short puff at the cigar, Al said, "They hire hands when they harvest. Do you have equipment that operates in muck?"

"No. Sounds like I'll be wasting my time. Anything going on in Belle Glade?"

"Not much. The muck gives off a bad smell. I've only been there a few times. Don't plan to eat there." He paused, as if deciding, before he said, "Did you serve?"

"Yeah, regular army. Italy, England, France, and Germany."

"I took a grenade at Anzio. Sure you can tell. Those British nurses were awfully nice to me. Didn't care for the Brit guys."

Asking if he knew the farm girl who became a nurse, who treated me awfully nice, might start a longer conversation. I had dangerous business ahead.

He puffed at the cigar again before saying, "I'd go again."

"Me, too," I agreed and shuffled to leave.

"Good luck in Muck City; you're going to need it."

Prophetic? "Good luck with the nags."

We nodded at each other and I left.

Back on the road, I fought off thoughts about the war, the mother and daughter from the farm, and Al's glass eye and scar.

If it all worked out, would I end up being a farmer? I decided farming wasn't for me. Being a private detective wasn't for me. First, I needed to stay alive, then I could decide what I wanted to do with the rest of my life.

It's strange what I thought about when everything was on the line. Maybe it was a defense mechanism meant to distract me from going into something crazy and deadly. I'd go in with two guns. Addie, my wife, would have a gun. Who knows how many other guns there would be? Yet, everything that had happened, including the threats, needed to be resolved.

Most of all, I hoped I wouldn't have to depend on the good luck Al wished for me. Did depending on good luck ever work out for the best?

Chapter 49.

I swung by the warehouse, leaving Addie to wait for me at one location, while Earl waited for me at the closer, other location. Another half hour shouldn't cause either much worry. I wanted to see the place before I checked it out with Earl.

If I wasn't expecting the sour decay smell of muck, it might not be as obvious. The locals must have become accustomed to it. The muck gave me ideas: good place to bury bodies and screw up murder evidence when the sugar cane was harvested and bodies were found. Maybe that's why the location was chosen? Maybe Joey Bacca, Jr. was already in the muck.

In the broad daylight of late afternoon, the warehouse looked abandoned. It boasted weeds, dirty windows and bricks, rusting metal, but no vehicles or signs of life. Maybe only a note to another location was inside. Earl might play it that way, run the opposition all around to learn what the opposition was really bringing to the party.

Vera was dealing the cards. I'd known her only briefly. She didn't impress me as especially smart and crafty. Her abilities lay elsewhere. The word *lay* almost made me smile.

It was Earl's brains that had kept her alive for so long. Earl would have come up with the trap and ambush in Cuba. Earl might be setting up another trap and ambush. Only this time, keeping me alive to be a go-between wasn't important. Whatever his plan, either the one I knew about or a double-cross, Addie was my ace in the hole. My wife might have to save me.

I left Sal's Ford parked behind her Chevy and climbed into the car from the passenger side.

"What took you so long?" she said with understandable nervousness.

"I wanted to see the warehouse first, on my own. I picked a place for you to hide and watch. If everything continues to look okay outside, Earl will enter, expecting me to enter after a ten count. I'll wave you down, so you can enter after me, say a five count."

"How do I count?"

"One Mississippi, two Mississippi…"

"If I don't wave, don't stick around. Drive back to Columbus and disappear with our son, Uncle Josef, and Aunt Babs. Promise me."

She said, "I promise," but I didn't believe her.

I got back in my car with the briefcase of ransom money. Ten minutes later, I crept up a fire escape against the east wall of the warehouse, while Earl checked out the other side. I hoped to find a window only partly caked with grime on the outside.

If Earl had been play-acting and about to betray me, I didn't see it. He was nervous and all business. He asked me to check my Browning twice. He opened the briefcase three times, as if the cash might magically disappear. Though I believed he was straight with me about everything, I was prepared for it to go wrong.

Three stories high, I hoped the rusting fire escape would support my weight. Moving smoothly, though quickly, I reached for the windowsill before my balance was too challenged. Falling off the railing, I could break an arm, leg, or neck.

My strong hands paid off again for me. While one hand gripped the windowsill, I wiped at the window with my right sleeve. The grime, probably having something to do with the muck, was black and greasy. Only dust seemed to cover the inside of the window. I squinted, as if my focus could pierce the dust. I could see a steel mezzanine. Beyond that to the wide-open floor space was a crap shoot. A large dark blob could be a car, which made sense and told me the opposition was inside. I thought I saw something in motion. It could be a person or a dog. I doubted whether I could make out something as small as a rat.

After observing for a while, I was convinced at least one person was inside waiting for Earl. I turned my head to the fire escape and wondered how I would safely and quietly get back to the three-stories-high metal platform. I doubted whether I could let go of the sill, balance for a moment, and hop back down to the metal platform. If I made the two moves successfully, how much noise would I make? A loud sound coming from outside would surely alert anyone inside.

Perhaps if I walked my hands down the brick wall from the window sill… I wasn't sure what I would gain being half bent over.

It must have been five minutes of indecision and doubt, looking for a reasonable option, when I looked down and saw Earl at the bottom of the fire escape. It had to be obvious to him I was in trouble, because he quietly came up the fire escape.

Like a revelation, it dawned on me I might be dead in a matter of seconds. If Earl wanted to shoot me, I was in no position to go for either gun, the Browning under my arm or the Smith & Wesson in the belt holster. Like a jolt of lightning, I rethought what I might be able to do. Hold the window sill with my left hand, go for the Browning with my right hand, whip the gun under my left arm, partly around my back, and take the one impossible shot I might be able to get off.

My eyes focused on Earl coming up the fire escape stairs toward me. His slightest move for his gun would make me go for the Browning and take the one-in-one-thousand shot, if my odds were even that good.

When he offered me his hand and helped me down, I knew Earl was being straight with me and still my friend. Now I only had to worry about how smart Vera and her new boyfriend were. I guessed the moving blob I saw was her new boyfriend. I sensed what I saw moving was a man, not a woman or a dog.

We made it to the ground. Vera had told Earl to come through the unlocked side door marked "Office," and follow the signs to the main warehouse area.

Earl seemed to stand straighter, while holding the briefcase at his side in his left hand. The weather was warm, but the rivulet of perspiration running over his right temple was something more than the heat.

He turned to me on his right and whispered, "Make it an eight count."

With the Browning in my right mitt and pointed to the ground, I nodded.

When he faced the door as he took deep breaths, I glanced past him and left to see Addie's hand go quickly up and disappear. She was in position.

Earl turned the door knob, pulled the door open, and walked inside. I was counting as I watched Addie hurrying toward me. She was agile and moved quickly for a girl, my girl, my wife.

Chapter 50.

With the office door slightly open, I turned my head back to look at Addie close behind, hoping I wasn't seeing her for the last time. She smiled as if everything would be okay. She gave me a quick kiss on the lips.

When I entered, too much daylight came through the door opening. If anyone was watching, I would be dead. I crept to the next door marked "To Warehouse." I saw more light enter the office and turned to see Addie enter. What happened to a five count?

The office reception area darkened when the door quietly closed again. Addie was at my back when I peeked through the interior door. I wasn't surprised to see a hallway and another door marked "To Warehouse." To the right I saw metal stairs, leading to the mezzanine catwalk three stories above the warehouse's main area.

I let the door quietly close and turned to Addie. "There are metal stairs to the right. They lead to a mezzanine above the main warehouse. Go up and stay crouched against the wall until you find a good spot."

"What if I run into someone?"

"I didn't see anyone when I peeked inside. If I'm wrong, don't hesitate. Shoot." I hated myself for saying what I said and getting her so involved. "How good a shot are you?"

She waved the short barrel Smith & Wesson in an unsafe and unprofessional manner. "I'm good at thirty feet. Better at twenty feet."

For a moment I flashed back to our days at the agency. Addie would come into my office and speak professionally about the finances of the business. She would have papers and pencils and sound very smart. After having my baby, she now held a revolver. If I heard gunplay from above, whatever I was doing wouldn't matter, I would go to save Addie.

From behind the interior second door, I watched her climb to the top of the metal stairs. She waved like everything was okay.

Mostly shielded by the door, I pushed it ajar, stuck out my Browning and yelled at the same moment I saw a guy with his back to me, "Grab air!

Punk!" When his hands went up, I yelled, "Drop the gun! Now, if you want to live!"

Past the guy with his back to me, I saw Earl standing above the open briefcase of cash on the floor. Past Earl, I saw Vera standing to the left of where Tony Bacca, Jr. was tied to a chair with her gun against his right temple.

At least Bacca was dressed this time. He looked more dead than alive. His face was swollen with bruises and dried blood. He didn't seem to have the energy or life force to acknowledge anything that was happening.

"Hi, Harry. Long time no see," Vera said in almost a joyful manner. "If you want this piece of shit alive, drop your gun, Harry. Go on, Ronny, pick up your gun," she said to the guy with his back to me.

The moment he started downward, I fired two bullets into his back. The loud gunshots echoed in the empty space. He hit the concrete floor with a dead thud.

My action froze Vera with sudden shock. Fear, panic, and hate filled her face at the same time. Gone was her snickering attitude. "I'll kill Tony!"

"Go ahead. I don't care. Looks like he's nearly dead anyway."

Bacca's head lifted maybe a quarter inch, all he could bear doing.

She turned her eyes on Earl. "I thought you loved me."

"I did. I do. After everything we had and I did for you, you betrayed me."

Vera turned her fiery eyes back on me. "Maybe I was meant to end up with you, Harry. Wouldn't you like to find out why so many men…" her words trailed to nowhere. "We can make a deal. There's enough for both of us."

"Both? What about Earl?"

She pointed her gun at Earl. "Sorry, baby."

The next shot was loud, echoed. The slug entered at the top of Vera's head and never came out of her body. She seemed momentarily stunned, like a bird dropping had hit her head, and then she went down fast, face first, like a building being demolished by dynamite.

I looked up to Addie still pointing the gun, her face set. She loudly said, "That bitch had to die."

Earl's eyes were up on Addie, who was walking on the metal catwalk without caring about the sound it made. "Harry, I always told people you were smarter than you looked. Where did she come from? I never saw her."

When Earl looked at me, he was surprised to see my weapon trained on him. "Thumb and forefinger on the butt. Take out your gun slowly and softly put it on the floor and then take three steps back."

"But Harry, we're partners and best friends."

"Do it."

Once he had followed my instructions, I said, "Addie has been across from me at the Aztec, eating sandwiches and drinking soda pop. When that bastard," I slightly waved my gun in Bacca's direction, "abducted me from the farm, Addie started practicing with a gun."

"Resourceful," Earl marveled. "I should have known from the start of this business. She'd make a good private eye. Didn't we say that then?"

To my left, I heard a blood curdling scream, "Kill him!" When I looked at Tony Bacca, Jr., he had passed out, using whatever energy he had to utter the shout.

Earl's voice was fifty times quieter when he said, "Maybe you should kill him. We can bury them in the muck. Do you know about this area? Sugar cane grows in muck. We'll split the money three ways. Addie deserves a full share."

Addie came up to us moving fast, though not running. I'm sure she had heard what Earl said.

I said to her, "Do you have anything in your car to help that poor son-of-a-bitch?" I nodded in Tony Bacca, Jr.'s direction.

"Yes," she answered and immediately left for her car.

"That bastard had Joey and Gus killed. I don't even have to talk about what he had done to Vera."

"She brought it on herself, stealing the books and money. Where are the infamous books?" Looking around a yard or so from where Bacca was tied to the chair, I saw a stack of what looked like journals and a leather bag.

Earl said, "You're looking at them and all the cash we have. What happens now?"

"I'm not sure. First, we're going to get Bacca back to half alive, so I'm sure he sees that she's dead. I can always kill him later, if that's the way this turns out."

"If he stays alive, he'll want me dead. You heard him. He might have you killed for not killing me."

"I'm taking all of that into consideration."

Chapter 51.

While Addie tended to Tony Bacca, Jr., Earl and I took the last hours of daylight to look for places to dispose of the bodies in the muck and their vehicle in Lake Okeechobee. Finding muck deep enough was more of a problem than sinking the vehicle in the lake. Different spots for the three seemed to make some sense, so they could be found separately at separate times and might not be linked together by the authorities.

Knowing I would also toss the murder weapons, Addie's and mine, in Lake Okeechobee, gave me a sentimental pause. Plenty of guns were left for me to keep control of the situation, yet … it was my Browning Hi-Power. I should have buried it on the farm after the hotel shootout. Again, I was thinking too much about too little. It was only another gun.

I expected the bodies to be found. No one knew any of us had spent a few hours in Muck City. A fellow vet named Al might remember a brief conversation with a guy looking to sell farm equipment. Why would he tie me to two mostly decomposed bodies found in the muck in six months, nine months, or whenever?

Earl came up with the idea of shower curtains to move the bodies and buckets of muck to cover the blood on the warehouse floor.

When we returned to the warehouse to wait for nightfall, Tony Bacca, Jr. was miraculously doing much better. He was bandaged with strips of a skirt I'd never see Addie wear again. She said that a half hour after slowly being given soda pop, she was able to feed him half a sandwich. Her ice chest idea was becoming an even better idea. I wondered if Bacca wondered, when he first saw the ice chest, if his finger and ring were in it. I guessed not; he was fighting to stay alive, though he might think of it later.

If nothing else, Tony Bacca. Jr.'s voice and full consciousness had returned. "I'm still tied up over here. If you won't shoot him, untie me, and I will. You can keep all the money for doing either."

I was about to tell Bacca to keep his yap shut, when Addie said it more nicely, "You should keep quiet for now."

When Earl and I went to wrap up Vera's body in the shower curtain, I said to Bacca, "Take a last look. She's dead. Remember it."

He said, "I want her head."

"That's not going to happen. Your memory will have to do," I finished, before Earl and I finished wrapping both bodies.

"What about the blood?" Addie asked.

"We'll cover it with the muck we brought in those buckets. Earl's idea. Can't imagine mopping it, using towels, and finding water to do it all."

Bacca's attitude was fully recovered. "Yeah, Griggs is a smart one. When do we talk turkey, Harry?"

I was about to say something smartass like *not until Thanksgiving*, but impressing anyone with my patter after what had happened seemed like a waste of breath. "After we get rid of the bodies."

Earl played it smartass with his patter. "Harry needs my help before he decides which of us dies."

His comment seemed to push Bacca back in the chair.

Earl and I worked like partners, like in the old days, though we had never hidden bodies in the muck of Muck City. We watched for car lights, moving from place to place, like we moved during the war. Neither body was too heavy for me, though Earl worked up a full sweat.

After watching Vera's new boyfriend's body sink in the muck like Vera's did, Earl said, "Like meatballs in a pot of tomato sauce."

As I drove us back to the warehouse, Earl pled his case. "You know I was crazy in love with her. Since before time, no one has been able to explain love. I never did anything to hurt you. You and Addie were in the mix since we first teamed up at the Vincent Hotel. I saved your life when I finished off the house dick. I saved your life in Cuba. I convinced Vera you'd be best to carry the ransom demand. And I played it straight going against Vera. Then there's everything before the war, during the war, and after the war, until Joey and Gus were murdered. There's the $25,000 for you, if things played out Vera's way. We can split the rest of the money, like I said before. Like I said before, we can go away and disappear."

"South Africa?"

"Not for me. Maybe France for me. If it wasn't for the death and destruction, I liked it there."

"Me, too."

"We could go together with all of your people – start a French detective agency. Bet we could learn the language in six months."

"Maybe you. I'm hard pressed using this language. Would you be able to plug Bacca?"

"I think so. He can go in the muck with Vera. Maybe they were meant to be together forever. C'mon Harry. It's me, Earl. You can't kill me. You can't turn me over to Bacca. You can't."

In a friendly manner, I said, "It's time for you to be quiet."

It was nearly ten when Earl and I walked back into the warehouse. I was as tired as any dog had ever been failing to catch the mechanical rabbit. The two kerosene lamps left by Vera and her new, dead, boyfriend had been burning for a while. I realized we had been there too long, been lucky no one had become curious about the lit dirty windows and called the cops.

I took a long look at Addie. Her eyes told me she trusted whatever I was going to do. Maybe no one has ever been able to explain what love was, but I knew how it felt.

"Earl. Take the bag of money next to the stack of books. I assume it's what's left of the money Vera stole from Tony and her husband, and your blackmail…and leave. Don't touch the ransom money. Do it now, before I change my mind."

"You're making a big mistake, Harry," Bacca said.

Before he left for forever, Earl extended his hand. I didn't hesitate. We shook hands. His eyes showed a different kind of love than he'd had for Vera.

Once he was gone, I turned to Tony Bacca, Jr. "Everyone has done wrong, except maybe me and my wife. Maybe you helped turn Vera into who she became, before she married that sap, Jameson. You were in the dope business with him against your father's wishes. Vera turned on you by stealing drug money and the books. Her blackmail scheme led to your killing Joey and Gus. I'm not God. I can't forgive you for that, but I can let it go, if you promise not to go after Earl. Your father is getting the ransom money back. You can have back the $25,000 that Addie and I have. You've had plenty of time to stare at Vera's dead body. You gave up a finger for it. Sure, a bunch of guys were killed by Cubans. Earl didn't actually do it. He had his gun on me. That's not much, since he planned the ambush. Maybe you'll give me your promise and it won't mean anything. Maybe someday you'll find Earl and make him pay for what he did. That's your problem, not mine. I'm taking you back to your father alive. My wife and I are taking our son and aunt and uncle back to the farm. We're done with this. If you want to come after me and mine at the farm, I'll be waiting. If you harm a hair on the head of anyone I love, better kill me first or I'll either kill you or die trying. That's the deal."

Addie had been watching me with something so special in her eyes, like the way no eyes had never looked at me before. She turned and spoke to Bacca. "It's a good deal. A fair deal."

"Do I have any choice?" he asked.

I said, "Not for a couple of days. But after that you'll be safe, protected, and staring at your missing finger. You'll ask yourself if enough happened to justify it. Only you will be able to answer that question." I paused before thinking of something else important. "One more thing. You have the power and influence to clear our names. We want to use our given names again. Make that happen, as an extra little favor to me."

He said what I didn't expect. "Keep the twenty-five large. You've earned it. If you ever want to make a lot of cabbage, come work for me."

"I'll keep that in mind, Tony." He knew I was only saying the words and would never work for him again. His words did make me think of what Gus had said about money tasting better than vegetables.

Everything appeared to work out in the end, but not really, not for four guys who survived the war but couldn't survive Vera, the wrong dame. I was the only lucky one. I ended up with a wife and family I loved. The $25,000 would help me start a new business, whatever it might be. It wouldn't be as a farmer.

We were about to drive off in separate cars. Addie was going to pick up Uncle Josef, Aunt Babs, and Ollie in Columbus and go back to the farm. I was driving Tony Bacca, Jr. back to his father.

Before getting into our cars, we held each other and kissed. Addie said, "I never get tired of kissing you. I always want more." We kissed again. She said, "Go and knock 'em dead, Harry." She rethought what she said. "I don't mean that literally. Just come back to me, Harry?"

"I will, precious."

"I'll let you get away with that this last time," she said and gave me the smile that always knocked me out and gave me every reason to make it back to her, Ollie, Uncle Josef, and Aunt Babs.

Driving with Tony Bacca. Jr. as my passenger, I said, "I'm going to talk to stay awake. We need to put a couple of hundred miles between where we stop to sleep and Belle Glade, also known as Muck City. Thought I would talk about Joey Alfonso and Gus Reese, two great guys. Maybe when I'm finished talking about them, I might change my mind about a few things."

Dedication

For my parents, Kay and Joe.

Mom, Dad, and me circa 1949

Credits & Copyright

Cover Image: iStock.com/Soubrette

Special thanks to Editor Maryjane Stout of Red + Blue Pencil

Next Harry Hamm Mystery Thriller:

Wrong About Harry

Made in the USA
Columbia, SC
03 November 2024

45578951R00135